# GANGS AND GHOSTS

BEYOND THE SHADOWS BOOK 1

KATIE MAY

EXPRESSO PUBLISHING, LLC

Copyright © 2019 by Katie May

All rights reserved.

No part of this book may be reproduced in any form or by any electronic or mechanical means, including information storage and retrieval systems, without written permission from the author, except for the use of brief quotations in a book review.

Cover Design by JODIELOCKS Designs

Edited by Meghan Leigh Daigle of Bookish Dreams Editing

*Dedicated to Grandma - Thank you for being amazing and supporting me unconditionally*

**CONTENTS**

| | |
|---|---|
| Prologue | 1 |
| Chapter 1 | 5 |
| Chapter 2 | 17 |
| Chapter 3 | 24 |
| Chapter 4 | 32 |
| Chapter 5 | 43 |
| Chapter 6 | 59 |
| Chapter 7 | 66 |
| Chapter 8 | 77 |
| Chapter 9 | 86 |
| Chapter 10 | 97 |
| Chapter 11 | 103 |
| Chapter 12 | 117 |
| Chapter 13 | 131 |
| Chapter 14 | 140 |
| Chapter 15 | 148 |
| Chapter 16 | 157 |
| Chapter 17 | 168 |
| Chapter 18 | 175 |
| Chapter 19 | 189 |
| Chapter 20 | 200 |
| Chapter 21 | 213 |
| Chapter 22 | 228 |
| Chapter 23 | 243 |
| Chapter 24 | 253 |
| Chapter 25 | 266 |
| *About the Author* | 273 |
| *Also by Katie May* | 275 |

# PROLOGUE

**Fourteen years ago**

The young couple stared through the glass screen, the fluorescent lights up above crackling at intermittent intervals. They held each other closely, an abundant number of emotions running rampant through them. Disgust, fear, pity, and an overwhelming sense of compassion.

"Is this her?" he asked the doctor. The 'her' in question was a petite figure. Dirt was smeared over her cheeks, and her body was unnaturally skinny. She was so tiny, so breakable, so *wrong*.

She was on her hands and knees on the ground, head tilted back as she howled at an invisible moon. Maybe she believed that the light *was* the moon.

"This is her," the doctor said. There was no sympathy in his voice. He was cool, calm, and collected—everything that the young couple was not. He glanced down at his clipboard and then back towards the small girl. "Are you sure about this?"

This question had been asked numerous times by

numerous people. His parents, their friends, complete strangers. It was his mom that had caused him to hesitate, her words heartfelt and sincere, despite the cruelness of them.

"Think about your son. She will hurt him. You saw the videos. She's a monster."

And he'd believed her, if only a for a moment. He would do anything for his family.

But the little girl...

She looked so innocent and tiny in the dauntingly large room. Her hair was unkempt, and her body was covered in soot. It was obvious that no one had bothered to clean her in the weeks she'd been here. His heart hammered in sympathy and something else.

Something almost like love.

He didn't know it was possible to love a little girl he'd only known for a few weeks and never talked to, yet he knew it to be true. This girl was meant to be his daughter. To be *their* daughter.

"Can we talk to her?" his partner asked, voice gruff. The doctor glanced at them, shocked by their request, but eventually nodded. He typed in a code, and the door swung open.

The couple tentatively ventured closer, and the child's head snapped up. She bared her teeth, eyes predatory.

"Hello, darling," he said, taking a step closer to her. She immediately scurried into a corner. He paused mid stride. The last thing he wanted to do was make her uncomfortable.

"Does she have a name?" This was addressed towards the doctor. The older man shook his head slowly, eyes trained on the feral girl.

"We call her Patient 214."

He bristled at the assumption that she was less than human, that she was undeserving of a name. That would change immediately once she came home with them.

"Hello, sweetie," he tried again. This time, he did not step closer. She could come to him if she wanted to.

She eyed his outstretched hand warily.

"Don't," she croaked out. Her voice was strange to his ears, an almost unfamiliar lilt to her vowels. "He doesn't want you to touch me."

"Who doesn't want me to touch you?" he asked, glancing over his shoulder at the stone-faced doctor. Had the doctor said something to her? From his apathetic expression and the stiff shake of his head, the man reasoned that he hadn't.

"Who are you talking about?" the man repeated.

The little girl stared up at him. Despite her young age, there was a coherence in her expression that was startling. When she spoke, her voice was a whisper.

"The Shadow Man."

# 1

**Present Day**

The house was...nice.

Not the most eloquent description, but there were no other words I could think to use. An immense structure with protruding rocks created the entryway, and the flower garden had row after row of carefully planted perennials. I personally believed that the house was trying too hard. The grass was green, manicured to perfection, and glinting with morning dew. A white picket fence separated the building from its neighbors.

I glanced up at the house in dismay, then glanced down the road at the dozens of other identical houses. Did the builders not believe in individuality?

One hand carrying a cardboard box and the other a garbage bag, I walked up the surprisingly steep staircase.

"What do you think?" Dad asked eagerly, fumbling to put the key into the lock. I chose, rather wisely, not to answer him. He was proud of this place, but despite its monotonous beauty, it was not my home.

*Only one year*, I told myself. *One more year until I could go back.*

To Dad, I queried, "Which room is mine?" I plastered a singularly beautiful smile onto my face to further emphasize my point. Colt had told me it was a smile that could make even angels fall. And then he'd proceeded to call me one of those fallen angels, so I couldn't really take it as a compliment.

"I call the biggest room." Karissa pranced by me, hands empty of any belongings. Knowing her, she expected us to carry all of her stuff inside. She probably even expected us to set up and decorate her room for her.

Twelve years old, and already a little diva.

"You don't get the biggest room." I rolled my eyes at her entitlement. I had always told my parents that they were too lenient with the little she-devil, too wishy-washy. She said jump, and they responded with how high. A petty version of myself might've been jealous of the way they treated her, but I'd long since accepted that her cuteness was impossible to defy.

"I call the basement," Colt called. He slung his duffle bag further up his shoulder, while his free hand gripped his familiar black guitar case.

"You don't get the entire basement," I said with a snort. In response, Colt merely flicked my ear.

"I need the space," he answered firmly.

"What you need is to get your own place and stop mooching off of Dads."

"Fuck off."

"Language!" The final member of our family, and the owner of that the strident voice, was Papa. A domineering figure with broad shoulders and a thick, red beard, Papa was an imposing man. Only his family knew that the giant beast was actually a big teddy bear.

"I can't get the damn key to work," Dad grumbled, hand turning the knob ineffectually. Papa took the key from his husband's hand and gently placed it into the lock. The door swung open instantly.

"Show off," Dad grumbled, but Papa simply grinned.

Choosing not to listen to the rest of their banter, I took off with a blistering speed towards where I assumed the living room was supposed to be. From Dad's explanation, there was a large hallway that branched off from this area with a cute room at the end of it. According to Dad, it had a secret door inside of the closet that led to another, smaller room. Apparently, the old owners had been paranoid of a break-in or something of the sort. Why else would they create a hiding place?

I heard the patter of footsteps as Karissa moved on the floor above me. Colt must've already claimed the basement, that bastard. Like the prima donna he was, he believed that he needed at least three rooms, a bathroom, and a 'studio room,' though I didn't understand how that differed from the 'three rooms' requirement.

"I'm a grown man now," he'd told me on the car ride over. "I need my space."

"You need your own house," I muttered for the one-hundredth time.

"I'm getting a job," Colt protested. "And going back to college."

I didn't have a response to that. I'd heard the same story thousands of times. He would come up with an excuse not to do any of that stuff, that I was sure of.

The hallway was long and barren, almost eerie in the artificial lighting. I noted, with some satisfaction, a bathroom adjacent to my desired bedroom. Hopefully, I wouldn't have to share with my siblings. Karissa made it a habit to leave her makeup and curling iron on the counter, and Colt was a slob. Laundry room? He hadn't heard of it. No, he apparently believed that the ideal place for dirty clothes was the linoleum tiles of the bathroom.

The door at the very end of the hallway was cracked open. Smiling with anticipation, I pushed it open the rest of the way.

It was small, though I hadn't expected anything else, and devoid of any trinkets or memorabilia. The flooring was a dark, mahogany wood that worked surprisingly well with the beige walls. A single window showed off our neighbor's house, brown siding obscured slightly by the tiny fence.

"I knew you would like this room," Dad mused from behind me.

"It's cute," I agreed. It may have been small, but it was positively darling. I could already envision where my furniture would be set up—head of the bed against the wall, dresser beside the closet, my bookshelf in the far corner. It wasn't Chicago, but it would have to do. It would never be my home, though. But maybe, just maybe, I could make it livable.

"The movers are bringing in the furniture," he continued. "I was thinking in a couple of hours, we could go out to dinner. Check out the town."

He shrugged helplessly, and something akin to guilt tore through my chest. My parents tried so hard to be the best that they could be. Moving across the country, getting a new job...they honestly believed that it was the best course of action for their family. I couldn't fault them on that, even though they'd ruined my life in the process. I knew I was being a brat and that I was making this whole situation harder than it needed to be. I vowed to myself, right then and there, that I would not shed another tear for the place I had left.

No, I only had to wait a year before I could go back. Once I turned eighteen, there would be no stopping me. Jaron and I had already talked about colleges on the east coast. Fiona would want to come too. It would be the three of us, my boyfriend and my best friend, against the world. As it should be.

I smiled wistfully at the fantasy, and my dad, mistaking my smile as acceptance of his proposal to go out for dinner, blew out a sigh of relief.

"I'll let your sister and brother know." He paused, fingers clenched around the doorframe. "We love you, Camila. You know that, right?"

I smiled at my father warmly.

"Of course I know that. I love you too."

And I did. My siblings might annoy the shit out of me and my dads might've been a bit too protective, but they were my family. They were the people I could count on when I thought about succumbing to the darkness. They were my light.

Dropping my boxes onto the floor, I froze suddenly. The hairs on the back of my neck stood on end as if bolts of electricity were coursing through my skin. My hands turned clammy by my sides.

I knew it was irrational to believe that someone was watching me, yet that pesky feeling wouldn't go away. It was almost as if I were standing on an elevated platform, stage lights glaring down on me—I was aware that there was an audience, but individual faces remained indistinct.

Glancing over my shoulder, I stared out the window. There didn't appear to be anyone in our yard, and I scoffed at how ridiculous I was behaving. Colt's conspiracy theories were finally getting to my head.

Still, the feeling that someone was watching me didn't diminish. If anything, it grew.

∼

"Nothing sounds good here," Colt fumed, glaring at the menu, as if his gaze could physically penetrate through it. I rolled my eyes, once again, at my brother's dramatics.

"Do you have to complain about everything?" I asked.

"Do you have to be such a bitch?" he fired back, earning himself a glare from both of my dads. Dad hated when we swore, especially with what he considered unnecessarily colorful language. I'd learned to get quite creative with my use of swear words. It was so fudging annoying. See? Even my mental thoughts were beginning to turn on me.

We'd found this restaurant downtown. We had to park at a meter a couple of blocks away, because there were no open parking spaces closer to the restaurant itself. Despite the numerous cars in front of the nondescript building, we were able to be seated right away, underneath a bear head.

Yup. You heard me right. A good old bear head, as if Yogi himself was judging what I ate.

Admittedly, the restaurant was cute, with a couple dozen wooden tables in the center of the room and a long bar opposite the door. The decorations adorning the walls varied from animal heads to dated newspaper clippings. There didn't seem to be a set theme to the diminutive diner, but the overall feel of the restaurant was homey. Comfy.

Our family had only garnered a few stares as we walked by. My dads were holding hands, and us children were trailing behind them.

Karissa, with her rich ebony skin and darker hair.

Colt, with his mane of blond hair and freckled face.

And finally, me, with my dark hair and tanned skin, thanks to my Latin heritage.

For the most part, the town had been friendly. The hostess had asked my parents how long they'd been together, the waitress discussed how beautiful us children were, and a couple patrons at the bar commented that they had never seen us before.

"We don't get a lot of tourists here," one of them had stated.

"We know everybody in this town," added another. I snorted at his small-town logic.

They seemed thrilled to discover that Papa was joining the police force and Dad had gotten a job teaching at the college a few towns over.

"I'm a deputy," one of the younger men said, extending a hand. "The name's Rick."

It wasn't bad. Not at all. One of my biggest fears was the bigotry of a small town. We would be judged, shamed, cast aside. It had happened once before. Instead, nobody batted an eye at my parents' marriage and their choice to adopt multiracial children. My respect for the town grew significantly.

Our food arrived, and I practically salivated at the crispy chicken wrap on my plate. I liked food. A lot. Could you blame me? Chocolate and fried chicken and everything in-between.

Fiona would often get on my case about my eating habits.

"Seriously?" she would say, lips curling in disgust. "Do you want to get fat?"

Sometimes, when I was feeling particularly vulnerable, I

would listen to her. Other times, I would tell her to piss off.

"How's the cheeseburger?" Papa asked Colt. My brother was picking apart his dinner. Bread was on one side of his plate, patty on the other. His nose was scrunched up as if the food were emitting a particularly pungent smell.

"I'm not hungry," Colt mumbled. The poor sandwich had been brutalized by my brother's repetitive knife slashing.

"Why did you order it if you weren't going to eat it?" I snapped. He did this shit every day. I'd long since stopped asking what went through that crazy head of his. "Is it because you're afraid the government is going to poison you? Is that it? You don't trust the meat?"

"When you die and I live, then we can talk."

"So are beers and chips the only food items not contaminated by the government?"

Colt merely glared at me.

After a few more bites of my wrap, I poked Papa on the shoulder.

"I have to go to the bathroom," I announced, waiting for him to slide out of the vinyl booth. Karissa, who was sitting on a chair at the end of the table, smiled innocently up at me.

"Do you have to go poop or pee?"

My sister was a real classy bitch.

"Don't be gross," I said, ruffling her hair.

"I'm honestly curious!"

"That's a demented thing to be curious about," Dad pointed out. Karissa huffed and crossed her arms over her chest.

"Bodily fluids interest me. Is there something wrong with that?"

Papa's face had turned green.

Dad patted the back of Papa's hand sympathetically. If there was one thing that could make the monster man squeamish, it was talk of pee and periods and all that fun stuff.

A useful weapon in my arsenal, if I did say so myself.

I made my way to the bathroom quickly, did my business, and washed my hands. Frowning, I considered myself in the restaurant's dirty mirror.

I was short for my age, almost embarrassingly so. It made my petite frame seem almost childish. My hair was an onyx black, hanging down my back in light waves. I wasn't model thin like the other girls. A slab of fat made my belly protrude over the waistband of my jeans. Not skinny. Not completely fat.

Not beautiful.

Not ugly.

Average.

I frowned at the face reflected back at me, hating every flaw on my brown skin and every tangle in my long hair. Why couldn't I have looked like Fiona? White and blonde and skinny?

Beautiful.

Why couldn't I be beautiful?

I pushed aside the self-doubt and quickly dried my hands. My psychiatrist had told me that I couldn't allow my thoughts to sink back into such dark territory. There wasn't a switch that I could just flip off, though. It took considerable effort to smother some of the darker thoughts and find my way back into the light. It was like tumbling through a riptide, my depression. I would sink beneath wave after wave of endless darkness, desperate to find a pocket of fresh air. Once I found it, I would be pulled back under yet again. The water would carry me farther and farther away from the shore, away from the light. I needed to stay above water.

I needed to stay in the light.

I decided to think about school instead as I headed back to the table. Anything to distract myself from the current direction of my thoughts.

I would be going to a new school. Was I nervous? Excited? What would Jaron think if—

My thoughts were interrupted as my body collided with a wall. At least I thought it was a wall. My anger quickly transformed into horror when I met the amused smirk of a handsome man.

His hair was dark, a few shades lighter than my own, and he had lightly tanned skin. Unlike mine, his skin color seemed to be a product of sunlight, not genetics. He wore a black jacket, tight over his muscles, and a white shirt that accentuated his chiseled chest.

"You made her speechless, Ty," a feminine voice said with a chuckle. A chorus of laughs greeted her statement.

I tore my gaze away from Tall, Dark, and Sexy and faced the table that the voice had come from. There were six of them—two girls and four guys. They all wore similar black jackets with skulls on the back and had numerous piercings adorning their skin. It was the girl with the lilac hair that had spoken.

"I'm sorry," I sputtered.

"Oh look," the man I bumped into drawled lazily. "It speaks."

The group broke into another round of laughter.

Feeling tears spring to my eyes, accompanied by the irresistible urge to run away as fast and as far as I could, I shouldered the stranger out of my way. Ty, I think the girl said his name was.

"She's so cute!" the second girl said. "Look at her waddle."

Ty, coming to stand beside me, mimicked the way I walked, hips swaying side to side in exaggerated movements. My face burned red. I'd dealt with bullies when I was younger, but they'd stopped after I befriended Fiona. The girl had a way of innately demanding respect and fear from anyone dumb enough to stare directly at her. Once I began dating Jaron? Nobody would dare even speak my name badly behind my back, let alone to my face. It was the type of power that both terrified and enthralled me. I felt as if I had the world at my fingertips. Were those feelings healthy? Normal? Sane? I wouldn't have been able to tell you. All I knew for certain was that I wished Fiona were with me now. She would know exactly what to say, what witty retort to come back with. I was inadequate compared to her. I couldn't even face my monsters alone.

"It looks as if she's going to cry!" Lilac girl squealed. "Aw. Poor baby."

Ty stopped moving almost immediately and turned towards me.

"We were just teasing you."

"How dare you?"

He opened his mouth to speak, but I cut him off with a flick of my wrist.

"How dare you stand there and tease me? Does that make you feel manly, teasing a girl half your size? Does it make your flaccid dick suddenly hard?" Hissing, I took a step closer to him until we were nose to nose. "You are an asshole. I don't even know you, yet I can tell that. Grow up. Or take Viagra to fix that little problem of yours."

"Wait!" he called.

Ignoring him, I made my way back through the dining

room and to my family. They were currently in a heated debate about the effectiveness of stools in the bathroom. Apparently, Colt believed that by elevating your feet when you were pooping, it would make said poop come out easier.

My brother was a strange man.

Papa's eyes zeroed in on my face immediately. He'd always been the most perceptive of my family members.

"You okay?" he asked, eyes scanning the room as if looking for any potential danger. I bit my lip, debating whether or not I should tell him about the rude teenagers. I decided quickly against it.

I would probably never see them again after today. People were dicks, especially kids. Besides, I didn't want my fathers to know that their words and teasing had affected me. They would ship me off to the nearest hospital if I so much as described the darkness I could feel brewing inside of me, the dark, inky tendrils that threatened to consume me whole.

I kept my mouth shut and enjoyed the rest of my meal.

# 2

"So, this is the bathroom wall. Isn't it cute? And over here, we have the hallway corner. As you can see, there's a nice crack right there."

I pulled the phone away from where I was displaying said crack and faced the screen.

Jaron wasn't even looking at me. His fingers moved over the controller of his gaming console, dark hair wildly disheveled. I glowered at my phone screen.

"Are you even listening to me?" I asked. Jaron jumped, glancing slyly at me out of the corner of his eye, before turning back to focus fully on his video game.

"I'm in the middle of a game," he answered evenly. "I told you when you called that I would be busy."

I groaned, moving back into my room to flop onto my bed. It was the only piece of furniture I'd had time to set up.

"You're always busy," I grumbled.

"Well, what did you expect? Between football after school, student senate, and my gaming group, I don't have a lot of time."

I bit my lip against the flurry of insults that wanted to

escape me. I wanted to tell him that, as my boyfriend, it was his job to make time for me. I wanted him to say that he missed me and loved me. Was I petty and selfish to want such a reaction from my boyfriend?

I decided to turn the subject around. Jaron hated discussing me, but he loved talking about himself. I couldn't entirely fault him on that. His life was exciting and adventurous, while mine...well, it wouldn't exactly get a five-star review.

"How did football practice go?" I asked.

And finally, *finally*, I got the hint of a smile on Jaron's full lips that I loved. The next hour was nothing more than him bitching about anything and everything. I tried to listen and respond accordingly, like a good girlfriend would do. As Fiona always said, Jaron was way out of my league. I would do anything to capture and keep his attention. If that meant nodding nonchalantly as he complained about his coach, then I would do so happily.

When he finally trailed off, I hoisted my phone up on my pillow and against the headboard.

"I miss you," I admitted softly. Jaron grunted under his breath, attention still fixated on his television screen.

"Miss you too, babe."

"I want to show you how much I miss you." I waited until I had his attention, his eyebrows raised above bemused eyes. I smiled wickedly at him. Without breaking eye contact, I slowly began to unbutton my blouse.

As I said before, I would do anything to capture and keep his attention.

His eyes turned heated as my fingers nimbly unbuttoned my shirt. I took comfort in the fact that I was the one that had put the lust there. Not some skinny, blonde-haired beauty like Fiona or Lilac girl, but me. Camila.

"Cami," he groaned. He had finally discarded his controller, attention trained solely on me. One could relish in his attention, drown in it.

Still smiling in what I hoped was a seductive manner, I slid the shirt off of my shoulders.

"J! I brought Chinese!"

I froze at the voice, high-pitched and familiar. Jaron froze as well, eyes flicking to someone I couldn't see.

"What are we going to do tonight?" the voice continued, either oblivious to me on the phone or choosing to ignore it.

"Fiona?" I asked in disbelief, shrugging my shirt back on.

There was a long, pronounced pause before Fiona stuck her head into view of the screen.

"Cami! I didn't know it was you on the phone!"

Fiona looked just as perfect and beautiful as I remembered her to be. Blonde, silky hair like molten gold. Emerald green eyes framed by thick lashes.

Perfect. Beautiful.

Not me.

"Hey, Fi. What are you doing here?" I asked. I tried to smother the accusation resting on the tip of my tongue. If I couldn't trust my best friend and boyfriend, then who could I trust?

Fiona rolled her eyes.

"What do you think? It's a Friday. We have a movie night every Friday."

My lips involuntarily pulled down into a frown. It was true, though it had never been just the two of them.

"I didn't know you guys were going to continue that tradition," I responded lightly. Fiona gave me a long look.

"Of course we would." She absently brushed her fingers

through her shimmering hair. "What did you think would happen? That we would both just stop our lives now that you're gone?"

I blinked, momentarily taken aback by the bitterness in her voice. I hadn't thought that at all, but I also hadn't expected Jaron and Fiona to continue hanging out together without me as a mediator. The two had always hated each other. They only tolerated one another because they both loved me.

So this...this *friendship*...it was strange.

"I'm happy that you guys are hanging out," I answered through the tightening in my throat. I could feel the beginning of tears in my eyes, but I willed them away. Fiona told me once that real women didn't cry.

"In today's society, we have to be strong," she would say with an imperious set to her chin. And I would always believe her implicitly. Fiona was the strongest, most confident woman I knew. If she claimed that crying made you weak, I had no choice but to believe her.

"Well, we should probably start the movie," Fiona said. "Bye, baby! Love you!"

"Love you, too," I whispered. And then, louder, I added, "Love you, Jaron."

He mumbled something in reply.

I stared at the now black screen of the phone, mind reeling. I told myself that I was being irrational. Fiona and Jaron were just friends. Nothing more. I trusted my boyfriend.

Didn't I?

Turning my face into the pillow, I let out a muffled scream. The darkness continued to churn in my stomach, growing stronger and more demanding as the seconds ticked by.

After a few more screams, I rolled onto my back. The

fan on the ceiling spun rapidly, providing much needed circulation in the stuffy room. I focused on the repetitiveness of each propeller as it circled and circled and circled. The monotonous movement made my eyelids begin to close.

And then, they snapped back open.

I had the feeling again—the feeling that I was being watched.

I sat up in bed, casting a quick, anxious look in both directions. My bedroom door was shut, as was my closet. I still had yet to explore the mysterious hidden room, but I figured I would do that tomorrow. Was that where I felt the eyes come from?

I dismissed that immediately. There was nobody in my closet. I was being ridiculous yet again. My conversation with Jaron had made me paranoid.

Slowly, I turned towards my bedroom window, and my heart juddered rapidly in my chest at the sight before me.

There appeared to be a silhouette sitting upon the fence. I couldn't make out any decipherable features, but I would guess it was a male from his broad shoulders and muscular body.

I blinked, and the figure was gone.

Frowning, I squinted at where I thought I'd seen the man. Either he had dematerialized into thin air or I was going crazy.

Maybe the darkness was finally winning.

∽

I SLEPT RESTLESSLY THAT FIRST NIGHT. THE WIND RATTLED against the side of the house, the sound eerie in the unfamiliar landscape. When the sun finally began to peek through the open blinds, I was wide-awake and more annoyed than I could ever remember being.

Yawning, I pulled open box after box until I finally found the one that contained my toiletries. After a long car ride the day before and hours of sweat, I needed a shower.

I began to hum softly under my breath. It was a song that I had written many years ago, when I was a child. The words had absolutely zero meaning, but the tune was catchy. I was so preoccupied with my one-woman show that I failed to see the Barbie car until my foot collided with it. I let out a string of curses as I fell to the ground.

"Damn it, Karissa," I mumbled under my breath. Was she trying to kill me?

And why would she even play with her toys so close to my room? She had her own damn room. And wasn't she too old to being playing with Barbies?

I would have to have a long discussion with her about where she could and couldn't play. My room and the area surrounding my room? Off-limits.

Scowling, I hurried to the bathroom.

The house came pre-equipped with a toilet, sink, and shower. I had added toilet paper, a rug, and a shower curtain. Tossing my towel onto the sink—I had yet to set up my towel rod—I stripped out of my pajamas.

I waited impatiently for the shower to heat up, steam covering the bathroom mirror.

The shower was nice. Relaxing.

I closed my eyes against the spray of water before sinking down to my knees. Only in the shower, away from wandering eyes and curious expressions, would I let myself fall apart. Piece by piece, I fell to shreds in the tiny enclosure of the shower. I envisioned the broken shards of myself being washed down the drain.

The darkness.

I willed the darkness away.

I didn't know how long I sat there, crying, but by the time I finally turned off the water, I was freezing cold. Rubbing at my eyes, I reached blindly for my towel.

No more tears would be shed. Not for Jaron or Fiona or my life that had drastically changed. As Fiona had said numerous times, strong girls didn't cry.

Stepping out of the shower, I quickly rubbed my skin raw with the towel. The physical pain had always been a manifestation of my mental one.

I had just hung the towel over the doorknob to dry when I caught sight of the mirror.

Written into the condensation was one word.

*HI*

# 3

"So, we need to talk about privacy and space," I started, pouring myself a bowl of cereal. Karissa glanced up from her own bowl, eyebrow raised.

"Huh?"

"Privacy and space," I stressed. "First, I don't want you leaving your toys near my bedroom. I almost tripped over your damn Barbie car this morning." Karissa opened her mouth to speak, but I cut her off before she could. "Second, don't you dare go into the bathroom while I'm showering again."

I kept my voice firm, something I'd learned I had to do when talking to Karissa.

Her eyes were narrowed at me, and she dropped her spoon back into the bowl with a loud clunk.

"First," she sneered mockingly. "I didn't leave my stupid car outside your room. I haven't even unpacked my toys yet, and I have most definitely not played with Barbie dolls in years. Second, I didn't go into your bathroom. That's weird and creepy." She shuddered delicately, face contorted into a grimace, but I merely rolled my eyes. My sister could deny it all she wanted, but she had lies a mile long. She spun her web, and I would be damned if I became stuck in the bindings like my fathers.

Still, I attempted to keep my voice calm and placating. "You're not in trouble. Just don't do it again."

"Why are you blaming me?" she asked. Her dark eyes were locked with my own, hers narrowed with an elemental fury. Her anger was almost palpable.

I let out a sigh.

"I'm not blaming you." I resumed eating my cereal, aware of her incandescent gaze burning a hole through my skin. "I'm just saying..."

"Whatever." Karissa grabbed her half eaten bowl of cereal and stomped up the stairs. I watched her retreating form warily. She was my sister and I loved her to death, but sometimes, she annoyed the shit out of me. She had this tendency to lie about mundane and stupid stuff. Would it kill her to be honest for once in her life?

"Why is Karissa so upset?" Papa asked, walking into the kitchen. His hand was warmed by a steaming cup of coffee. He must've already unpacked the coffeemaker, though that was not necessarily a surprise. Papa drank more coffee than water. He practically inhaled the dark liquid.

A headache was forming between my eyes, and I rubbed at the sensitive skin.

*Because she's evil*, I wanted to say.

*Because she hates me.*

Instead, I shrugged.

"Who knows what goes through her mind?"

Papa gave me a look that suggested he didn't entirely believe me, but he chose not to say anything. He pulled out a bar stool and sat down beside me.

"I was thinking that we could head to the store today.

Get some school supplies and maybe a new outfit," he suggested gruffly. He wouldn't quite meet my gaze, especially when I turned to stare at him in alarm.

Don't get me wrong. Papa was the best dad that anyone could ask for, but he wasn't the "go out and shop" type of person. That would most definitely be Dad. Papa was our family's protector, silent and sullen with a fierce expression on his face.

It was always Dad that took me shopping for clothes or school supplies, never Papa.

I couldn't help but eye my father suspiciously.

"You want to go shopping? With me?"

The words were almost comical.

In answer, Papa merely grunted a nonsensical reply.

"Like actual shopping?" I repeated. "And not online shopping?"

Now Papa finally turned to stare at me.

"Don't be a smart-ass," he said, rolling his eyes. A hint of a smile touched his face, though.

"I'm sorry. I'm just confused. Did hell freeze over last night?"

Papa shrugged, but I thought I saw his cheeks burning red behind his thick beard.

"I know this move has been hard on you. Your father and I just want you to be happy."

I opened my mouth to tell him that I was happy, but quickly snapped it shut. That would be a lie, and he would know it immediately. I was away from the life I had always known, away from my friends and boyfriend, away from my bedroom with the window that squeaked whenever Jaron would come visit me. I was roaming an unfamiliar landscape, terrified that one wrong move would send me tumbling over an edge.

Straight into the darkness.

"So, you're trying to bribe me?" I jested, only half teasing.

"I'm trying to help you." He rubbed a hand through his hair in agitation. My father always struggled at expressing his feelings. Deciding to save him from any more awkward ramblings, I captured his large hand in my own.

"I would like that. A lot."

I wasn't certain if my words were a lie.

∼

I MADE MY FIRST PAINTING WHEN I WAS FOUR YEARS OLD. I don't remember what inspired me to make it. Dad believed that it was a product of my old childhood, before I came to live with my new family. I don't remember anything about my life with my birth parents, but I figured it had to be demented for me to create such a drawing.

My first one had been of a little girl, me I assumed, standing in what looked like a forest. Next to a tree stump, was a figure.

Not a human. Not an animal.

A monster.

It was a black shadow in the shape of a man with red, vibrant eyes. According to Dad, I had smiled happily at the picture.

"That's my new friend," I had apparently said. "The Shadow Man."

For years, I would draw this mysterious figure. My parents said that all of my bad decisions were blamed on the Shadow Man. Stealing cookies? He made me. Lying about a fight? He told me to. Sneaking out of the house? He came with me.

I don't remember any of that. My earliest memory was of being six years old and falling off the jungle gym. The doctor had said I'd hit my head, losing those earlier memories.

Honestly? I was relieved. Whatever had happened in my childhood had made me messed up. A Shadow Man? Seriously. Younger me had no imagination.

Still, drawing was my escape. I could transport myself into another world. A world of my own creation.

There was no rhyme or reason to my drawings. They were merely lines on a page—abstract, some would say—but they spoke to me like it was its own language.

"You're doing it wrong." The belligerent voice came from across the yard. I turned, startled, and dropped the paintbrush onto my lap.

A boy's head had materialized over the top of the picket fence that connected our two yards.

"Um...I didn't realize you could do art wrong." Tentatively, I grabbed the paintbrush once again, grateful that I had remembered to wear an apron, and dipped it into a mound of burgundy paint.

"You can if you're in Mrs. Hatch's art class," he continued.

"Mrs. Hatch?" I asked, remembering the name from my class schedule. I had her third period, just before lunch. Setting my paintbrush onto the canvas, I swiveled fully on my stool to face him. I had set up a simple display on the decorative yard table, the stereotypical fruit bowl, and had taken it upon myself to scavenge my old easel from one of the many unpacked boxes.

The boy cleared his throat and began to speak in what I suspected was an impersonation of Mrs. Hatch's voice. A poor one, at that.

"Dots. We do dots. Dots here. Dots there. Dots everywhere. Dots."

I stared at my painting in apprehension. All of my beautiful work...

"She would want us to make a fruit bowl out of dots?" I asked in disbelief. "What if we don't want to? What happened to artistic freedom?"

"What happened to a lot of stuff?" The boy folded his arms over the top of the crooked fence, resting his head in the crevice that they made. "They don't teach us anything that matters in school. Like taxes and student loans and how not to be a dick to one another. You know, the normal things."

I frowned once more at my painting before throwing it to the ground.

"I'm Camila, by the way."

The boy smiled. "Dorian."

On closer inspection, I saw that he had messy blond hair, just down to his shoulders. He looked boyish, perhaps only a year or two older than me. His smile went to his eyes, causing the skin around them to crinkle.

"Do you go to the public high school?" I asked stupidly. Because of course he went there. How else would he know about Mrs. Hatch?

He surprised me by shaking his head.

"I used to, but I changed schools a couple of years ago." He was silent for a moment, surveying me with his large green eyes.

"I actually used to live in that house," he admitted at last, nodding towards the looming structure just behind me.

"My house?"

"Well, it was my house at the time..." He chuckled at his own joke, a fact that demoted him from intimidating to approachable. Any boy who could laugh at himself received a gold star in my book. "But my parents moved the second this house opened up."

I considered the two houses. Same dark coating of paint. Same entryway. Same size. Probably the same floor plan.

"Why would they do that?" I asked with a raised eyebrow.

Dorian, my neighbor apparently, offered me a shit-eating grin.

"I'm surprised you haven't figured it out already." Still flashing me a wicked smile, Dorian began to walk the length of my yard. A momentary gap in the fence allowed me to see the white tank top he was wearing with a pair of low-slung jeans.

"Figured out what?" I asked, averting my attention away from his impressive physique. I reminded myself that I was dating Jaron. Though I wasn't doing anything besides talking to this Dorian fellow, it felt wrong to admire him. Dirty, almost.

"That your house is a gateway to Hell," he answered at last.

I stared at him.

And then burst into hysterical laughter. He was either a nutcase or a comedian. But I had to give him some credit—I most definitely needed that laugh.

"You're a dramatic dude, aren't you?" I said, covering my mouth with my hand to conceal my chuckles. If Dorian was offended by my observation, he didn't show it. Instead, he continued to offer me that same knowing smirk.

"Just keep in mind that I lived in that house. I know about the darkness." He paused, turning to face me fully. The smile was gone from his face, replaced by an impassive expression. "Don't come crying to me when you discover that your house is haunted."

I snorted yet again. The house looked as if it was made only a couple of years ago. An old mansion in the middle of nowhere? Okay, maybe I could get on the whole haunting wagon. This house? In a spacious neighborhood with a freaking swimming pool? Laughable.

Before I could retort, Dorian ducked behind the fence and was gone.

# 4

"Are you sure you don't need a ride to school?" Dad asked, shoving a mound of papers into his briefcase. He had always been disorganized, so it was a wonder he was able to find anything at all.

"Don't worry!" I shoved a muffin into my mouth as I spoke. Of course I had overslept on my first day of school. Of fucking course. "Besides, school is in the opposite direction of the college."

It would add about fifteen minutes to his already long drive. Not horrible by any means, but long enough that guilt had me refusing his offer.

"Papa will take you then," Dad insisted, and I rolled my eyes. Papa had already left for work an hour ago. He would have to drive home, drive to school, and then drive back to work.

"I'll be fine," I insisted again, plastering a smile on my face. I knew my father was worried about me walking alone. He had always been overprotective. It was one of the things I loved about him. "It's not that far of a walk."

I had walked every day to and from my school in Chicago. I enjoyed the wind whipping my hair, the sleek, icy roads, the fallen snow creating a fluffy canvas on the sidewalks. I had never been scared. I'd felt almost safe, which was utterly ridiculous. The streets of Chicago were ten times more dangerous than the streets of Roseville, yet I'd never felt any fear walking alone at night. Nobody bothered me.

I knew that I had gotten lucky, most women didn't fare as well as I had, but it almost felt as if I had my own guardian angel.

Silly, I knew, and completely irrational.

"Maybe I could ask Colt..." Dad trailed off when he caught sight of my annoyed expression.

"Colt would rather stab himself in the eye than get up early to drive me to school."

I knew my brother too well. He would quite frankly laugh at the suggestion and then say to me, rather rudely, "Don't get murdered."

I would be getting no help from my nice big brother.

"Besides, he has to be here to send Karissa off."

Unlike high school, elementary and middle school had a bus system. The bus would pick her up at the end of the driveway at approximately seven twenty-eight according to the slip of paper Dad had received. I, on the other hand, had to either find a ride or walk to school. I cursed myself for not getting my license sooner, but there had been no point to it while living in Chicago. Everything was in walking distance or a short bus ride away.

We didn't have that same luxury in this small town.

"I need to go before I'm late."

Dad watched me helplessly, indecision evident on his face.

"But..."

"Need to go!"

"Cami..."

"Need to go!"

I flashed him a smile before turning towards the full-length mirror in the hallway between the kitchen and living room. I wore my favorite green shirt with a pair of black leggings. The outfit concealed my stomach nicely enough, and the leggings made my legs look toned. I had swept my hair into a fishtail braid that stopped mid-back. Usually, I didn't take the time to wear makeup. Fiona would tell me that I looked trashy and slutty with it on.

I figured today I could afford to heighten my bland face. Simple mascara to make my eyelashes pop and to bring out the gold flecks in my eyes, and a small amount of pink lip gloss. Personally, I thought I looked cute.

I had sent a selfie to Fiona and Jaron earlier that morning. Jaron hadn't responded back yet, but Fiona had sent a vomit emoji. I tried to decipher whether or not she was kidding.

Choosing not to read into her text, I quickly grabbed my backpack and began the long walk to Roseville High.

Papa and Dad had driven past the school a few nights ago, on the way home from the restaurant. It was a modest brick building with row after row of unwashed windows. Frankly, it was the stereotypical high school that you would see on television—flagpole near the front entrance, steep staircase leading to bright red doors, a football field a short walk away. Roseville High was the epitome of an American high school.

Fortunately, we lived only a few blocks away.

My nerves were running haywire as I trekked down the

neighborhood street and crossed the road. I didn't know what to expect on my first day of school.

Would I make friends? Did I even want to?

It didn't escape my attention that I planned to leave this hellhole as soon as I reached eighteen. Any friendships I made here would no doubt be insignificant when compared to my relationships with Fiona and Jaron. After all, Fiona had been my best friend for years, and Jaron and I were practically engaged.

Practically. Hopefully.

Maybe.

I didn't want to think about Jaron right now.

Or ever, if I was being completely honest with myself.

Shaking my head to clear my muddled thoughts, I focused on the scenery around me.

Chicago had been busy. It had been a continuous stream of people and transportation. There had been no silence, no serenity, only noise. Walking down this wooded road, I was reminded of the ethereal beauty that was in nature, in silence.

It had rained only hours earlier, and puddles still resided in the crevices between the road and the sidewalk. The sun beat down, reflecting off the translucent pools. The sky itself was a metallic violet color, the sun unable to completely chase away the lingering darkness.

I was in awe.

A car engine broke me out of my reverie, and I jumped, turning towards the sound. A large pickup truck was barreling towards me.

Instinctively, I brought my hand up in a small wave. I didn't know why, it just seemed like something that a small-town person would do.

And I, apparently, was now one of those small-town people.

The truck veered awfully close to where I was standing on the sidewalk, its rear tire kicking up water from the puddle I had noticed earlier. I didn't have time to move before I was completely drenched.

Sputtering, I glanced up at the car with wide eyes. The passenger window rolled down, and two familiar faces stared back at me.

Lilac girl and the jerk from the restaurant, Ty or something.

It was the guy who was behind the wheel, his expression amused.

"It's not even raining," he said, clicking his tongue. "How did you get wet?"

"You're awful, Ty," Lilac girl said, but she was laughing as well. Turning towards me, Lilac raised a pierced eyebrow. "Do you need a ride?"

"I don't want my car to get wet." Ty smirked at me yet again. It was an annoying smirk, the type of smirk that made me want to punch him repeatedly. In the nuts. With a sledge hammer. Until he began to bleed...

Good Lord, I was turning into my psychopathic little sister.

Schooling my features, I forced out a smile.

"No thanks," I declined through clenched teeth. "I'm fine with walking."

"Where are you heading?" Lilac queried, choosing to ignore my unspoken plea that demanded they left me alone.

"School."

Without another word, I began to walk faster. The wind, which I had once found so appealing, was freezing cold against my wet skin and clothes. I was humiliated, but I would not allow these bullies to see me shed tears. I would be strong.

Like Fiona.

The truck, unfortunately, kept pace with me as I resumed my walk.

"Roseville High?" Ty asked. "Are you new?"

I chose not to answer him, hoping that he would either get tired of harassing me or get the message and leave me alone. I had never been that lucky.

"Oh my gosh! A newbie! What grade? Freshman? I thought for sure you were in middle school." I didn't know if Lilac girl intended to be rude or not, but I found myself bristling with indignation at her comment.

Before I could stop myself, I snapped, "I'm a senior."

I bit my tongue to keep from ending with "assholes."

Lilac girl clapped her hands together.

"We're seniors too! I'm Phoebe, and this is my brother Tyson."

I knew that this was the point where I was supposed to say my name, shake hands, and then sing a song around the campfire with them like merry old friends.

However, I was soaking wet, embarrassed, and pissed as all get out. The last thing I wanted to do was buddy up to the devil siblings. No, they both could rot in hell for all I cared.

Or, according to Dorian, my house. Apparently, the two were one and the same.

I snorted, amused with my own inner joke.

"I have a change of clothes," Phoebe was saying cheerfully. She really was an obtuse girl. "You're probably freezing."

Before I could stop myself, I said, "No shit! And I wonder whose fault that is?"

The last sentence was accompanied by a glare directed at Ty. Instead of looking ashamed like I expected, he simply shrugged.

"I just wanted to make sure you were okay. I didn't see the puddle."

I might've believed him if I hadn't noticed the mischievous glint in his eyes. He knew damn well that there was a puddle only a foot away from me.

We turned a corner, and another car appeared behind Ty's. I smiled with satisfaction, knowing that they couldn't just loiter on the side of the road any longer.

However, Ty grinned at me once again before putting his hazards on. The car immediately passed him.

"What the hell are you doing?" I hissed, my already thin patience splintering.

"We just want to make sure you get to school safely," Ty answered mockingly. Phoebe nodded her head earnestly, and I had to wonder if she understood that his inflection held no sincerity.

Glaring at both of them, I hurried my pace.

Five more cars passed us before we turned into the school parking lot. There was a car drop-off near the side entrance, and a few kids were milling around outside. Most were no doubt already inside, away from the bloated gray clouds that threatened rain.

Ty was finally forced to leave me in order to find a parking space, and I took that opportunity to run inside. I didn't trust Ty and Phoebe. Maybe she had good intentions. Maybe he wasn't as big of a dick as he seemed.

Or maybe, and this was the most logical explanation, they were both demons who'd escaped from hell.

The hallway was crowded with kids when I entered. Unlike in the movies, nobody glanced at me or began whispering amongst themselves. I was just another face in a sea of too many names to remember. I was nothing remarkable, so nobody would remember a short Latina girl with wet clothes and smeared mascara. And if they did remember me, the reasons wouldn't be good.

I garnered a few sympathetic stares as I made my way to the bathroom. My first order of business was to dry myself off. From there, I would make my way to the office.

Despite receiving my schedule, I had to meet with Principal Hudson. I didn't know why, and I didn't bother to ask. I figured he—or she—would give me the standard speech about behaving appropriately and the whole shebang.

Grabbing paper towel from the dispenser, I made quick work of drying myself off. My mascara wasn't smeared, a small miracle, but my hair was beginning to curl where it had escaped the braid. It wasn't a bad look, but it made me appear slightly disheveled. Still, I hadn't thought to bring a brush and my hair was impossible to tame without one. The braid would have to do.

After drying myself off to the best of my ability, I ducked out of the bathroom and into the hall.

The warning bell wouldn't ring for another five minutes. Hopefully, I would be able to see the principal without being tardy to class.

I only had to ask for directions once before I stopped in front of a large window that housed the offices. A secretary sat behind the desk, talking into a phone. I pushed open the glass door and took a seat in one of the many chairs adorning the back wall.

After what felt like hours, but was probably only a few minutes, the secretary put the phone down and offered me a small smile.

"Can I help you?" she asked.

I opened my mouth to answer but quickly clamped it closed. My hands began to tremble in my lap.

Most times, nobody could tell I had anxiety. Other times, it took control of my body and innately commanded the attention of everyone in the room, be they teachers, authority figures, anyone of the opposite sex. My brain would turn into liquid.

I wanted to run out of the door, never stopping, never slowing down.

The need to escape was overwhelming me...

Suffocating me...

One of the office doors opened, and a kid stormed out. He was tall and muscular, with buzzed blond hair and a scowl marring his handsome face.

"I hope you'll at least take it into consideration," an older woman was saying. The boy glared at her before storming towards the door. As if he felt my eyes on him, his head whipped in my direction.

And he did not look pleased.

Shrinking into my seat, I watched his retreating back warily. I hoped I never had to see that angry man again. He scared me.

"Ms. Rollings?" the woman asked softly. She had light skin and dark hair smoothed back into a low bun. She looked sophisticated and elegant, especially when compared to my sopping wet self.

"That's me," I muttered, standing up. She smiled, showcasing perfectly white teeth.

"I'm Principal Hudson. Would you step into my office?"

Gulping, I tried to tamp down the rising flames of anxiety. She was the principal, not a sadistic serial killer. Why did I feel so uneasy?

Nodding, I followed the woman back into her office,

noticeably relieved when she didn't shut the door behind her.

I had never been a fan of small spaces.

"How has the new house been?" she asked, settling into the leather chair across from me. Her office was tidy, papers stacked neatly upon each other and a small bookshelf against the far wall. Her desk was devoid of any clutter besides a small picture frame facing her direction and a computer.

"Good," I muttered, feeling immensely awkward. I had never been good at the whole small talk thing.

Pulling my lip through my teeth, I waited for her to speak again.

"I know that it's probably stressful moving to a new school in the middle of the year, but we're here to ensure your success. Any questions or comments whatsoever, I want you to feel free to ask. My office door is always open to you. As your neighbor, I take personal responsibility for your well-being."

I raised my eyebrow at her but didn't speak. This principal was definitely friendlier than the one back in Chicago. That one had been an aging man that hadn't even bothered to learn my name, despite the fact I had been a student worker since my freshman year. And she was my neighbor? Did she happen to be the mother of that weird guy, Dorian? I didn't know whether it would be rude of me to ask.

"I appreciate that," I answered honestly. And I did. School was terrifying, and I was forced to conquer it alone. No friends. No boyfriend. No family. Colt had already graduated a few years earlier.

"I hope to see you again soon," Principal Hudson declared with another overly bright smile. I nodded in acknowledgement, trying to ignore the twisting of my stomach.

She was just trying to be nice.

So why was my gut warning me to steer clear of her?

I frowned at myself. My gut also told me to stay away from Jaron and Fiona.

Apparently, it was wrong more often than not.

# 5

My first class of the day was chemistry.

I had taken it a few years earlier, when I was a sophomore, but it was apparently required for students to take two years here—normal chemistry and honors chemistry. I was in the latter.

I made it to the room the second after the bell rang. Fortunately, I wasn't the only one wandering in late.

The room was surprisingly large, given the diminutive size of the school. Ten black tables were set up in the classroom, five on each side. Each one, I noticed, only sat two people.

I waited hesitantly at the front of the classroom, unsure where I was supposed to go. The last thing I wanted to do was steal someone's seat in the middle of the semester.

But I also didn't want to stand at the front of the room like a freak.

See? It was only first hour, and anxiety was already making me its bitch.

Mr. Henry, a middle-aged man with a receding hairline, glanced up from where he was scanning the textbook.

"You must be Camila," he said, extending a hand. "I'm Mr. Henry, your chemistry teacher for the rest of the semester."

I shook his sweaty hand, barely resisting the urge to wipe my own on my pants when I pulled away.

"I know that you're joining the class in the middle of the semester. Hopefully, we'll be able to catch you up." He handed me a textbook and a small stack of papers. "We have short readings every night for homework and a quiz the following class to see how much information was retained. Don't worry about the quiz today, though you are welcome to try it if you would like. I have a short outline of all of the material we have covered so far. Think of it as SparkNotes for chemistry. Of course, I would highly recommend borrowing one of your fellow student's notebook, but this will work for now. I also have here your syllabus for the year. It pretty much states what I already said. The person you sit next to will be your partner for the rest of the year, both for outside assignments and labs. We have labs every Tuesday. Today, I am assigning an out of class assignment that should take you and your partner a couple weeks to finish. Do you understand everything, or do you have any questions?"

All I could do was blink up at him. Had he even breathed once during that little spiel?

Realizing that he expected a response, I managed to nod.

"Great! Now, we have an empty seat next to Kieran. Second row, at the very back."

Nodding, and secretly grateful that my seating dilemma was clarified, I shuffled down the aisle and into my assigned seat.

The second occupant, Kieran apparently, was noticeably absent. Shrugging, I placed my backpack on the floor and flipped through the notes Mr. Henry had given me. For the most part, I recalled learning the information my sophomore year of high school. Hopefully, this class would be nothing more than review for me. Even the textbook was the same one I had used.

"You're tardy again, Mr. Splicer," Mr. Henry snapped. I glanced through my fringe of lashes to see a tall, muscular boy walking down the aisle. He looked familiar, and it took me a moment to figure out where I had seen him before.

The boy from the office—the scary one with the buzzed hair and scowl. That same scowl was still on his face as he glared down at me.

"You're in my seat," he hissed. His voice was low, far deeper than a normal teenager's, and it caused goosebumps to erupt on my arms.

"Kieran, this is Camila. Your new lab partner." Mr. Henry nodded his head towards me, as if that small gesture provided all the clarification needed about who I was and why I was here. Kieran continued to glare at me.

Feeling small, like a bug moments before it was squashed, I squeaked out, "I could move to the other stool."

Kieran frowned, then glanced at Mr. Henry before tossing his backpack onto the table and sitting on the stool beside me. He was so large that his bicep brushed my arm whenever he moved and his thigh pressed against mine.

I instinctively shied away, attempting to make myself as small as possible. Not exactly hard, considering I stood at a solid five foot.

The lesson was a blur of periodic elements and atomic masses, but I barely paid attention to the teacher at the front of the classroom. My attention was entirely focused on the angry boy beside me. He would cast me the occasional glare every couple of minutes, as if it were my fault I had been placed beside him.

I supposed that, in a way, it had been.

When I wasn't fearing for my life, I was glancing anxiously at the ticking clock behind Mr. Henry's head. It was the longest hour of my life.

Ten minutes before class ended, Mr. Henry clapped his hands together with a cheerful expression. I was beginning to realize that Mr. Henry lived and breathed science. His face practically seemed to glow.

"As you know, we have a term project coming up."

There were a few groans.

"I know. I know. You guys are all so excited. I can see your enthusiasm from here." He chuckled. "For this semester's project, you will be conducting one of the experiments listed on this sheet. We have a couple of different options for you to choose from, all of which will be conducted inside the laboratory. However, you and your partner will have to create a lab report and poster over your findings. As you know, the project portion of this class will count for forty percent of your total grade. Right now, I have a tentative deadline of two weeks to complete this. We will have the lab tomorrow, so you and your partner will have to decide which experiment interests you by tonight. Email me your decisions by midnight."

The class bell rang, and the students immediately began grabbing their bags.

"Midnight!" he reminded the students hurrying around him.

Sighing, I turned towards Kieran, who stood beside me, shoving his book into his bag.

"So, do you want to exchange numbers or meet up..."

Before I could finish my sentence, Kieran quickly exited the classroom. I watched his retreating back, mouth agape.

How rude! What a freaking asshole!

Who exactly did he think he was?

I glared at the door he'd just exited. Yup. A complete and total asshole.

Shrugging my backpack on, I headed reluctantly into the hallway. Only an hour in, and I already knew that this year was going to blow.

∼

The next two classes were relatively uneventful, if not painstakingly boring. Dorian was right about the art class though.

If you weren't using dots, you weren't creating art.

By the time the bell finally rang, signaling lunch time, I was both physically and emotionally exhausted. The day had taken its toll on me, and my body was heavy with fatigue.

Jaron had finally decided to text me back with a quick reply to the selfie I sent him.

*Cute.*

Cute. Not beautiful. Not sexy. Cute.

I told myself that he was probably busy and didn't have time to say more. I told myself that he was probably stressed over the history exam I knew he had today. I told myself that repeatedly as I walked down the hallway, flipping through my Instagram feed.

My finger paused on a picture of Fiona. Her light hair was put into an elaborate twist on the top of her head, and her unblemished skin wore very minimal makeup. It wasn't so much the picture that had captured my attention, but the comments. One comment in particular.

Jaron: Gorgeous!!! So beautiful.

My stomach clenched painfully as I read his comment on my best friend's post. One time. Two times. Three times. I thought I was going to vomit. I wanted to.

I tried to reassure myself that they were only friends. Fiona was gorgeous, and a friend would say as much.

I took a deep breath in a feeble attempt to control the unsettling direction of my thoughts.

I would call Jaron tonight, I decided. I would ask him pointblank if anything was going on with Fiona.

My heart aching for the first time that I could remember, I followed the crowd to the cafeteria.

Most days, at my old high school, I would pack a lunch. The food was atrocious there, to put it mildly. However, I had completely forgotten about that little issue before I'd left for school this morning.

Frowning, I pulled a couple of crumpled bills out of my pocket. Hopefully, it would be enough for lunch.

I piled pasta in Alfredo sauce onto my plate and then added a salad to the side. There were a few fruit options, and I grabbed a banana from the selection. I knew I wouldn't be able to eat all of it, but I also knew that I would get hungry again later on in the day. It was always a smart move to have a snack on hand. High school 101.

Pushing my tray to the front of the line, I watched the sweet-looking lady punch my order into her computer.

"Three dollars and twenty-five cents," she said at last. I frowned at my pile of money, all three dollars of it.

"I don't have the twenty-five cents," I admitted. Her smile turned sympathetic.

"Are you sure you don't have a quarter in your backpack? We don't allow students to have a debt. Do you have any money in your account?"

"No," I said, shaking my head. "I'm new."

"I got her, Mrs. T," a familiar voice exclaimed from behind me. I glanced over my shoulder, unsurprised to see Ty's cocky smile. Without breaking eye contact, he handed the lunch lady a quarter. To me, he said, "I suppose you could say that I'm your hero."

Snorting, I rolled my eyes and grabbed my tray. He didn't deserve even a thank you. The boy had made me soaking wet on my first day of school. If anything, he deserved a punch in the gut.

I could hear his laughter behind me as I quickly made my way through the throng of kids. Unfortunately, I faced another dilemma almost immediately—where to sit.

You might not think it was that big of a deal, but for a person with anxiety, the decision was monumental. You had this fear of sitting beside others, yet you also feared sitting alone. You feared rejection, but you also feared acceptance. The contradicting emotions battled one another inside your already fragile brain, but there was never a clear winner. If anything, your thoughts sank deeper and deeper into despair.

I moved to a table where a group of girls sat, smiling at one another, before quickly hurrying away. I couldn't garner the courage to speak to them. Fear prohibited me from partaking in such a simple action.

A leaden, miserable feeling settled deep in my stomach as I surveyed the various groups.

Where did I belong?

There was no Fiona to guide me anymore, no Jaron to be my anchor when I wanted nothing more than to float away at sea.

Eventually, I spotted an empty table near the back of the cafeteria. I watched it for a couple of minutes before determining that it was unoccupied. If there was one thing I knew about high school, it was that everyone had their designated seat. I wasn't stupid enough to break the unspoken social rule on my first day of school.

Sliding into the empty seat, I let out a noticeable sigh of relief. That relief instantly transformed into terror when I considered my current predicament.

I should be out there socializing, not sitting by myself like a loser. What would people think of me?

I turned my attention towards my pasta, the faded graffiti on the table, the crack on the wall, anything besides the inner turmoil of my mind. I was in a room full of people, yet I ironically felt more alone than I would've been by myself.

"You must be the new girl. Not the we're creeping on you or anything. Not at all. That would be weird, and we're not weird." I glanced up, stunned, to see two identical boys hovering over my table. They both had a shock of red hair and freckled skin. Their bodies were lithe and nicely muscled, one wearing overalls with a bright pink shirt underneath, and the other dressed in a faded T-shirt and jeans. The one with the pink shirt also had on a fedora, doing little to conceal his mane of garnet red hair.

"I'm Leroy," the pink shirt guy said with a wave. He nodded towards the identical, and more modestly dressed, man beside him. "And that's Luke."

Before I could respond, Leroy threw himself into the seat across from me. Luke remained standing, arms folded over his impressive chest.

"I heard that you moved into the house on Butterfield. You know, the haunted one."

I spit out the milk I had been sipping.

"What?" I asked, eyebrows furrowing. Good Lord, the people of Roseville were insane.

"We've been studying that house for years," Leroy continued excitedly. "Ever since the first haunting was recorded."

"Haunting?" I parroted dumbly.

"You haven't heard the superstition about that house?" he asked in disbelief. "Seriously?"

"Lee, man, chill out." Luke put a hand on his brother's shoulder. "You're freaking her out."

They weren't freaking me out. Not entirely.

Instead, they were making me question the sanity of the entire town. Hauntings? Superstition? They were probably friends with that crazy nut Dorian.

"My house isn't haunted."

Leroy opened his mouth, no doubt to argue with me, but clamped it closed with one look from his twin.

"We—my brother and I—are actually a part of the ghost hunting club here at school," Leroy admitted at last. He touched the edge of his fedora, the movement hinting at his anxiousness. I stared at him like an imbecile.

"Ghost hunting club?"

Leroy nodded, completely unashamed, but I saw Luke's cheeks tint a dark red, almost identical in color to his hair. He quickly glanced away.

"We've always wanted to set up in your house. See if we can find any ghosts."

"Ghosts," I repeated. When Leroy just continued to nod enigmatically, I added, "You do realize how insane you sound right now, right?"

The blush on Luke's face deepened, but Leroy smiled, unconcerned.

"You may not be a believer yet, but you will be. I'll give you two more nights in that horror house before you come crawling to us for our help. Besides, your eyes already look *haunted*."

He sounded so sure of himself, so damn confident, that the anger I had been holding in since my confrontation with Ty and then Kieran exploded out of me.

"I wouldn't ever ask for your help. If it were haunted, what makes you guys think that you could do anything besides sprinkle some salt on the doorstep while chanting in Latin? Seriously, this isn't *Supernatural* and you aren't Sam and Dean."

Leroy and Luke both stared at me, expressions indecipherable. I felt my cheeks flame when I realized what I had said.

"I am so sorry," I muttered, quickly glancing down at my food. "It's just been a long day."

Despite the gazes I could feel on my forehead, I refused to look back up.

*Way to go, Camila. No wonder you have no friends.*

It wasn't them, honestly. I was just tired of alpha asshole guys and their alpha asshole behaviors. One, I could deal with. But four?

Nope. I didn't sign up for that.

"I know that you're *dying* to ask us this question," Leroy said, breaking the silence that was growing unbelievably awkward. I dared to glance up, my hair providing a shield between me and them.

"You think, brother?" added Luke, stirring a cup of coffee with his straw.

"Oh, I know so. She's curious."

I took the bait that they'd thrown out.

"What am I curious about?" I asked with a huff. I took a tentative sip of my warm apple cider. Hmmm. Not bad. It needed something sweet. Caramel.

I made a mental note to grab a packet of caramel next time.

"You're wondering if these hot and sexy twins have souls."

I sputtered, nearly choking on my drink. Luke absently patted my back, but Leroy continued to grin at me with a wicked glint in his eyes.

"Do we have souls, twin?" Leroy turned towards his brother.

"We used to have a third...a triplet," he pointed out.

"Oh yes. Lance. What happened to Lance?"

"We ate his soul," Luke deadpanned.

What the actual hell was happening?

A laugh, unbidden, escaped from my mouth, followed immediately by an undignified snort. I placed my hand over my face to muffle the sound, but the twins had already heard it and were roaring with laughter.

It was a loud sound, gruff and almost husky. A few tables nearby cast us confused looks. Nope. That wasn't a hyena dying. It was just the twins laughing.

"Speaking of questions..." Leroy waggled his eyebrows suggestively. And I finally realized what they were attempting to do—distract me from the tumultuous thoughts that were continually washing over me like a tidal wave. "I'm curious what the biggest dick size is."

Now it was my turn to throw back my head in laughter. Luke's lips twitched at the sound.

"Maybe you should look up the smallest dick to see if you broke any world records," he joked, throwing a grape at his brother. Leroy caught the grape in his mouth.

"We're identical twins, dumbass."

I giggled, especially when Luke's face went up into flames.

"I think the real question," I said, drawing both of their attention to me, "would be how to look it up using the school Wi-Fi without us being accused of watching porn."

The twins wore identical contemplative expressions. Leroy placed his elbow on the table and tapped his finger against his lips.

"But it's merely research."

"Research," Luke agreed.

I mimicked their movements, a stupidly large smile breaking over my face.

"Research," I parroted.

"And it's not watching. It's reading. Can people even read porn?" Leroy asked.

Luke leaned across the table to whack his head.

"It's called erotica."

"And you know this because...?"

Feeling somewhat comfortable, I took a chance to tease him as well. "What types of books have you been reading Luke?"

Leroy began to laugh again, and even Luke chuckled softly. When Leroy held up his hand for a high five, I gave him one eagerly.

Maybe, just maybe, the twins weren't so bad after all.

It was in my fifth hour that everything finally imploded. The class was math, my least favorite subject, and I arrived at the classroom five minutes after the bell rang. It was just my luck that I'd gone to the wrong classroom at first, then took the staircase up, only to realize that I had to go down two levels. By the time I arrived, I was breathless and red-faced.

And embarrassed, of course, especially when the entire class stared up at me.

I recognized the ginger twins almost immediately, sitting in the front row. The asshole Kieran sat a few seats behind them, glowering into his notebook. In the back of the room, Ty sat with the rest of his *Brady Bunch* friends.

"Camila, I presume," the stern faced teacher acknowledged. I nodded mutely. "Try to get to class on time. I don't know how you did things in Chicago, but here, we respect our teachers."

The class broke into muffled chuckles, and I felt my cheeks redden even more. I didn't think it was physically possible.

I was going to explode. It was official—I would be the first girl to die from embarrassment.

"Have a seat." He nodded towards the crowded classroom.

"We have a seat back here!" Phoebe shouted. She waved her hand in the air as if I had somehow missed seeing her. I mean, I was pretty sure I would have to be blind to miss her vibrant, lilac hair sticking out like a black dot on a white sheet of paper.

Cheeks still flaming, I shuffled to the seat she indicated. Fortunately, it was on Phoebe's left, while Ty was on her right. I really wasn't in the mood to deal with that asshole today.

Ty didn't bother to pay me any mind. Instead, he was leisurely stroking an unfamiliar girl's back. She was practically purring, body arched at an awkward angle to ensure maximum...stroke? That did not sound right.

"How has your first day been, bitch?" Phoebe asked.

I frowned at the nickname but answered with a shrug.

"It's been all right. Besides dealing with, you know, assholes." I hoped that she didn't miss the intentional diss I'd thrown at her brother. Phoebe smirked.

"My brother only teases girls he thinks are hot. You should be flattered."

"Annoyed, more than anything."

"My brother may be a dick, but he's honestly a good guy once you get to know him."

I couldn't help but chuckle at that.

"First, I don't have any intention to get to know him. He has enough girls as it is." I nodded my head towards the male in question. The girl behind him was giving him a massage while he fingered the bra strap of the girl in front of him.

Phoebe shrugged.

"So? That's Mallory and Ali. They don't mean anything to him."

Changing the subject, I nodded towards where Kieran was hunched over his notebook.

"Do you see that dude? The big, scary one with the blond hair?"

"Kieran?" Phoebe asked, eyes widening in alarm. "What about him?"

"Besides being an asshole?" I began before realizing that it probably wasn't a smart idea to insult Phoebe's classmates. For all I knew, Kieran was her boyfriend or another brother.

"You're right about that." Phoebe tossed a glare at Kieran's back. "He is an asshole. What did he do?"

"He's my partner for chemistry, and he completely blew me off when I tried to discuss our project. Like, walked away when I was in mid sentence."

Phoebe scowled but did not necessarily look shocked by my declaration.

"No surprise there," she whispered back. She cast a conspiratorial glance towards the math teacher, still unaware of our muttered conversation in the back of the class, before turning back towards me. "He's the quarterback of the football team. Won three back-to-back state championships. Complete and total asshole. Cocky as all can be. Hell, he doesn't even talk to the players on his team."

My lips pursed at that. What type of person felt so entitled, so imperious, that they were incapable of making friends? I didn't know whether to loathe him or pity him. Either way, I knew I had to put up with him. Ugh. Stupid science and stupid partners.

"You're actually kind of cool, new girl," Phoebe mumbled out of the corner of her mouth. "I wish we could be friends."

"Why can't we be?" I asked, startled by her phrasing.

She nodded towards the crowd around her, all dressed in similar black jackets with the skull on the back.

"Our group has strict rules." She shrugged. "It makes it a bitch to date, though. I actually met this really cute guy on Tinder. We're going out tonight."

"Phoebe! Camila! Do you have something you would like to share with the class? Perhaps you would like to answer the problem on the board." The teacher, whose name I still hadn't caught, was glaring at us from the front of the room. Every eye was trained on Phoebe and me, varying degrees of amusement in their expressions. The twins winced in sympathy, and Kieran just glowered.

"Ahh..." Phoebe stuttered.

"X equals the square root of nine over four," I answered immediately. The usual whispers had diminished like a flame being blown out until the room was utterly silent. You could've heard a pin drop.

"That is correct," the teacher muttered numbly. I wanted to disappear inside of my seat. I wanted the floor to swallow me whole.

I may have hated math, but I was damn good at it.

# 6

I left school immediately after the final bell rang. I didn't want to risk running into anyone. No, what I wanted to do was take a nice, long bubble bath while I simultaneously stuffed my face with ice cream.

The walk home was, blissfully silent. There were no rusty pickup trucks to stalk me or cute guys to make me wet.

And no, I didn't mean that as a sex joke. Get your head out of the gutter.

The first thing I heard before I even opened the door was the blaring music. The first thing my eyes unfortunately saw was my brother dancing around in the living room wearing nothing but a pair of sleep shorts. A pungent smell immediately assaulted my nose as I stepped farther into the house, and I instinctively brought a hand to my nose.

"God, Colt. Did you shower today?"

Colt paused mid dance—though calling it a dance was too generous of a term—and turned towards me.

"Hey, sis! How was school?"

"Fine," I replied dismissively, tossing my backpack onto the sofa. Dad would get on my ass about not putting my stuff away, but fortunately, he wouldn't get home until after dinner. Both of my parents worked late. "How was your day?"

I eyed my older brother distastefully. It was obvious that he hadn't even bothered to get dressed, despite it nearing almost four in the afternoon. His hair was disheveled, and the shadow of a beard lined his rounded jaw. My frown deepened.

"Working on band stuff." Colt practically had to yell to be heard over the roaring music. Sensing my displeasure, or at least noting the fierce glare directed his way, my brother grabbed the remote and turned down the speakers.

"Band stuff?" I crossed my arms over my chest.

"Band" was a loose term for what my brother did. Back in Chicago, he performed with his ex-girlfriend, Crystal. He would play the guitar, and she would jam out on the piano. Sometimes, my brother would drag me along to sing with them.

When they broke up, Colt had decided that it was imperative that he kept the band together. As a one-person show. Without any gigs or songs or followers. Or talent.

Yup. Completely logical.

Rolling my eyes, I began to walk down the hallway towards my bedroom and bathroom.

"Whatever. I'm going to take a bath."

"'Kay. Karissa should be home from school in about an hour. I'm going to be heading out in a couple of minutes."

Hopefully fully dressed. And hopefully to get a job.

I loved my brother to death, but there was only so much the world could give him until it swallowed him whole. His actions had consequences, and the sooner he realized it, the better off he would be.

I didn't bother to go into my bedroom. Instead, I sat on

the edge of the bathtub and allowed blistering hot water to fill it. I placed my hand beneath the steady stream of water, waiting until the temperature was to my liking.

Stripping out of my clothes, now dried from the incident, I sank into the only half filled tub. The relief was immediate, glorious.

They should seriously make a bath holiday.

A...wait for it...bathday.

I mentally slapped myself.

When the water reached the tip of the tub, I finally turned off the faucet. I didn't know how long I intended to soak, only that I would use the time as an escape. The tranquil water swirling around my body wiped away all of my sins, mistakes, failures.

I didn't have to think about Jaron and Fiona and the assholes at school.

Closing my eyes, I warned myself against falling asleep. I knew how dangerous it was.

Yet the pull of sleep was hypnotic, and I found myself obeying its seductive call.

∼

I woke up with a gasp.

Black.

The first thing I noticed was the color black.

Everywhere.

The water, once a translucent shade tinged with pink from my soap, was now completely black, like a cauldron of ink. I raised my hand through the suddenly thick liquid and held it to my face. It felt like tar beneath my pruned fingers.

What the hell?

Gasping, I threw myself out of the tub. The drastic movement sent me panting, bare-assed, onto the cold tiles of the bathroom.

"Colt!" I screamed, reaching absently for my bathrobe. I tied it quickly around my waist and pulled open the door.

Then froze.

My breath left me in a whooshing exhale. I found that I was suddenly unable to breathe, utterly transfixed and terrified by the sight before me.

It was still my hallway. I recognized the crack in the far corner and my room adjacent to it. That was where the similarities ended. Long, black strings swooped down from the ceiling, each appearing silky in texture. It reminded me eerily of a spiderweb, but each string was significantly thicker than that of a web, and the color was the shade of molten obsidian stones.

And the voices...

I could hear them reverberating through each created web, each string. Talking to me. Urging me.

"*Come.*"

"*Help us.*"

"*Do you see...?*"

Horror and curiosity warred within me, each one fighting for dominance. I knew that, logically, I had to be dreaming, yet the entire scene felt almost tangible. I was positive that I would be able to reach over and pluck one of the numerous strings.

After a moment of indecision, I did just that.

"*Please...*"

Yes. My initial assumption was correct. The voices were coming from each string.

Bracing myself, I plucked another one.

"*See you...*"

I had played the violin throughout middle school. These

strings, the voices, almost reminded me of that instrument. Each was a different note, a different song, a different story.

It was my job to play them.

Some of the strings felt dark. I wasn't stupid or naïve enough to believe that the world was inherently good. I knew that there were checks and balances, good and bad, in every facet of nature. The malevolence emitting from some of the thrumming strings made my skin prickle.

Pluck.

*"Death..."*

Pluck. Pluck.

*"We're here..."*

*"He's coming..."*

One string was more vibrant than the others. It almost seemed to have its own shadow—a gray sheen contradicting with the monotonous blackness surrounding it.

It was that one that I walked to, head tilted curiously to the side.

Listen.

I had to listen.

Pluck.

*"Mom! Please no!"*

Pluck.

*"Please!"*

As I plucked, I followed the string. It led me down the hallway and to the staircase.

Pluck.

*"I'm not...!"*

Pluck.

*"No!"*

The string brought me to an upstairs bathroom, windows tinted by a suddenly dark sky. There was no light in this room.

As the door shut behind me, I became entirely engulfed in darkness.

A single light, like a spotlight being switched on, illuminated three figures. They were made entirely of shadows, so I couldn't discern any features. Two silhouettes were standing over a tub.

A third was sobbing inside of it.

As I watched, horrified, one of the standing shadows pressed down on the sobbing figure's head. The water began to bubble, and the drowned figure fought desperately to free himself from his captor.

"Be gone, devil!" the man shouted.

The water was turning red—red with blood. It was the only color in the room besides the customary darkness and the white of the tub.

It was overflowing, soaking my bare feet and the towels on the floor. I glanced down at the sticky liquid, shocked, before staring back up at the gruesome scene before me. All three figures were gone. In their place, was a tiny girl.

She had skin the color of burnt porcelain and dark hair cascading down to her knees. Her eyes, the color of liquid amber, were staring up at me.

I recognized the little girl immediately, though I had only seen her in pictures.

She was me.

I was her.

We were one.

"He's coming for you," younger me said fearfully. She wrapped her thin arms around her waist. The gesture wouldn't hold her together, no matter how much she willed it.

I would know.

"Who's coming for me?"

I was confused, but not because of the lack of information. I was suddenly overwhelmed with too *much* of it. I had so many pieces, so many answers, yet the puzzle and the questions were unknown.

"The Shadow Man."

# 7

Gasping, I sat straight upright in the tub. My body ached from falling asleep in such an unnatural position, and my skin had shriveled in on itself like grapes turned to raisins.

I knew that I'd just a strange dream, a dark dream, but I struggled to recall what had transpired. Something to do with spiders, perhaps?

I shuddered. Spiders were the devil's lovechild, and they deserved to crawl into a hole and die.

After the tub was drained and I was dressed in a pair of Hello Kitty pajamas—I had nowhere to go, don't judge—I wrapped my hair in a towel and padded downstairs.

Karissa was already home, hunched over a notebook. I heard inarticulate mutterings beneath her breath.

"You okay?" I asked, amused. She jumped, obviously unaware that I had been behind her.

"My stupid teacher already assigned me homework," she grumbled.

"What did you expect? A free pass on homework because you're the new student?"

Karissa stare at me incredulously. "Well, duh."

Moving around her, I peered into the fridge. My stomach was already growling. I would have to make dinner for Karissa and myself. I didn't know what time Colt was coming home, but I knew for certain that Dad and Papa were not going to be back until after nine.

"What are you going to want for dinner?" I asked, shifting through what little we had for groceries. I could potentially make some spaghetti in a pesto sauce...

The ringing of the doorbell made me jump. I yelped as my head banged against the shelf above me.

"Shit," I muttered, rubbing at the sensitive flesh. Karissa just chuckled.

"Dad's home early," she guessed, turning her attention back towards her notebook. A scowl was firmly back in place as she glared defiantly at her homework. Knowing Karissa, she would just beg Dad to do it for her, under the notion that he was "helping her." My parents were so whipped when it came to my youngest sibling.

"What do you think? Lost his keys, or can't get the door opened?"

It was an ongoing joke with my father. Back in Chicago, he would always, and I mean *always*, lose his keys. Papa had to make him at least twenty copies before he finally gave up. It was only when Papa declared we were moving to Roseville did Dad admit the truth—he had the key, but he couldn't figure out how to use it.

We would never let him live that down.

"Five bucks on lost," Karissa bet, smirking evilly. When I raised a brow at her, she nodded towards the kitchen counter. Sure enough, Dad's familiar keychain stood out against the granite countertop.

Chuckling, I headed into the entryway.

"I can't believe you forgot your—EHHHHH!"

It wasn't my dad staring back at me. Oh no. The fates didn't love me that much, apparently. Instead of my balding and slightly insane father, Kieran himself stood in the doorway, his hand raised as if he was about to knock a second time.

Kieran, with his cropped blond hair and penetrating gaze.

Kieran, with his customary scowl.

Kieran, who was...staring at my Hello Kitty pajamas with an amused expression.

On reflex, I closed the door in his face and pressed my back against the wood, my labored breaths coming in and out way too freaking fast for my poor lungs to handle.

*Breathe, Camila. Breathe.*

I tried to piece together everything that I knew. Hot guy standing outside my door? Check. Crazy girl dressed in only pajamas with a towel wrapped around her head? Check. Said crazy girl slamming the door in said hot guy's face? Check.

*Oh dear Jesus.*

Taking a calming breath, I opened the door once more.

*Play it cool, Camila. Play. It. Cool.*

"What are you doing here?!" I screamed. Okay, so maybe I wasn't the subtlest individual, but could you blame me?

Kieran gave me a long look, as if I were the one who'd randomly shown up on his front porch.

"Um...we need to work on our project?" His voice, which had started out strident, wavered towards the end, turning the statement into a question. He shifted nervously from foot to foot.

"How do you know where I live...? Wait, don't answer that. So you ignore me? Walk away when I'm speaking? Yet you think you can just show up on my doorstep?" I was rambling, I knew it, but this entire moment felt surreal. I half expected him to laugh in my face...and then stab me with the stick up his ass.

"Yes?" Kieran regarded me strangely.

"No!" I countered. "You need to do things the normal way. Get my number, ask what time we can meet up, and then go to the designated meeting place."

An undefinable expression crossed Kieran's icy face. It was there and gone too quickly for me to read.

"So can we work on the project?" he asked, hoisting his backpack farther up his shoulder.

"No! You didn't ask me for my number!"

What was wrong with me, you might ask? A lot. A whole freaking lot.

Kieran's expression had transformed from impassive to downright confused. I didn't entirely blame him. Even I still struggled to understand what I was saying.

"Can I have your number?" he asked tentatively.

"Nope."

Without another word, I slammed the door shut. *Take that, asshole! You ignore me, I shut the door on you!*

*Badass Camila.*

*Badass bitch.*

*Badass—*

My phone began to ring from where it was tucked into my waistband, and I pulled it out.

"Hello?" I asked.

Silence.

"This is Kieran. I got your number from Facebook," a gruff voice said over the line. I couldn't help the involuntary smirk that pulled up my lips.

"Kieran who?"

There was an exasperated grunt on the other line, but that only made my smile widen. Oh yes. This was sweet revenge. Who needed blood and death when you could cause greater damage just by annoying the shit out of someone?

"Your lab partner," he responded through clenched teeth. "I was wondering if you wanted to meet up to work on our project."

"I would love to. What time?"

"Now?"

I pretended to consider it.

"How about in an hour?"

There was a longer pause this time, and I could've sworn I heard him cuss me out under his breath.

"Are you fucking kidding me?"

"Would you prefer two hours?" I asked innocently.

Another prolonged silence. I awaited his answer with bated breath.

"One hour would be perfect."

"Great! So let's meet at your house! What's the address?"

"I was thinking we could meet at your house. I'm already in the area," he responded dryly.

I sighed dramatically.

"I suppose I could make that work. I'll see you in an hour!"

Before he could say anything else or argue with me for my admittedly childish behavior, I hung up the phone.

The bastard could wait outside for all the shits I gave.

~

I LIED.

I had too much of a conscience to leave the asshole outside for an hour.

After quickly changing into clean clothes and throwing my wet hair into a messy bun—I wasn't trying to impress the jerk—I hopped down the stairs and opened the door. Feigning nonchalance, I leaned against the wooden frame.

*Be cool, Camila.*

"Waz up?" I muttered, crossing my arms over my chest and offering the brooding man a nod.

*'Waz up'? Really? I said be cool, not a wannabe gangster.*

"You're here early," I continued, and then facepalmed myself.

You know that feeling you have when you want to curl into a ball and die a slow and painful death?

Well, guess who had ten fingers and wanted to curl into a ball and die a slow and painful death? I'll give you a hint—it wasn't Santa.

God, I was going to agonize over these stupid decisions for months.

Me, enjoying a nice coffee five years later.

"OHMYGAWD! Do you remember when you totally embarrassed yourself in front of that cute guy?" I would say to myself.

Just another perk of living with anxiety.

"Are you going to invite me in?" Kieran asked. His face was as stoic as usual, but I thought his lips were tipped up marginally. Maybe. Hopefully.

Probably.

*Oh God. Now you're staring at his lips. Think, Camila. Think. What did he ask you?*

"You're in front of my house," I blurted. "And you're wearing different clothes. From school. Not that I looked or anything. Because that would be creepy. And I'm not creepy. You know what? Just ignore me. And kill me. Please."

Now I was positive I wasn't mistaken. Grumpy Kieran's lips were most definitely curved into a tentative smile.

"I had football after school," he replied, answering one of my babbled questions. I had to give him some credit—I couldn't even remember what I'd asked. "I changed after my shower."

"Shower. Great. I just took a bath."

Desperate for something to do, for something to save me from this horrific clusterfuck I found myself in, I leaned once more against the doorframe.

Yup. Just me. Holding up the house.

Productivity.

"Are we going to go inside?" Kieran inquired. From his tone, I suspected it wasn't the first time he'd suggested it.

"Inside? Yes. In. And to the side. So inside." Realizing that I was still blocking the doorway, I hurried farther in. Kieran, eyes cautious, followed after me. "Welcome to *mi casa*!" I extended my arms to encompass the entire house.

And then I did a little dance.

Did. A. Little. Dance.

*Why am I the way I am?*

Face burning, I immediately turned in the direction of the study. The last thing I wanted to do was go into the kitchen with Karissa. I would turn my normal switch on, and we would work on our project like two normal individuals. It shouldn't be that hard, right?

"TAKE YOUR SHOES OFF!" I screamed at Kieran a second before he would've stepped onto the white carpeting. I hadn't meant to scream at him. I had actually meant to nicely suggest that it would be much appreciated if he didn't stain our new carpeting. However, my mind was an incoherent mess of words and phrases and emotions. It didn't know how to process my request for calm. Calm, apparently, translated to complete and utter psycho in my good old brain.

When Kieran's eyes widened, I died a little bit inside.

Died.

Flipping on the study light, I bit my lip to keep from commenting on the clutter throughout the small room. Boxes upon boxes were balanced precariously on top of one another, and a desk sat, half set up, in the center of the room, directly across an unlit hearth. The only thing that Dad had put into the room were two leather chairs and a small black couch. It was the couch I sat on immediately, tucking my legs beneath my body. Kieran surprised me by sitting directly beside me, despite the two chairs opposite us. I could feel his warm thigh pressing against my own.

"You know," I began, anxiously twirling a loose strand of hair that had escaped its binding around my finger. "This all could've been avoided if you would've just given me your number in class. We could've texted which experiment we wanted to do instead of meeting up."

And as if it couldn't get any more awkward...

God, I was awful at conversing with people. Fiona would have probably slapped me for my incompetence.

Kieran's face turned a few shades redder.

"Anyways..." I turned towards my backpack, only to realize that I had completely forgotten it in my haste. Well crap. "I've seemed to have misplaced my rubric. Do you have yours?"

Wincing internally at how stupid I sounded, I watched Kieran dig through his backpack. He had long fingers, I realized almost dumbly. The pointer finger on his right hand was covered in ink. Was it just his pointer finger? How creepy would it be if I asked to check out his hand?

Maybe I could stealthily trip into him and look at—

Shaking my head, I waited impatiently for him to pull out the rubric.

"Tomorrow, we're doing the lab portion," Kieran read, reiterating what we'd already been told in class. "And then the report and poster themselves are due in two weeks."

He handed me the paper, the long sleeves of his jacket brushing against my clammy skin. It was smothering hot inside of the house, but Kieran didn't seem inclined to take off his jacket. Not that I blamed him. He looked quite good in the letterman jacket, displaying the blue and gold colors of the school. Quite good indeed.

*Focus*, I mentally scolded myself, prying the paper from his fingers. I read through the examples the teacher had given us.

"I like this one," I admitted at last, pointing to a suggestion farther down the page. Kieran leaned towards me to see which one I was referring to, and I got a whiff of his spicy cologne. It was a manly scent, one that I would associate with ruggedness and being outdoors. Okay, so maybe my perverted mind pictured a lumberjack. Bite me.

Kieran could totally pull off the lumberjack look if he allowed his hair to grow out and added a beard...

"The dehydration of sugar," Kieran read. "Sounds easy enough."

"And actually kind of interesting. I would much rather work with sugar than alkali metals."

Kieran nodded, pulling a pencil out of his bag to circle the topic. He wrote a few notes in the margins, but I couldn't read his small handwriting.

"I'll email the teacher when I get back."

Without another word, Kieran began to put his books and binders back into his bag. Each movement made his arm brush against my own. I wondered if he was doing it intentionally. I mean, it was a pretty big couch. He didn't have to sit so close to me.

When he stood up and headed in the direction of the door, I blurted out, "Do you want to stay for dinner?"

I honestly couldn't tell you why I'd asked that. Maybe I wasn't that horrible of a human being.

Or maybe it was because of the sadness in his eyes, the despondency that hinted at something I couldn't even begin to understand. I wondered if he was fighting against the same darkness I was.

Kieran paused in the doorway.

"I really should get home," he responded after a moment. His voice was different than I had heard it before, gruffer, as if he was trying to restrain some emotion.

Shrugging, I followed him outside. The sky was turning gray, and the trees on the horizon looked almost menacing with their darkened silhouettes, like monsters extending their long arms. I'd always had an irrational fear of forests, especially at night.

"Do you have a ride?" I asked, noting the lack of cars in the driveway.

Kieran shrugged.

"I can walk."

"How far away do you live? I could give you a ride."

What I actually meant was that I could find someone to give him a ride. To be completely honest, it was kind of an empty offer. I would feel like a dick if he took me up on it.

"It's fine."

He quickened his pace, and a self-conscious part within

me wondered if he was trying to get away. From me. From my quirks.

"Thanks for visiting the Camila Hotel!" I called, waving a hand. I cringed at how idiotic I sounded.

Camila Hotel? Really?

I stood on the front porch, mentally berating myself over my own stupidity, until Kieran disappeared around the corner. I released my breath in a long exhale.

"Well, that was pathetic," a familiar voice observed slyly. I turned towards the fence, unsurprised to see Dorian's shaggy blond hair peeking over the top. "You are horrible at talking to people."

"And you're horrible at stalking people," I retorted. "Aren't you supposed to silently watch? I never asked for your input."

"But you sure do need it." Even from the distance, I could see that his face was twisted into a smirk. "Camila Hotel? Really?"

"Oh, shut up."

Turning on my heel, I stepped back into the foyer.

"Have you figured it out yet?" he called, seconds before I was going to shut the door. His words made me pause, my curiosity spiking.

"Figured out what yet?"

He rested his head on his arms.

"That your house is a gateway to Hell."

Of course.

Of freaking course.

Rolling my eyes, I slammed the door on my strange neighbor.

# 8

"Hey, bitch!"

I started at the voice, nearly dropping the books I was attempting to remove from my locker. Glancing over my shoulder, I met familiar azure eyes and vibrant, lilac hair.

"Hi, Phoebe."

Beside her, hands shoved into his pockets, was Tyson. His two "girlfriends" trailed along behind him. And behind *them* were the other few boys I recognized from the restaurant. They all wore identical, black leather jackets and had their hair slicked back. Obviously, they took their conformity very seriously here.

"Phe, we talked about this," Ty murmured indolently, eyes flicking over to me. He did not look impressed. "No talking with the new girl."

"Wow. You're a real piece of work, you know that, right?" I snapped, and there was a collective gasp from the remaining students in the hall. I could've sworn they were all staring at me, at us, waiting to see what would happen.

Who needed movies when you had sweet, little Camila shoving her foot into her mouth?

Ty's voice was cold when he spoke next.

"What do you mean by that?"

Ignoring the shake of Phoebe's head, warning me against saying anything more, I added, "It means that you're kind of an asshole."

I wasn't one for swearing, but Ty? I felt he deserved it. And more.

One of the boys in the Breakfast Club made a move as if to lunge for me. Instinctively, I pressed myself further against my locker.

What the hell was his problem? Was this the "insult one Breakfast Club member, insult them all" type of mentality?

Ty held up a fist, and the guy immediately backed down with a few choice words. It really made my asshole comment sound like a compliment.

Without breaking eye contact, Ty walked the remaining steps until he was only an inch away from me. I could see his eyes, a honey-soaked brown, and the faintest trace of a scar just above his lip.

"I would be careful about who you insult, beautiful." The word on his lips, in his voice, would've made any normal girl melt. It was raspy and sultry, caressing every bit of me. Fortunately, I was immune to cheesy endearments, especially when I knew them not to be true.

"Don't call me beautiful," I hissed. Because I wasn't.

Not even Jaron called me beautiful.

"Don't call me an asshole," Ty countered. He radiated a male smugness that I found immensely irritating. He wasn't charming, wasn't sexy.

He was just freaking annoying.

"I call them how I see them," I responded at last.

Turning back towards my locker, I grabbed my math book and shoved it into my bag. I wouldn't need it until after lunch, but the cafeteria was opposite the lockers in the school. There wasn't enough time for me to go back for the damn thing and still make it to class on time.

Ty lazily leaned against the locker beside me. I noticed, somewhat absently, that the rest of his little group hovered nearby. They weren't close enough to be in hearing distance, but they were well within eyesight.

And all of them were taking full advantage of that little fact.

The stares, and glares in some cases, penetrated my skin like thousands of tiny knives. I felt almost dirty under their combined weight.

Why wouldn't Ty just leave me alone?

"I think I know the real problem," he vocalized suddenly.

"And what might that be?"

Really, at this point, I was humoring him. The asshole was getting on my last nerve.

I felt his breath against my ear, and goosebumps erupted on my skin. It was an instinctive reaction. I dare any of you to have someone breathe on your neck and *not* break out in goosebumps. Seriously. Dare you.

"It's because I got you wet," he whispered. I most definitely did not miss the sexual innuendo in that simple statement.

Because, dammit, it was true.

"Real mature," I snapped. "I already thought of that joke yesterday."

My face burned once I realized what I'd just said. I wished that I had a time machine just to slap the stupidity out of me. Maybe that would spare me the embarrassment of my own words.

The shocked expression on Ty's face, though, as I finally gathered my bearings and walked away?

Totally worth it.

~

"Hello, lab partner," I greeted Kieran, sliding onto the stool in the lab. It was a small room, a couple doors down from the classroom, and had large black tables that held about twenty kids, ten on each side.

Kieran, the ever eloquent man, grunted in reply.

Apparently, we still hadn't moved from nonsensical noises to actual conversation and words. Maybe if I grunted in response, Kieran would respect me. I could totally get behind that. I could be the grunt champion. Grunt badass.

"So do you know what supplies we'll need for the lab?" I asked conversationally.

Kieran, of course, didn't respond.

"Cool story. Glad we had this chat," I added.

Still nothing.

Mr. Henry arrived then, wheeling in a cart with what looked like glass beakers and measuring cylinders on it.

He gave the standard lab safety speech before setting us free. I turned towards Kieran expectantly, only to find him... already gone.

Okay then.

I watched the larger man's nimble fingers gather the materials necessary for the assignment. He didn't say one word to me as he carefully began measuring sulfuric acid.

He didn't ask for my help once during the lab.

He also didn't say one word to me.

Second day of school?

Freaking peachy, thank you for asking.

～

OKAY, SO YOU WOULD THINK THAT I WOULD HAVE LEARNED MY lesson by now.

Before school? Annoyed by Tyson.

During chemistry? Ignored by Kieran.

During lunch?

Dah dah dum.

The twisted twins.

I had just placed my lunch tray down when I was immediately surrounded by Ginger One and Ginger Two.

Ginger One—Leroy, if I remembered correctly—was wearing bright red suspenders over a brown shirt. His red hair was covered by what I assumed was his customary fedora.

The other twin, Luke, wore a Superman T-shirt and ripped jeans.

Without waiting for an invitation, Leroy dropped his lunch bag onto the table across from me and sat down.

"Oh, what do we have today?" he asked, eagerly pouring the contents of his lunch onto the table. "A jelly sandwich. Yummy!" He hummed happily and began picking at the crust with his long fingers.

I glanced at the twin still standing, eyebrows raised as if to ask, "Is he for real?"

Luke just shrugged helplessly.

"Can I help you?" I asked after a long, oddly sensual moment of watching Leroy rub the crust between his thumb and forefinger.

He glanced up, as if startled that I was there.

"No...unless you're not going to eat that brownie. Then you could help by giving it to me. After that, *lettuce* have a conversation."

Without waiting for my response—but really? Should I have expected anything else?—he grabbed the brownie from my plate and shoved it into his mouth. I had to admit that I found the twins...endearing. And kind of adorable. They made the new girl feel comfortable, which wasn't an easy feat.

"I suppose you can have it."

There must've been something in the water here—something that made all of the men act very strange and erratic. That was the only plausible explanation I could come up with.

Or maybe I just attracted the crazies. Again, no surprise.

I flicked my eyes up towards Luke, still awkwardly standing with his tray of cafeteria food, before letting out a sigh.

"Sit down and eat. Don't just stand there acting as if I have cooties."

Luke blinked down at me, frowned, then obediently slid into the seat beside me. He made sure to sit as far away from me as possible, a nice change from Asshole One and Asshole Two I'd had to deal with earlier.

"So, did you decide to take us up on that offer?" Leroy, the fedora wearing twin, queried.

"Offer?"

All I could think about was their previous comments about penis size. Did they want me to...measure?

"About your house." He hadn't even bothered to look up at me while he talked. Instead, he began to shovel grape after grape into his mouth.

"My house isn't haunted," I insisted with an eye roll.

*Gangs and Ghosts* | 83

Yup. Definitely the water.

"Oh yeah? Are you sure about that? Luke, the facts." Leroy tapped his fingers against the table, and Luke pulled a mound of papers out of his bag. Without a word, he slid them in front of me.

"What am I looking at?" I asked, glancing from twin to twin. Luke's face was sullen, but Leroy's was alit with a mischievous smirk.

"Proof, my beautiful new friend."

Again with the endearments.

With a sigh of defeat, I flipped through the pages displayed. Most of them were printed newspaper articles and police reports. Did they expect me to read all of them in the half hour of lunch?

Really, I was more of the "skim through" type of person.

"You're not going to read them, are you?" Luke asked softly from beside me.

"It's just a lot of words," I muttered meekly. A lot of words while I was functioning on only one cup of coffee. No thanks.

Leroy made a sound of indignation and pointed to the first article. It appeared to be an older one from the picture, and one check at the date confirmed as much—1889.

It was odd to see a black and white, slightly blurry photo on a printed sheet of perfectly white paper. It was like new and old existing in an almost uncanny harmony.

The picture appeared to be that of a church, though certain areas of the photo were faded. Besides that? There was nothing of interest on the page.

And no, I didn't read the words.

Shut up.

"June 11, 1856. A church was built directly where your house is at. Years later, on July 27, 1889, all of the churchgoers, all thirty-two of them, were found dead—eyes gouged out, teeth removed, arms disconnected from their bodies."

"Well, that's pleasant lunch conversation." I stared at my pizza slice in dismay.

Ignoring me, Leroy continued, "There were no witnesses. Police found their burnt bodies days after the incident. There were bugs everywhere, crawling out of floorboards and the eyes of the deceased. All of the people had somehow been burned, yet the building still stood."

"Okay, so they were attacked by a serial killer. I don't see how that—"

"The man who found the bodies claimed that he saw their killer. He claimed that the killer spoke to him. He told the police that it was a shadow man," Leroy finished, and my body grew cold. That name...

It was just a coincidence. Besides, he referred to it as *a* shadow man, not *the* Shadow Man.

"A shadow man," I repeated.

Leroy pointed to another picture, this one of a family standing in front of a wooden door. A mom, a dad, and two beautiful little girls.

"On December 12, 1932, the littlest daughter murdered her entire family. Their house? Right over the plot of land where you're currently living. When she was questioned by the police, she kept repeating that the Shadow Man made her do it."

There was a constant buzzing in my ears. It was getting louder and louder as the seconds dragged on. He had to stop talking. My heart thumped at an irregular rhythm inside of my chest, and my stomach threatened to expel what little food I had eaten for lunch.

"March 22, 1956. An entire family was found with their throats slit. There were no witnesses, and neighbors claimed that they hadn't seen anyone around the house. The police couldn't find any sign of forced entry."

The pounding in my head was intensifying.

"October 15, 1973. A young couple claimed that they were haunted by the ghosts of the deceased. They said that they could see women in fancy dresses walking with their arms detached from their bodies. Little boys with their throats cut. Men with—"

"That's enough!" Luke snapped coldly.

"—ropes around their necks—"

"I said that's enough!" Luke's voice broke through the chatter like the crack of a whip. Leroy's mouth clamped shut immediately. "Don't you see her face? She's as white as a fucking sheet!"

Leroy finally glanced up from where he was analyzing the articles. He winced at whatever he saw in my expression.

"I'm sorry," he mumbled, rubbing at his neck.

I felt as if I was going to vomit.

So much death. So much destruction.

*It was just what he always wanted.*

I didn't know where that thought came from, and that, more than anything else, scared the crap out of me.

So much death...

The darkness inside of me purred happily.

# 9

My brother bombarded me the second I stepped inside of the house after school.

Thankfully, he was actually dressed this time, though the stained white shirt and ripped pants were a very questionable choice for clothing. His hair was tousled yet again, as if he hadn't bothered to put a brush through it.

"Little sis!" he called, picking me up and spinning me in a circle.

"Put me down, you idiot!" I pounded his back, and he obediently set me on my feet.

You see, ladies? Even assholes like my brother understood when no means no.

"What do you want, Colt?" I demanded, throwing my backpack onto the couch. I was starving, and my stupid stomach growled in agreement. I most definitely needed a post-school snack. Preferably something with chocolate.

"Why can't I just be excited to see my baby sister?" Colt reasoned. He followed me into the kitchen and leaned against the counter. I rolled my eyes.

"So you don't want anything from me?"

With a gleeful whoop, I pulled out a container of chocolate ice cream. Dad must've been busy, because the entire kitchen was now fully stocked with every type of food imaginable—fish fillets, what looked like glazed strawberries, ripe bananas.

Thank you, Dad.

"Okay, so maybe I do want something."

"Wow. You don't say?"

I grabbed a bowl and spoon from the cupboards and proceeded to scoop out the chocolate heaven. If I could just live off chocolate without getting fat, you would never see me eat broccoli again. Seriously, I had a complete distrust for any and all broccoli lovers. That shit tasted like...well, shit.

"So my girlfriend is coming over tonight—"

"Crystal? I thought you guys broke up?"

"Not Crystal." Colt gave me a look that suggested I was an imbecile for even thinking such a thing. Well, excuse me. How was I supposed to know that my brother had gotten a new girlfriend in the four days we'd been here? The man worked fast. "She plays the piano, and she knows someone who plays the drums."

"I still don't understand what that has to do with me," I stated, taking my ice cream back into the living room. Colt followed behind me, yet again, like a helpless puppy.

"Well, I know how you like to sing..."

"Stop right there." I spun on my heel and jabbed a finger into Colt's chest. "I'm not going to sing for you."

The expression on his face was almost comical—lower lip protruding into a pout, and eyelashes feathering against his cheekbones rapidly. He looked as if he hadn't even considered me saying no.

"But—"

"I don't sing."

I had stopped months ago, ever since Jaron had teased me about it. He'd told me that my voice was too raspy, too seductive, and it was embarrassing to listen to. He'd also told me that people would assume I was a whore if I sang the songs I did, the way I did.

Fiona had agreed.

"What can I do to get you to change your mind?" He snapped his fingers, as if he had a grand epiphany. "How about we pull out the old wig? Do you remember it?"

I frowned. Of course I remembered it. It was nearly impossible to completely eradicate the way I felt when I put on the fake blonde hair. The darkness cooed happily low inside of my belly at the memory.

I shivered involuntarily. The seductive pull of the darkness was getting stronger and stronger. Just the thought of transforming into my other self, my darker self, sent pinpricks of desire through me.

"I'll consider it," I said at last, knowing that those were the only words besides an exact yes that could appease my brother. And I also knew that I would never say yes. Something that appealing could be considered a drug, and drugs could only lead to death.

∽

After finishing my math homework, I finally gained the courage to explore the rest of the house.

First stop? The closet and secret room.

I hadn't bothered to hang up any of my clothes yet, so the white wall and steel rod were the first things that greeted me when I opened the wooden closet door. The apparent "door" in the closet was easy to spot—a rectangular outline near the bottom of the wall.

Crawling on my hands and knees, I felt the sharp outer edge of the door. The plaster moved easily away, revealing nothing but darkness. I used the sparse flashlight on my phone to illuminate the diminutive hole.

The "room" was small, significantly smaller than even the closet. It barely fitted two people, and even then, the two people would have to sit practically on top of one another.

I groaned.

Really? All that buildup only led to that?

I shouldn't have been surprised or disappointed. What had I expected? An indoor amusement park with Zac Efron as their only employee?

Still, I couldn't help but glower at the hole.

Positioning the plaster so it once again settled snugly against the wall, I sat back on my heels.

Well that was...disappointing and entirely anticlimactic.

"Cami! Get your ass down here!"

I jumped, startled by the strident voice reverberating from somewhere downstairs.

"What do you want, Colt?" I yelled back.

"Get down here, and I'll tell you!"

"No! Come up here and tell me!"

"Seriously, get down here!"

I knew one of us would have to cave. We both had strong personalities, magnetic personalities as my parents would say, but like any magnet with the same charge, we clashed. Propelled ourselves away from one another, both physically and emotionally. I loved my brother, but I would never understand him.

Still, I could be the bigger person.

Grumbling beneath my breath, I shut my closet and headed towards the basement door. It was the one level of the house I hadn't entered. Colt had claimed that it was "his space" and "his space only." Those were exact quotes. My brother tended to speak in the third person when he got overly excited.

I knocked on the door, foot tapping with increasing speed as the seconds dragged on and Colt still didn't answer. I was going to murder him.

Finally, *finally*, the door opened, and my brother's golden blond hair appeared.

"Camila! Come!"

Without waiting for a response, he hopped down the staircase. I just barely resisted the urge to throw a shoe at his head.

"What's so important that you couldn't walk upstairs and tell me yourself?" I huffed, following him down.

The basement was dimly lit, a dangling bulb flickering at intermittent intervals in the center of the room. My brother had set up a couch against the far wall and a simple cot against the other. There were still numerous unpacked boxes balanced on top of one another. The single table was completely covered with empty chip bags and beer bottles.

It was in the "studio"—a closet-sized room with a drum kit, an amp, and a small keyboard—that I saw them.

Well, him. I recognized her lilac hair, of course, but she was barely a dot on my radar.

No, my perverted mind was utterly focused on him and him alone.

The sweat dripping down his tattooed, bronzed skin.

The disheveled hair pushed away from his face.

His long fingers tapping an unfamiliar pattern against his jean-clad leg.

My inner self immediately began to whine.

Why did all of the assholes have to be so hot?

"Camila!" Phoebe screamed when she noticed me. I was immediately engulfed in her tiny arms, the pungent smell of her perfume nearly overwhelming.

I patted her back awkwardly.

"Hi, Phe."

Once she finally released me, Ty took a step towards me.

"Don't I get a hug?" he asked.

"I'm sure Colt will give you one if you ask nicely," I quipped, carefully avoiding looking at all of that skin on display. I would not be caught staring at him like some drooling fool.

One would think I had never seen a naked chest before. Besides, it wasn't that impressive at all. Just...an eight-pack. Not sexy. Nope.

Jaron had a better chest. A sexier chest. And he had man nipples.

Not that Ty didn't have man nipples or anything...

*Jaron. Think of Jaron.*

That thought instantly cooled me down.

Turning my back to the asshole, I glared up at my brother.

"What's all this?"

"So I told you about my girlfriend—"

"Girlfriend?"

Phoebe and Colt?

Stranger things had happened.

"I'm not technically your girlfriend," Phoebe piped up. "The rules are strict. You know that."

Rules? Was she was referring to the Barney and Friends club or something else entirely? Did it have something to do with the asshole? I may not have known her that well, but I would most definitely get involved if I discovered he was emotionally abusing her. I didn't care if that made me a nosey bitch. Women always seemed to have this mentality that we had to stab one another in the back. I'd never understood such dark thoughts. We were victims in a society that had us low on the totem pole. The only way we would survive would be if we stood together.

"Anyway," Colt drawled, reverting my attention back towards him. "I played them that song you wrote. 'Summer Love.' They agreed to join Fire Ball!"

First, yes, I did try to convince my brother to change the band name. No, it did not work.

Second, I knew exactly where he was going with that little spiel. He knew how I felt about singing. He knew how vulnerable I'd felt ever since Jaron had shattered my self-esteem.

"You know I don't sing anymore."

"Because one asshole made you cry!" Colt snapped, and I blanched at the venom in his voice.

"Who made her cry?" Ty asked, though he sounded as if he couldn't care less. Well, screw him.

Not screw him. Ew. No.

"Her stupid boyfriend, Jaron." Colt hissed his name as if it were acid on his tongue. As if it were a curse word and he was in church. I knew that Colt had never been a fan of my boyfriend, but I had never heard such hostility before. I blinked up at him, startled by his behavior.

"You have a boyfriend?" Phoebe squealed. Ty had straightened from where he was indolently leaning against the wall. His eyes were narrowed.

"What did he say?" he questioned dangerously.

"It doesn't matter what he said," I evaded, and my eyes dared Colt to contradict me and continue the conversation. My brother glared right back. It became a contest of wills—

my dark eyes locked with his light ones. The energy was almost palpable in the air. It was me who looked away first, internally cursing myself for being weak.

"Fine. One song," I said with a growl. Colt let out a gleeful squeal. The glorious smile on his face made a tentative one tilt up my own lips. I loved seeing my brother happy, even if I had to be miserable for him to be so.

"Do they even know 'Summer Love'?" I asked, nodding towards Phoebe and Asshole.

I had decided that Tyson wasn't worthy of being referred to by his name. From this day forth, he would forever be called Asshole.

"We have the music! It's amazing!" Phoebe gushed. Ty—excuse me, Asshole merely shrugged.

"It's okay."

"Well, your face is okay," I retorted.

*Real smooth, Camila. Really smooth.*

Face burning, I turned towards the microphone stand in the center of the room. It was directly in front of the drum set. The room was so small that my butt would practically be in Asshole's face.

The microphone didn't actually work. That, along with the stand, were bought for my brother a few years earlier for Christmas. He had broken them only three months later. Now, he used them as a tool for me to "get into character."

As if he expected me to...

"I found this in your drawer," Colt said, grinning impishly. He held up a blonde wig.

"You went through my drawers?"

"Well, duh." He didn't seem at all perturbed by my outrage. Stupid brother.

*Have a big brother*, they said.
*It'll be fun*, they said.

*He'll protect you*, they said.

No, what they failed to mention was that big brothers farted on your face until you passed out and locked you out of the house for five hours in a snowstorm. Those little details were just conveniently left out of the pamphlet.

"You have a wig," Asshole declared.

"Real perceptive, asshole," I muttered. He made a sound in the back of his throat, but I couldn't decide if it was anger or amusement.

"You don't have to perform with us ever again," Colt hurried to assure me. "I just need you to sing this one time, for them to get a feel of the song. Please?"

He began to pout again. Grown men really shouldn't pout. It made them look ridiculous and slightly constipated.

"Fine!"

I could sing one song. I could put on the wig for three minutes.

Grabbing a ponytail off of my wrist, I threw my hair into a messy bun. Then, heart pounding, I put on the wig.

The feeling was exhilarating. Suddenly, I was weightless. The world no longer scared me. I had the strength to fight off the monsters.

The wig had always given me confidence. I knew it was only a mental thing, but the elation it brought with it was all too real.

"There she is," Colt exclaimed happily. I flashed him a smile.

"Here she is."

Without waiting for his response, I sauntered towards the microphone. Colt moved towards his guitar, and Phoebe trailed her fingers over the piano. Ty remained standing, staring at me with a raised eyebrow.

I gave him a sultry smirk and a wink.

"Are you just going to stand there, or are you going to put your stick to good use?"

His eyes widened, but I had already turned away.

"Try not to screw up too badly," I muttered.

Colt began to strum the guitar immediately, followed by the familiar notes from the piano. Finally, Ty joined in.

I tapped my foot against the ground, the music rising within me. I could feel each beat, each note, as if they were an extension of my body.

Finally, I began to sing.

"*Do you feel the wind? The air? The rain? The roaring in my face as I wait for you. Do you taste my skin, in the heat, in the dark? Do you remember what it felt like when you had my heart?*"

My body swayed to the music.

"*Summer love, guide me away. Summer love, I have no say. Love me, and please me, and take me in your arms.*"

As I sang, I began to lightly run my hands over my body. Jaron had always hated when I did that. He'd said it made me look slutty and needy.

One could argue that I did it for those exact reasons.

Grabbing the microphone, I pulled it off the stand.

Instinctively, my eyes slid towards Tyson. He wasn't even watching the drums—his gaze was fixated solely on me.

Feeling powerful and sexy, I continued to meet his stare as I sung about a tryst on the beach. My hands slid lazily up my body, hitting the side of my breasts.

I swore that he wasn't even breathing.

We didn't break eye contact until the very last note. I licked my lips, and his eyes zeroed in on that motion.

Offering one last smile, I turned my back on the strangely seductive man.

Fortunately, Colt and Phoebe seemed unaware of the

awkward exchange between Ty and me. They were too busy eye-stripping one another.

Ew. Ew. Ew.

"Wasn't that amazing?" Colt screamed.

"Holy shit! Your voice is incredible!" Phoebe added.

Aware of the eyes still on my back, I shrugged.

"Wasn't my greatest performance."

"Wasn't your... Holy crap! You have to sing with us for our first show!" Phoebe was practically vibrating with excitement.

"This was a one-time thing," I reminded. My voice was still low and husky. Sultry, almost. Putting a little extra sway in my step, I waggled my fingers as a goodbye. I knew that Ty's eyes were on my ass. I could physically feel them caressing my skin. It was erotic and empowering at the same time.

It was only later, when I finally removed the blonde wig, that shame and regret filled me.

Oh god. What had I done?

I had sung, something I had sworn to never do again. And I had also flirted with Tyson. No words had been spoken, but none needed to be. How could I have done that to Jaron?

Gasping at the consuming pain, I tried to ignore the gleeful cheer from the darkness inside of me. The darkness relished in the attention, in the power of Ty's stare.

It only made me hate myself more.

## 10

The rest of the week was agonizingly long.

Each morning, Ty would park his truck outside of my house. He would always ask if I wanted a ride, and I would always refuse. Instead of taking the hint, he decided to ride slowly beside me, chatting about anything and everything. Sometimes, Phoebe would be with him, but other times, he would come by himself. He always ended our morning routine begging me to consider joining the band.

The band. He said it as if it was his band, as if he hadn't just joined a couple of days earlier.

On Friday, he surprised me by taking our interaction a step further. He walked me to my chemistry class and sat down beside me. I caught a few glares from the other girls. Even his group of friends—the Mickey Mouse Clubhouse—would glower at me. I still had yet to understand why they disliked me talking to Ty and what exactly their group was.

During chemistry, I exchanged only a few words with Kieran. Despite his lack of communication skills, I thought that the big, scary man was warming up to me. If anything, he didn't scowl at me as often. We still had yet to meet outside of class to work on our assignment, though I wasn't overly worried. I had come to realize that Kieran was a genius at chemistry. The Friday Ty had walked me to class, Kieran had arrived early as well. I found that surprising. The man almost always walked into class the second before the bell rang. When Kieran took note of Ty sitting beside me, his eyes narrowed into thin slits. The two engaged in a heated standoff, Kieran towering over Ty, while the other man's almost elemental fury made up for his submissive posture. Ty waited until the bell rang before reluctantly grabbing his bag and flashing me a wink.

"See you later," he'd said, and Kieran's expression had darkened even further.

At lunch, I sat with the ginger twins. When they weren't bugging me about my house, I found them to be quite enjoyable. Leroy was hilarious. He had a natural wit that presented itself in every word he spoke. Luke was more soft-spoken than his eccentric brother. More reserved.

"Did you know," Leroy began conversationally, his fingers drumming against the table, "that the youngest parents are five and six years old?"

"How would you know that?" I asked, just as Luke said, "Don't tell her your life story."

Leroy gave me a look. Today, he was wearing a black suit coat, his signature fedora, and brown pants. Luke wore another superhero T-shirt, this one Batman, and blue jeans. The twins, I began to realize, were as different as night and day.

"I read it on the internet," he defended indignantly. I exchanged a look with Luke. It was our standard "what is wrong with him?" expression.

"The internet isn't always true," I pointed out, offering

him the brownie on my plate. That was another one of our daily rituals. I never understood why Leroy didn't just buy a brownie himself, but there was a lot about Leroy I had yet to understand.

"Don't look now, but Tyson Michaels is staring at you," Luke muttered under his breath.

"Michaels? Is that his last name?" I asked. I didn't know why I was surprised. Of course he had a last name. I supposed I just expected it to be Asshole or Douchebag or something of the sort. Michaels just made him seem more... human. Normal.

Non-assholeish.

"Wait? Do you know him?" Leroy was staring at me as if I had suddenly sprouted wings, grew three heads, and began stripping.

"I suppose." I shrugged, taking a tentative bite of my turkey sandwich. The "turkey" was more red than pink, but I was too hungry to care. "He and his sister are over at my house almost every day. They joined my brother's band, and Phoebe's dating him." I shrugged yet again, confused by their incredulous expressions. One would think I was talking about the devil doing a Dutch dance in my backyard.

"Look, Cami..." Luke began. Leroy, for once, was struck speechless.

"What? You guys are acting weird."

Well, weirder than usual, that was.

"Phoebe and Ty don't hang out with anyone outside of their group. Ever," Leroy said. For once, there was no humor in his voice.

"So they have their friend group. What's wrong with that?" At my old school, everybody had their clique. The volleyball girls, the football guys, the cheerleaders, the partiers. School was its own separate entity, its own separate world, with various divides. Why would this be any different?

"You don't understand," Luke stressed, lowering his voice. I gave him a "duh" look. Of course I didn't understand. I didn't speak in riddles.

"Oh for the love of..." Leroy leaned across the table. "They're in a gang."

Well.

I hadn't expected that.

"What?" I asked, blinking rapidly. I must've heard him wrong. This was a small town, after all. There weren't any gangs in small towns. Hell, I had barely seen any gang members in Chicago, though I did go to a private school.

Was it just a term the twins used to describe Ty's friend group?

"A gang," Leroy repeated bluntly. "They live on the east side of town—the bad side. They call themselves the Creepers. There are about fifty different members."

"A gang." My voice sounded strange to my ears.

"Tyson and Phoebe are practically royalty," Luke added. He glanced anxiously over his shoulder, as if he was afraid he would be overheard. "Their parents are Molly and Big Pete."

Okay, that was almost comical. Molly and Big Pete. Really? Why not Little Molly?

"Am I supposed to know them?" I asked.

Luke leaned closer to me until his breath was caressing my ear.

"Molly and Big Pete are the leaders."

The onslaught of information was staggering. Colt was dating a gang princess? And what exactly did their gang do? Rape and murder and pillage? Or was that reserved for pirates? I had never heard of these Creepers before, even with my dad being a cop. I knew that the twins had a tendency to overexaggerate things, but there was something about their words that rang true. It would most definitely explain Phoebe's hesitancy to become my friend and Ty's imperious behavior. It would also explain the aggressiveness and protectiveness of the group, especially when I insulted Tyson.

The word was almost comical. Gang. I automatically envisioned prison felons with teardrop tattoos. It was odd for me to associate the crude term with someone as vibrant as Phoebe. Even Ty didn't seem to fit the mold and stereotype attached to that term.

Gang.

Could it be true?

Well, shit. I really wasn't in the mood to piss off a gang prince.

"Their rules are really strict," Leroy continued, oblivious to my inner turmoil. "They aren't allowed to develop relationships with people outside of the Creepers. If they do, the partner must be inducted or the member risks banishment."

"But Phoebe's dating my brother," I protested. From what I could see, they seemed to really like each other—in a way that two people who have only known each other a few days could like each other.

"Maybe she plans on getting him to join," Leroy suggested with a shrug. That thought made me nauseous.

Colt? In a gang? A few days ago, I would've laughed at how ridiculous that sounded. The worst thing he had ever done was accidentally steal a turkey the day before Thanksgiving. In his defense, he'd put it in the bottom of the cart and merely forgotten to pay for it when he'd reached the checkout lane. It wasn't intentional by any means. But this?

Willingly joining a group that called themselves the Creepers?

Did I even know my brother?

Was he aware of who his girlfriend actually was?

And why was Tyson continually pestering me? If what the twins said was true, he wouldn't be able to fully join the band nor develop a friendship with me. What was his angle?

*God, he must be so lonely.*

"They're rivals with this other gang called the Black Hawks. Like, *murder* rivals."

Shaking my head, I picked at the crust on my sandwich. My mind spun in circles, developing question after question that demanded answers I wouldn't, and couldn't, receive.

"I don't want to talk about gangs anymore," I said shakily. "Let's talk about something else." Before Leroy could respond, I added, "And no ghosts either."

Gangs and ghosts and assholes.

Those topics should be banned from conversation.

## 11

The Friday night lights were the only familiar thing in my life.

Every Friday, without fail, I would paint my face green and gold with Fiona. We would stand in the student section, me holding a large poster with Jaron's number painted on it and Fiona wearing her boyfriend-of-the-week's away game jersey. The lights, the sounds, the excitement.

It was as familiar to me as breathing.

But there was no Fiona to talk to. No Jaron to cheer on from the crowd.

No, according to Fiona's Instagram account, she was wearing *his* jersey to tonight's game. The thought made me feel sick, but not in the way that I'd expected to be. I was more annoyed than anything else. I wasn't stupid enough to believe that nothing was going on between the two of them, but did they have to announce their affair so bluntly?

And why wasn't I more upset? Shouldn't I be crying hysterically?

I'd loved Jaron only a week earlier. At least I'd thought I did.

Shaking my head to clear my muddled thoughts, I focused on the game.

Phoebe was right—Kieran was good. Really good. He had a strong, accurate arm, and he was surprisingly fast, despite his lumbering frame. When I heard that Kieran played football, I'd expected him to be a linebacker or a center. The guy was huge, muscle upon muscle accentuated clearly through the thin shirts he always seemed inclined to wear. I hadn't expected him to be their starting quarterback, much less be amazing at it.

By halftime, the score was forty to zero. Our school had decided to go for the two-point conversion after all five touchdowns. With Kieran as our quarterback, we had no trouble getting into the end zone.

"That boy has an arm," Papa observed, clapping along with the rest of the fans as the team retreated into the locker room for halftime.

"Speaking of football, how has Jaron been doing?" Dad inquired. He reached over me, towards Colt, and grabbed a handful of popcorn. Colt glared at my father for stealing a snack paid for by his "hard-earned money."

That was sarcastic, by the way. My idiot brother had found three quarters in the couch when he helped set it up and one quarter in his pocket. Apparently, that was considered "hard work" now in my brother's distorted mind.

Phoebe sat next to Colt, her lilac hair pulled back into a braid. Ty was sitting in the row behind her.

Directly behind me.

I could feel his knees pressing against my back with each movement I made. The stadium was crowded at tonight's game, and there was barely any room between bodies.

I tried to ignore Ty. His presence, as vibrant as a flame in the dark. His musky scent. His voice with its deep timbre. His gruff laugh.

I knew, even without looking, that he had a girl on either side of him—two female members of his gang, if I believed the rumors.

Papa automatically reached for a handful of popcorn, but Colt pulled the bag away.

"Get your own!" he snapped.

"I would love some popcorn," Karissa, ever the opportunist, said, smiling brightly. I could see the exact moment when my parents caved. See? Karissa was impossible to resist.

I didn't know why we had even bothered bringing her to the game. She'd complained the entire way to the stadium and then continued on for the first quarter. It was only after she'd found a pen and began doodling in the margins of the roster that her grumbling finally ceased. I'd tried to convince my parents to leave her at home, but they had instantly refused.

Apparently, they didn't trust her to stay home alone by herself.

"She's only twelve," Dad protested, stunned that I would even suggest such an absurd thing.

I wanted to point out that I had stayed home alone once or twice when I was that age but decided it wasn't worth an argument.

Thus, I had to deal with my sister's complaints. At least she saved me from having to talk about Jaron. That was the last thing I wanted to do.

"Do you have any money, Jeb?" Dad asked, turning

towards Papa. Papa rummaged through his pocket, grabbed a handful of crumpled bills, then standing up. Dad followed, grabbing his husband's hand.

I was momentarily frightened by the small gesture. While the first night in town had proved the people here to be accepting, I knew that not everyone was open-minded when it came to same-sex couples. If I had to, I would educate the shit out of whoever complained.

When no one, not even asshole Tyson, made a quip, I allowed my body to relax.

"Do you want anything?" Dad asked, turning towards me.

"Chips and cheese, please," I sung.

"You and your cheese." Papa shook his head, amused.

"Whatever."

Karissa shoved her roster into her pocket and followed them down the stadium steps. Colt had moved farther against Phoebe's side, nearly three feet separating us.

I was alone...with Tyson.

I felt his hands on my shoulders, and my body instantly stiffened. Before I could yell at him, his fingers began kneading at the knots in my neck. I heard one of the girls behind me gasp, but I didn't bother turning to see which one.

Okay, so he may have been an asshole, but his hands were bliss. Complete and utter bliss.

Before I could do something stupid, like moan, I came to my senses and yanked my body away from Tyson's all too tempting fingers.

"What are you doing?" I snapped, swiveling on the bleachers to see him. "And why are you smirking at me?"

"Smirking? I was merely smiling. The fact that you

thought I was smirking suggests that maybe you're not as immune to my charms as you claim to be."

I snorted and rolled my eyes, but he continued before I could respond.

"You seem tense. What's wrong?"

"Nothing's wrong. Just watching the game."

He considered me thoughtfully, head tilted to the side.

"You seem to know an awful lot about football."

I tried to ignore the fact that he had obviously eavesdropped on my conversation with Papa and Dad. I would get my revenge on a later date.

"I should know. I went to all of Jaron's games."

He was silent for a moment, and I turned back towards the field, believing the conversation to be over.

"Jaron. Is that your asshole boyfriend?" His voice sounded funny, almost as if he was speaking through clenched teeth. That only made me even more livid. He didn't know Jaron, and he wasn't allowed to have an opinion on somebody he'd never met.

Sure, Jaron might not have been perfect, but he was what I'd always wanted in a boyfriend. Even if he didn't like my singing voice, he would show up to every one of my shows. He would hold my hair back when I got sick, and he comforted me when I was sad. I didn't know what was going on between him and Fiona, but he was still my boyfriend and I still loved him.

Maybe.

I *maybe* still loved him.

"You don't even know him," I snapped, throwing a glare at Ty over my shoulder.

"I know that he made you cry after one of your shows because he called you a whore. I know that he never bothers to ask you about your day, yet he expects you to ask about his. I know that he refuses to do anything that interests you."

I blinked up at him, stunned.

"How...how do you know all of this?"

I hadn't admitted that to anyone. Not Fiona. Not my parents.

Hell, not even to myself.

He leaned closer to whisper in my ear. His voice was muffled by the roar of fans, but he spoke slowly enough so each word was emphasized.

"Your brother is more perceptive than you think."

I had expected him to admit to stalking me, maybe even being a mind reader.

But to call Colt perceptive? To imply that my brother actually cared enough about me to complain about my boyfriend?

My heart began to hurt.

Colt *had* been perceptive, and I had been oblivious. Dumb.

Driven by this image of what I believed love to look like.

I'd been told you would know the exact moment love found you. It would be like a thousand bricks pulling you below water. Unlike a normal drowning, this death would be peaceful and welcoming. Love, I'd heard, took you by surprise. It was staggering in its intensity, pulling you under wave after wave until you were dizzy with the madness of it all. Love wasn't supposed to hurt, despite the endless ride it took you on.

The last time I'd called Jaron, we had talked for hours about his history test and then football practice. When I tried to bring up my new school, he'd claimed he had to go.

I treated him like he was my world, and he treated me like I was the ground he walked on.

It had just occurred to me that I was afraid of falling in love, of investing myself so deeply into another person, only to discover that they didn't feel the same way. That was how you could die while still breathing.

It was impossible to tell whether or not you fell for the wrong person until it was too late and your heart shattered.

I couldn't admit that. I *wouldn't*. Not to Ty.

"You don't know what you're talking about." Each word was a gasp. I could barely speak around my suddenly dry lips.

"I know that I would never treat you the way he does."

His words, his voice, did funny things to me. They were most definitely *not* things I should've been feeling while I had a boyfriend.

"You don't even know me."

"I know enough. And, Cami?" His voice was dangerously close to my ear. He just had to lean forward an inch and his teeth would be touching it, nibbling on it.

Heat pooled low in my stomach.

"I always get what I want."

Before I could respond, somebody called Ty's name. It was one of the girls I'd noted earlier. She and her friend must've gone to the bathroom or something during halftime. They reclaimed their seats on either side of him.

"One thing you should know about me, Ty," I whispered, my voice as soft as his had been, "is that I'm not something you want. I'm something you need."

With that, I turned back to the game.

∽

WE WON. NO SURPRISE.

Kieran was a beast on the field. He was also a beast off

the field, but I wasn't about to tell him that. After the cheers had finally diminished, I stood up to stretch my sore muscles.

And stupid Ty began to tap my shoulder, the ever persistent asshole.

"What?" I snapped, not bothering to turn around. Papa gave me a strange look. As a general rule, I barely ever raised my voice, let alone to people outside of my family. My parents considered me too nice.

It wasn't an attribute I cared very much about. Don't get me wrong—I believed wholeheartedly that everybody should be kind to one another.

But I hated that people only ever knew me as the "nice girl."

Was that what I wanted on my tombstone? *Here lies Camila. She was nice.*

"I was wondering if you were going to the Soak," Ty answered, unperturbed by my less than impressed attitude. I threw him a dirty glare.

"What the hell is the Soak?"

"A weekly ritual," Phoebe answered, coming to stand beside her brother. Her arm was linked with Colt's. "And you are *so* going."

"I am?"

Ignoring the disbelief in my voice, Phoebe gave me a quick once-over.

"And we're going to have stop at your house first. You need to change."

~

"I LOOK RIDICULOUS," I GRUMBLED, CROSSING MY ARMS OVER my stomach. Phoebe laughed.

"You look hot! Show off that cute bod and have some fun!"

Phoebe had insisted on riding home with me. Colt, much to my displeasure, went with Tyson. I didn't trust Ty with my brother. He had too many secrets, too many demons, for me to feel comfortable around him.

After quickly changing clothes, I allowed Phoebe to drive me to our destination—an immense mansion in a completely ignored stretch of woods. People were everywhere—lounging on chairs, dancing in the yard, and swimming in the pool. The air was uncharacteristically warm today, but I still would've preferred a snow suit over my current outfit.

A red, strapless bathing suit.

Phoebe had tried to convince me to wear a bikini, but I had quite literally laughed in her face. I didn't want to blind the students of my new school. Despite my bathing suit being more modest than some of the others, I still felt as if I were walking into the party naked.

A group of boys hollered at me, and another guy whistled. The urge to run was overwhelming.

"I don't think I can do this," I whispered to Phoebe. Eyes. There were eyes everywhere. Watching me. Judging me. Hating me.

Fortunately, this didn't seem to be an exclusive "gang" party. I saw a few familiar classmates, as well as members of the football team. However, there was more than one glare directed at me from the Creepers, a representing name, if you asked me. I didn't know if I believed all of the "gang" rumors, but I most definitely did not want to get on their bad side.

I recognized the two girls that had been fawning over Ty —Ali and something. The guy next to them was a large, unfamiliar man who looked as if he was a few years older. College, perhaps? He wore the black leather jacket standard for all members of the group and black jeans that displayed firm muscle. He, too, was glaring at me. Beside him was the sleazeball that had wanted to attack me for insulting Ty. I think his name was Johnny or something.

"I really don't think I can do this," I repeated, but Phoebe was already sashaying away towards Colt. I knew that if my anxiety got too bad, Colt would reluctantly take me home.

But I could do this.

It was a party, and I had been to parties before. I could smile, dance a little, and drink some water, right? I didn't need Fiona and Jaron holding my hands.

Straightening my shoulders, I steeled my resolve.

I could do this. I had to.

"Hey, hot stuff!" someone called, and my face burned.

I couldn't do this. I most definitely could *not* do this.

What I could do was head back home, curl up under my blanket, and watch Netflix until my brain exploded. *That* I could do, and I would do it with pride.

Crossing my arms over my chest to ward off the sudden chill that had nothing to do with the weather, I sat at the edge of the pool. People were dancing against one another, two girls were making out in the hot tub, and the smell of beer was sharp and pungent in the air. I noticed Kieran a little bit away. He glared at the wall, two girls on either side of him. They seemed to be trying desperately to get his attention, and he seemed to find that wall particularly interesting.

I snorted.

Typical Kieran.

I'd half hoped to see the twins here, but I quickly squashed that idea. For one, they most definitely did not seem like the partying type. For two, they had a horror movie marathon planned for the night. When they had discussed it during lunch, a wistful part of me had wanted them to invite me. I loved horror movies, but I never got to watch them since they made Fiona pee and Jaron thought they were too lame. I also wanted my friendship with the twins to develop, though I would never admit that aloud. It had seemed as if they were going to invite me—Luke had brought it up in a roundabout way, and Leroy had asked if I would want popcorn if I ever did come to their movie night —but the invitation was never explicitly stated. I shouldn't have been surprised. The twins really only spoke in one language—riddles.

My chest began to vibrate, and I quickly grabbed my phone out of the confines of my bathing suit.

One pro about having big boobs—a walking purse. Seriously, it was like a clown car down there. I never knew what I would pull out next.

Frowning, I read the text message on my screen.

JARON: CALL ME.

THIS MESSAGE WAS FOLLOWED BY TEN MISSED CALLS. FEELING slightly anxious, I stood and walked towards a dark corner, away from the teeming partiers and their curious ears. I dialed the number I knew by heart.

Jaron answered on the second ring.

"What's wrong?" I asked immediately. I couldn't remember the last time Jaron had called me first. He was always so busy that I would have to be the one to plan our dates and take the initiative to start a conversation. I couldn't fault him on that. His parents were constantly bugging him about perfecting his grades and going to an Ivy League school.

"You haven't called in a week," Jaron snapped as soon as the words left my mouth. I froze.

"Huh?"

"You used to call every night, but you haven't called since last weekend. Is everything okay?" He sounded more annoyed than anxious. I wished desperately that I could see his face.

"I'm fine. Just busy with school and stuff."

"Where are you? I can barely hear you. Let's FaceTime instead."

Before I could respond, my phone buzzed yet again to indicate that Jaron was requesting a FaceTime. I grimaced but accepted the request.

Jaron's handsome face appeared on my phone screen, hair tousled, cheekbones sharp in his already arresting face, and large eyes framed by annoyingly thick lashes. Seriously. I would've killed to have those lashes.

Jaron took one look at me and scowled.

"What the hell are you wearing?" he demanded.

"A bathing suit."

"Let me rephrase my question." Jaron pinched the bridge of his nose. "Why are you wearing that?"

"I'm at a pool party." I turned the camera so he could see the house I was at. He used to always go to parties when I lived in Chicago. Sometimes, I would go with him. Other times, I would choose to stay at home. I'd never been overly fond of parties. The people, the music, the noise—it was sometimes too much for my poor brain.

"You should change," he snapped, and I felt myself bristle.

"Why the hell would I do that?"

"Seriously? Do you need me to spell it out for you?"

I quirked a brow at him. Spelling it out would be fan-fucking-tastic.

"Fiona wears ten times more revealing clothes to church than I am right now," I pointed out, trying not to lose my patience. Jaron didn't seem to have the same mentality as me, though.

"Fiona isn't my fucking girlfriend," he exploded. I took a deep breath.

Calm. I needed to remain calm.

"Do you want her to be?" I asked. There was no accusation in my voice. It was merely a question.

The expression on his face was almost comical—wide eyes, gaping mouth, clenched jaw.

"Why the hell would you say that?" he hissed through gritted teeth, and I frowned.

"So you're not denying it?"

"Don't put fucking words in my mouth, Cami. You always do shit like this."

"Like what?" I challenged.

"Jump to conclusions!" He paused, breathing heavily, before letting out a long exhale. "Look, just head home, change your clothes, and we can discuss this like adults."

"Or we can discuss it now. Why should I have to change?"

"Because you look like a whore!"

The words were a slap to my face and only reiterated every fear and self-doubt I'd ever had. My breathing was stilted, and his words replayed continuously on a loop in my mind.

Whore.

Whore.

Whore.

Before I could respond, the phone was snatched out of my hand, and the line was disconnected. I glanced up, stunned, to meet Kieran's icy gaze.

"How much of that did you hear?" I whispered.

He responded, "Enough."

I didn't like the way he was staring at me—with pity. I didn't need to be pitied.

So I had a little disagreement with my boyfriend? That was completely normal. Every couple had hills they needed to climb over.

There was no reason for him to be staring at me like... like *that*. Like I was a vase of porcelain that had fallen off the table and shattered into thousands of pieces.

Without another word, I turned away from the brooding man and headed in the direction of the party. I needed to get drunk.

Fast.

## 12

The music reverberated through my body, almost like a physical force.

"I loveeeee this song. Loveee it," I slurred, my body swaying to the beat. The world around me was bright and cheerful. The walls? Bright and cheerful. The floor? Bright and cheerful.

The man's lap I was sitting on while simultaneously dancing? Bright and cheerful.

The world was so freaking bright and cheerful.

The man's name was Johnny, and he was a member of Tyson's gang. Gang slang. Gang shebang. Gang…bang?

I snorted at my own stupid joke. Actually, it wasn't even a joke. It was just my own stupidity.

"Quit wiggling, girl," Johnny hissed. His palm was flat against my stomach.

Pouting, I wiggled again. I couldn't understand why he was freaking out over my dance moves.

And what was that hard thing digging into my back?

"I…danceeeee…" My attention diverted to the flashing strobe lights.

So. Freaking. Pretty.

What if I became a light? A beautiful, shiny light?

Would I be...snort...bright and cheerful?

I began laughing hysterically yet again. Johnny didn't laugh, but that was okay. I was hilarious.

Groaning, Johnny buried his head into my hair.

"Seriously. Stop. Moving. Or else I won't be able to control myself."

"Control yourself from doing what?" I asked. We were in the living room, sitting on the musty floral couch. I didn't recognize the other couples in the room, nor did I expect to. I didn't really know a lot of people yet.

That had to change.

"Helloooo!" I cooed to a couple that was making out beside us. The male looked towards me, frowned, and then turned back towards his partner. The XY chromosome members were test-osterone-ing my patience. Snort.

See? Freaking hilarious.

Stupid Jaron, and his stupid XY chromosomes, and his stupid face, and his—

Johnny pressed his lips against my neck. I had always loved when Jaron would kiss me there. Warmth would radiate through my body, and heat would churn in my lower stomach.

Johnny? Jaron? Did it really make a difference who was kissing me?

I turned in Johnny's lap, claiming his lips eagerly with my own. His lips were soft, like a pillow. A comfy, soft pillow.

Now, I was craving my own bed. To sleep in. Hmmm...I was so tired.

And also still kissing a boy. Kissing a Johnny.

Not a Johnny, but *the* Johnny. Right? Or one of the Johnnys. I was sure more than one Johnny existed in this world.

"Hey!" a strident voice bellowed, and Johnny was ripped away from me. My lips immediately tried to chase after his like the pathetic creature I was.

Shocked by the intrusion, I met a pair of light blue eyes.

They were soooo pretty.

Beautiful eyes. Sooooo beautiful.

The man was unfamiliar, but he was almost ethereal in beauty. Hard jawline, high cheekbones, dark hair.

"You are so pretty," I told him. My hands instinctively reached out to caress his face.

"And you're so wasted," he pointed out, throwing a glare in Johnny's direction. To me, he asked, "Do you have a ride home?"

"They left...a while ago...before the room began to spin." I hiccupped. Phoebe and Colt had bid me farewell shortly after my phone call with Jaron. They hadn't told me where they were going or when they would be back, but I hadn't seen them since.

"Okay. I'm going to take you home." Without another word, the stranger lifted me up. My arms automatically circled his thick neck. Turning towards Johnny with an almost incandescent fury, the man seethed, "And what the hell were you thinking, man? Taking advantage of a drunk girl? Ty will kick your ass when he finds out!"

Johnny's face paled.

Of course, I began chuckling. He looked like a ghost. A —Oh, shiny!

My attention became fixated on the glimmering rings of a girl.

"Who are you?" I asked the man carrying me. That

seemed like important information to know, considering the fact he was, well, carrying me.

"I'm Ian," he introduced, his voice flowing thorough me like the sweetest bourbon.

How did she even get so many rings? I only had, like, two. I needed to buy rings. Rings sparkled in the light.

I would sparkle.

I would be a vampire.

"I'm Camila," I slurred. "And I'm also really drunk right now. And tired. And I think you're really hot."

"I can see that," Ian agreed with a chuckle.

"You can see that you're hot?" I asked. "You're so vain!"

Ian said something else, but his words went through one ear and then out the other.

Walking down the long driveway, we stopped at a small black car with tinted windows.

"You live in the Hell House, right?"

"How do you know that?" I muttered. Sleep was begging to claim me, but I resisted. Nope. I would not sleep yet.

There could still be more sparkles for me to see.

"Everybody knows about the cute girl that lives in the murder house. Ty doesn't shut up about you."

He chuckled darkly and opened up the back door of his vehicle. Very gently, he set me down on the leather seat, being extra careful with my unbearably heavy head. The movement made me want to vomit.

"Ty's an asshole," I muttered sleepily. When did the world start spinning?

And when would it stop?

"Yeah, he is," Ian agreed. He put his jacket over me as a makeshift blanket. The smell of engine grease assaulted my nose.

"You're a member of the gang," I murmured in realization. Well, half realization. The other half of my brain was trying to figure out how plausible it would be to buy a dog. "The Creepers."

"Where did you hear that?" he asked. He still sounded as if he was suppressing a smile, so I figured my questions weren't going to get me stabbed.

"Idunawannatalk," I mumbled. If he understood me, then he was officially my favorite human ever.

Sighing, Ian gave my foot a squeeze.

"I'm going to—"

Whatever he was "going to do" was cut off by the sound of flesh hitting flesh. I tried to sit up, tried to see what was happening, but my body felt leaden.

"What the hell do you think you're doing?" a familiar voice demanded. Ty.

What was he doing here?

"I'm taking her home!" Ian defended.

Ty continued, "I swear to god if you did anything to her while she's like this, I will murder you!"

There was what sounded like a scuffle.

"I would never do anything like that!" Ian sounded as if he was spitting. And not the sexy kind of spit either.

Because...spit could be sexy. And shiny.

Shiny, sexy spit.

It took considerable effort to refocus my attention.

"If you're going to kill anyone, kill Johnny. I caught the bastard with his tongue down her throat and his hand on her boob."

I snorted. Boob. He said boob.

And did Johnny have his hand on my boob? I couldn't remember.

The rest of their conversation was lost to me.

Darkness obscured my vision like blinds being drawn, and sleep finally claimed me.

~

I BOLTED UPRIGHT.

What the...?

I was back in my room, in my bed, with moonlight filtering through the blinds in ribbons of silvery gold.

Everywhere I looked, black strings created an intricate web. Voices, muffled as if spoken underwater, reached my ears.

Tentatively, I crawled out of bed and took stock of my surroundings. I was still wearing my bathing suit, but the last thing I remembered was being at that stupid party. How had I gotten home?

I shook my head, as if that could somehow make my scattered thoughts more coherent. At least I didn't feel sick. That was more surprising than anything else.

But where did these...*strings* come from? I didn't know what other word I could use to describe them.

Almost instinctively, I reached out to pluck the one closest to me. It was dark black and almost seemed to be vibrating, as if electrical currents were running through it.

Music emitted from the string. Soft, soothing music.

I plucked it again.

The string led me downstairs and out the front door. Despite being only clothed in a bathing suit, I didn't feel cold. If anything, my body was radiating heat.

Pluck.

Pluck.

I frowned when my foot touched freshly manicured grass. Before, there had been houses upon houses, all identical in appearance and expanding half a mile in each direction. Now, there was nothing but a throng of trees on either side of me. The forest looked menacing in the darkness, as if each branch was a claw preparing to devour me.

I spun in a circle, awe mixing with fear, but paused when I caught sight of the building I had just exited from.

It was no longer my house. No, the building in front of me was now a structure with white boards and a steep roof.

A chapel.

The black string began to thrum erratically beside me.

Music, becoming clearer and clearer as the seconds dragged on, wafted from the open church doors. I didn't recognize the song, but I heard the words "Lord" and "love."

I had always felt safe in church. Protected. My parents were firm believers in God, despite being a same-sex couple. They insisted we go to church every Sunday. Colt would complain, but I actually enjoyed it.

Safe. The church made me feel safe.

But this building? Terror shot down my spine, encasing me in a block of impenetrable ice.

My hands were trembling as I climbed up the stone staircase and peered into the musty room. Sunlight filtered through the stained-glass windows, revealing row after row of dusty pews. Each pew was filled with people, all wearing clothes that looked as if they came straight from a Halloween catalogue.

As if I had somehow transported back in time a hundred or so years ago.

Fear strangling me, I plucked the string.

I walked inside the small building with two windows on either side. The flooring, as well as the walls, were made entirely of wood covered with white paint.

Even with the windows open, the church was stiflingly

hot. There didn't seem to be any remedy to smother the blistering heat. Sweat drenched my neck and dampened my hair.

There were numerous people sitting in the pews, each dressed in elaborate gowns and suits that could've been taken out of a historical romance novel. I felt immensely out of place in my...bathing suit. Yup. Still wearing the hideous one-piece.

I was grateful when no one paid me any mind.

The pastor's strident voice reverberated throughout the small building. Every pew, every aisle, every Bible was practically shaking with the pure willpower that he displayed.

He was an older man with an oval head and beady, dark eyes. Peppered hair, surprisingly colored, despite the rest of his haggard appearance, was trimmed carefully around his asymmetrical face.

"*When thou goest out to battle against thine enemies, and see horses and chariots, and a people more than thou, be not afraid of them: for the Lord thy God is with thee, which brought thee up out of the land of Egypt. And it shall be, when ye are come nigh unto the battle, that the priest shall approach and speak unto the people, and shall say unto them, Hear, O Israel, ye approach this day unto battle against your enemies: let not your heart faint, fear not, and do not tremble, neither be ye terrified because of them; for the Lord your God is he that goeth with you, to fight for you against your enemies, to save you.*" He paused, allowing the words to sink in to the willing crowd. He looked as if he was made for this moment, standing on the stage, spinning his web, telling his stories. He had an all-consuming personality that made me lean closer to hear what he had to say.

Only when the silence grew excruciating did he continue, "Deuteronomy 20: 1-4." He stepped out from behind the pulpit. His movements were agile and graceful, which was surprising, given his age. "We pray for our brothers in battle. Our sons. Our fathers. Our husbands. This war has been fought for too long."

There was a collective cheer from the assembled masses. Betty Thomas, whose son was fighting overseas. Jorge Malley, who had lost his father. Those were just two names out of many. I didn't know how I knew those facts, only that I did. I knew them just as I knew my own name and age.

The country was face to face with death, and it, death, was staring at them with pinprick black eyes and a coercing smile. It beckoned them towards battle like an unnerving siren.

All eyes turned to stare at dainty Sophia Warren. She was only eight, plump for her age, with rosy cheeks. They had received word that her father had died only last week. Her mother, driven by grief, had thrown herself off a cliff.

How had I known that?

The world had always been full of death, but the people here were only just beginning to comprehend it. With death, there was no second chance. There was no opportunity to wake up in the morning, say goodbye to that first love, kiss your husband, your wife, your children. It was the finality of all things life.

To the church, it was a transition from one world to another.

Before the pastor could continue on, the church doors blew open.

Dozens of figures marched into the church. They wore long, black cloaks that obscured their features. Each one was holding a torch.

The fire burnt steadily, a flickering flame of orange and red and yellow. Sometimes, the fire would morph itself into a startling blue, the same color the sky became as day transitioned into night.

Collectively, they stopped in the aisle and turned towards the petrified crowd. My own breathing had stopped entirely. I was frozen with fear and something else. Something that I would almost call curiosity.

The tallest figure, and the one in front, dropped his torch onto the ground. Immediately, a small fire began to burn. People began to scream, but there was no exit. No escape.

The cloaked figures surrounded them.

Their robes obscured their faces, but their hands were clearly visible as they tossed a single object into the fire.

A bone.

*"Effundetur sanguis Filii. Hoc donum tibi offero meipsum. Pelli autem imponitur pro maledictione mea cum obtulerit sanguinem disperdet eos."*

It was almost uncanny, their voices, as if each individual was speaking a distinct musical note. But nobody would consider what they were saying music. It was like a slash of a knife as it cut through flesh. The growl of a beast before it sprung. The murderer that wasn't just out for the hunt, but for the kill. Malevolent. Despite the ambiguity of the words, anybody within hearing distance could detect the predatory-like hunger. I didn't recognize the language, but goosebumps erupted on my flesh. I wanted nothing more than to run away.

Yet I stayed and watched.

*"Effundetur sanguis Filii. Hoc donum tibi offero meipsum. Pelli autem imponitur pro maledictione mea cum obtulerit sanguinem disperdet eos."*

It was Betty Thomas who felt the effects first.

The Bible she was holding slipped from her fingers,

hitting the ground. Even as every eye turned to stare at her, she fixed her gaze straight ahead. Her brow had been furrowed, almost as if she were contemplating a very difficult math equation, but it suddenly smoothed over.

And then she began to scream. It was a scream that I'd never heard before. Agony. There was no other way to describe it. She screamed as if her spine was being torn from her body.

Her eyes flashed white as they rolled back into her head, and she began to cough violently. From afar, it would appear as if she were coughing up blood.

Only upon closer inspection would you realize it was spiders.

"*Effundetur sanguis Filii. Hoc donum tibi offero meipsum. Pelli autem imponitur pro maledictione mea cum obtulerit sanguinem disperdet eos.*" The chanting was growing louder, reaching a crescendo. It was still tame enough where one wouldn't consider it a scream.

Their pale hands poked out from the sleeves of their cloaks, strange symbols etched into their skin.

Sophia Warren screamed next as if a thousand needles were being stabbed into her head. She held her body, as if that physical gesture could somehow keep her insides together.

She opened her mouth to scream again, but something got caught in her throat. Something long and slimy and crawling towards her teeth. Out of her lips. Down her chin.

A centipede.

I couldn't look away.

She curled in on herself like old, brittle paper. Pain. Pain everywhere. She was aware of nothing else except for this pain. I knew that. I could almost feel the remnants of her pain caressing my skin. Something was crawling through her hair, down her neck, across her legs.

The fire erupted in a flash of color. The newcomers in black robes did not step back as the flames engulfed them. They didn't seem shocked, almost as if they'd expected this to transpire.

The fire was attacking their bodies, and the bodies of the churchgoers, in an array of colors like a kaleidoscope.

It was beautiful and horrifying.

Fear continued to strangle my voice, and my breath alternated between sobs and wheezes. I blinked away the frightened tears and focused on the fallen figures, flames fully covering their skin.

I only had a second to fear that I would get burned alive, that they would find my charred remains, before I was pulled out, panting. I was back in my room.

The threads continued to vibrate with their unanswered pleas.

*Listen*, they seemed to say.

*Listen*.

I couldn't focus on them, though. All I could focus on were the fallen bodies. The bugs leaving their months. The flickering flames.

And the cross.

It stood behind the pulpit, tall and proud as if God himself was physically looking down on his children.

But somehow, during those robed men's strange chants, the cross had turned itself upside down.

~

I woke up with a gasp. My head pounded, and my body ached as if I'd been run over repeatedly by a semitruck. Fun times.

I had never gotten drunk before. Sure, I'd had a few sips here and there when I would hang out with Jaron and Fiona, but rolling on the floor, hysterical laughing, vomiting on my shoes drunk? That wasn't me.

And where...?

I tried to sit up, tried to see where I was, but the pain in my head prohibited such a movement. Still, I recognized the white propellers of my bedroom fan and the chipped paint on the walls. I couldn't recollect how I'd ended up back in bed, nor how I had even ended up at home. The last thing I remembered was...Jaron. And some dude named Jonathan. Or something. Maybe Johnny?

What had happened?

I vaguely recalled a nightmare I'd had only moments earlier, but it continued to slip away from me. It was like trying to cup water—impossible to grasp. After a moment of furrowed brows and narrowed eyes, I chose to forget about the strange dream. If I couldn't remember it, then it probably wasn't important.

I had other things to worry about.

Like my pounding head. My sore body. The inevitable grounding I was bound to receive. And my...my hand?

Okay, so I might not be an experienced drunk, but I was like ninety-nine-point-nine percent sure your hand wasn't supposed to ache. Pushing aside my blankets, I surveyed the skin in the light.

Tiny shards of glass were embedded into the palm of my hand. My knuckles were red and scabbed, tiny specks of blood coating the surrounding skin.

What the hell?

I most definitely did *not* remember losing a fight to a blender.

Trembling, I sat up completely in bed. My vision blurred, and the world began to spin. I squeezed my eyelids shut to push down the rising nausea.

*Think, Camila. Think. What happened last night?*

Try as I might, the memory refused to come to me.

I knew that I needed to talk to my dads. They would help me. They would comfort me.

And that was what I needed—comfort.

And aspirin. Lots and lots of aspirin.

After making quick work of destroying my bedroom's garbage can with vomit—joy—I gingerly crawled towards the door. It was only then that I took note of the wall above my bed.

Written in blood—my blood, most likely—was a simple sentence that sent pinpricks of terror coursing throughout my body.

HE'S COMING FOR YOU.

## 13

I told myself it was a joke. A prank.
Drunk-me must've done it.
That was the only logical explanation.

Logic. I needed to focus solely on logic. What it could do for you, and what it could mean. I squeezed my eyelids shut as if that could somehow block the words I'd already seen, the words etched on my eyelids like a demented tattoo. It was a warning, wasn't it? From whom?

From *me*?

And who was the ominous "he"?

I had so many questions but so little answers. The puzzle pieces did not seem to fit together, try as I might. Frowning once more at the wall, I chose to bury my emotions so deeply that not even a necromancer would be able to raise them.

After quickly bandaging my hand, I decided to throw on a pair of gloves to hide my busted knuckles. I know, totally not suspicious to be seen wearing gloves inside.

Sue me.

I threw my hair into a ponytail, splashed water onto my

face, and changed into a pair of sweatpants and a baggy sweatshirt. Once I was certain that I no longer resembled the epitome of drunk teenager, I tentatively made my way down to the living room.

The clock above the fireplace mantle said it was after twelve. I must've slept the entire morning away. The television was on, and I caught sight of the back of Dad's dark hair as he sat on the couch. Papa wasn't anywhere to be seen, which struck me as odd. I knew for a fact that he had this Saturday off. We had made plans to go shopping this afternoon after our previous one got postponed. Perhaps he was doing yard work or was in the kitchen?

But that didn't seem right. Papa's favorite college football team was supposed to be playing today. Hell would freeze over before you could force him away from the TV during that time.

My foot accidentally stepped on a particularly loud floorboard, and I winced as Dad swiveled to face me.

"I know I'm in trouble!" I began, holding up my hands as if I were a prisoner approaching a cop. "And I'm so sorry, but I just wasn't thinking and..."

I trailed off as I caught sight of Dad's face. The skin around his eyes was red, and his cheeks were puffy. Dad wasn't as impassive as Papa, but it was still rare to see him cry.

Before I could inquire, Dad jumped from the couch and engulfed me in his large arms.

I had expected a severe reprimanding, maybe even a metaphorical ass kicking, but not this. Not a...hug.

My confusion grew the longer my dad held me. When he began crying into my hair, the confusion transformed into fear.

"What's wrong?" I pushed him back, scanning his body

anxiously for injuries. "Is Papa okay? Is Colt? What about Karissa?"

I could feel myself beginning to panic. The familiar signs of a panic attack made themselves known—erratic breathing, difficulty concentrating, twitching of hands. Dad must've noticed that as well, and he hurried to reassure me.

"They're fine. They're all fine."

"Then why were you crying?" I queried. Now that my panic has ebbed, I was able to focus more clearly on my distressed father.

"When you didn't come home last night..." He trailed off, hands tightening on my shoulders. I quirked an eyebrow at that. When I hung out with Jaron and Fiona, it would be a rare event for me to arrive home before midnight. Did Dad expect things to be different now that we were here?

Seeing my confusion, Dad tightened his hold on me. I would've considered it painful if there hadn't been something near pleading in his dark eyes. I felt as if he needed to hold on to me, needed to anchor himself to my sinking ship.

"A student went missing last night. From the party Colt said you were at."

I blinked, stunned by the news.

"What?"

"Police—Papa arrived at the scene. We couldn't find you, and..." He pulled me towards him again, and I allowed myself to sink into my father's comforting embrace. I felt safe and loved and protected. The world couldn't harm me when I was with my fathers. "Once they found the body..."

"The body?" I exclaimed, pulling away yet again to see his face. His eyes welled with tears as he recounted the events.

"The missing teen was found murdered in the woods. I

don't know a lot of details, it hasn't been released to the public yet, but Papa said it appeared to be a ritualistic killing. Weird symbols and torn limbs." Dad shuddered. "And we couldn't find you. Some kid claimed that only seconds before the police arrived, he saw you getting carried away by some strange man."

Those words brought back vague memories of a handsome face with light scruff on his jawline. And Tyson. He'd been there too, hadn't he?

"He dropped you off at the house." Dad's hand clenched into a fist where it still sat on my shoulder. "Papa insisted that we bring him down to the station to make sure nothing had been done while you were unconscious."

"And?" I prompted, chewing on the tip of my fingernail. I didn't feel like anything had been done to me, at least with him. The more I thought about it, the more I became certain that the stranger drove me straight home.

"Checked the traffic cams. He drove straight from the party to the house," Dad stated, reinforcing what I'd already suspected. "Good kid. A little pissed we got him arrested though."

Well, no shit.

If my faulty memory was correct, then the Good Samaritan was a member of the Creepers. That realization made the blood drain from my face.

Holy crap. I'd accidentally gotten a gang member arrested.

My fuzzy mind sorted through all the information I was given before it settled on one thing.

"The teen who died? Can you tell me who it was?"

Indecision flickered across Dad's face. I knew Papa had told him, and I also knew that they weren't allowed to tell me. Still, I needed to know.

For some reason, I already had an idea.

"His name was Johnathon," Dad admitted at last. "Johnny, to his friends. We believe that the murder could be gang related, but nothing has been confirmed."

Before he had even finished speaking, I was pulling away from him. He said something to my retreating back, but the words were inaudible, due to the roaring in my ears. Each jerky movement made me want to vomit. Still, I managed to forge ahead, throwing open my bedroom door and charging to my dresser.

The strange dreams. The bruises on my knuckles. The blood.

*He made me do it.*

My fingers trembled as I grabbed out my blonde wig.

It was coated in blood.

~

Breathing was difficult.

I gripped the edge of the bathroom sink, as if that minuscule movement could somehow keep my life from falling apart. My entire body trembled, and all I could do was stare at myself.

Face pale, eyes feral, lips pulled back.

Who was this girl?

I tried to tell myself that it was a coincidence, that I had nothing to do with Johnny's death, but the darkness purred happily inside of me. It was content, for the first time in its life.

As if...as if it had just been fed.

Shaking, I released the counter and collapsed onto the floor. I pulled my knees up to my chest and then wrapped my arms around my legs. It was almost as if I hoped the physical comfort would help soothe my mental anguish. I knew the effort would be futile.

There was something severely wrong with me.

After what felt like hours, I finally dared pull myself up. My eyes were red-rimmed, and my head pounded, both from the crying and the alcohol earlier.

I surveyed myself once more in the mirror.

The girl staring back at me was familiar.

But also unfamiliar.

Same dark hair, same tan skin, same puffy eyes. But unlike me, her lips were pulled back into a sinister smile. Blood stained her teeth, dribbling down her chin. As I watched, horrified, she held a single finger to her lips.

Shhh.

*I'm not crazy. I'm not crazy. I'm not crazy.*

I repeated that to myself as I stumbled out of the bathroom and into my bedroom. I slammed the door shut, slowly sinking down to the floor.

*I'm not crazy. I'm not crazy.*

My eyes widened as I took in the state of my bedroom. Clothes were discarded across every available space, each one completely destroyed. I noticed my favorite dress had been cut into shreds. My shirts all had holes in them, meticulously sliced as if they had been done with a sharp knife.

*I'm not crazy. I'm not crazy.*

I squeezed my eyelids shut, as if that could somehow erase the images already imprinted on my brain. My breath came out in shallow pants.

*I'm not crazy. I'm not crazy.*

Sitting on my bed, almost as if it was being displayed, was a familiar black outfit—leather corset, miniskirt, lace stockings, and knee-high boots.

It was my outfit. The other me's outfit.

The dark me.

Beside it all, mocking me in the afternoon sunlight, was the blonde wig.

∽

"Dorian!" I screamed, pounding on the neighbor's front door. "Dorian!"

I imagined I looked crazy. Perhaps I actually was crazy. I couldn't decide. The lack of coherence in my life—and consequentially, my mind—terrified me in ways I hadn't thought to be possible.

I waited at the door, foot tapping with increasing speed as the seconds dragged on, before stomping down the driveway with a few choice words.

"Were you looking for me?" a familiar voice inquired slyly, accompanied by a mop of disheveled blond hair. He leaned against the fence, arms crossed over his well-defined chest. "Did you know," he began conversationally as I stormed towards him, "that this fence is actually built on your property? Your lawn technically extends a few feet past it."

Ignoring his cryptic words, I slammed to a stop just centimeters away from him. My panting would've been embarrassing if I had the wits to care.

"You said that you used to live in my house, correct?"

He raised an eyebrow but did not bother to acknowledge me. I tampered down my annoyance and continued on doggedly.

"You said that it's a gateway to Hell, right? You said that it was haunted. Do you actually believe that crap, or were you just pulling my leg?"

His entire body stiffened at my words. Only his eyes

moved to trace my features—my wide, fearful eyes and pale skin. His brows furrowed in confusion.

"What did you see?"

"Just answer the question!" I hadn't meant to get testy with him, but my anger was running rampant within me. I was a volcano just waiting to explode. It wasn't necessarily anger I was feeling, though that was what the emotion felt like.

It was fear.

After a moment of careful consideration, Dorian nodded.

"Yes, I believe it to be real. Now, what did you see?"

"I believe my house is haunted."

*Or I'm completely losing my mind.*

I couldn't decide which one I wanted to be true.

"Stuff keeps getting moved, and I'm having these dreams—"

"What kind of dreams?" Dorian interrupted.

"I can never remember them once I wake up. But, Dorian? They terrify me."

And they did. I couldn't remember any explicit details, but fear clung to me like a second skin when I woke up. The fear only grew when the darkness inside of me growled its approval each and every time.

"Okay. I think I know something that could help." He nodded his head slowly, eyes sweeping over my face without sticking on any particular feature.

"I would do anything," I whispered. I knew that there was a real possibility he was playing me for a fool. I half expected him to laugh hysterically at me for believing his horror story. Despite all of this, I was desperate.

For answers.

For an escape.

My eyes flicked to my bandaged hand, concealed in the black glove.

I needed answers, even if I wouldn't like what they were.

"You're going to have to go to sleep," Dorian asserted, and I blinked at him. Yup. I had been played. Disappointment reared its ugly head. Dorian, oblivious, continued to tap a finger against his lips.

I decided to humor him.

"How exactly would that help me?" I asked scathingly.

"You claim you can't remember your dreams, right?"

"So...?"

"So, I have a solution."

I clenched my hands into fists so I wouldn't tear out my hair. Or gorge Dorian's eyes out of their sockets. Both were immensely tempting.

"Which is?"

"I'm going into your dreams with you."

## 14

"This is so stupid," I muttered. Dorian stood over me, eyes sparkling with amusement and a hint of fear. The two contradicting emotions caught me off guard, but I kept my mouth shut.

"Trust me," he murmured, placing a palm against my forehead.

"I don't even know you."

I was annoyed, yes, but not frightened by his presence. My intuition always warned me when I was in danger, and right then, it remained calm. There were no red flags or warning bells.

I trusted my instincts with my life.

"Okay, how does this work?" I asked grudgingly. I fully believed that Dorian was batshit crazy, but I was also beginning to believe that I was as well.

"Just close your eyes and let me work."

"Are you like a witch or something?" I asked. The "something" translated to a complete psychopath in my head.

My fears weren't soothed when he said, "Or something."

Psychopath it was, then.

*And you're alone with him, Cami? Real smart.*

I had brought him into my bedroom, being extra careful to avoid any rooms that my father may be in. Fortunately, he seemed to have left the living room, so I didn't have to broach the awkward conversation of why I was inviting a boy into my room.

"Oh hey, Dad! This stranger says he can see into my dreams. Considering the fact that I'm going completely insane and seeing things, I decided, what the hell! If I'm not back in five hours, then I'm probably dead! Okay...love ya!"

I should've just told him we were filming a porno. That would've been easier to explain.

"Close your eyes, and relax your mind," Dorian muttered.

Was I really doing this?

Apparently, I was. My body obeyed his commands rhythmically. First, my hands unclenched, then my muscles loosened, and finally, my brain shut off.

I heard him mutter something, his shockingly cold hand still pressed against my forehead, before darkness consumed me.

∼

I SAT UPRIGHT.

I was back in the spiderweb room. String room. Whatever-the-hell-it-was room.

And I wasn't alone.

Dorian stood beside my bed, glancing from side to side in awe.

"It worked," he muttered, and I frowned at him.

"Oh, great. And now I'm dreaming about sexy, crazy men. Just what I needed."

Throwing aside my covers, I padded over to the nearest string. It was already emitting a soft, soothing song. My hand ached to pluck it, to hear its story.

"I don't know which question I want to ask," Dorian mused from behind me. "That you think I'm sexy? Or that you didn't believe I would be able to go into your dreams?"

I snorted, turning back around to survey the handsome man. My imagination had most definitely done him justice. Everything about him was identical to the actual Dorian, the one back home.

"You can't go into dreams," I deadpanned, rolling my eyes. "It's not possible."

"Then how do you explain this?" he asked. He spread his arms out to encompass the entire room.

Moving around him, towards another dark string, I said, "You're a figment of my imagination. Obviously, I fell asleep, and since we were talking about you entering my dreams, my subconscious put you into it."

The words made sense to me, but Dorian's smirk only grew.

"You literally just admitted I'm in your dreams."

Dream-Dorian was a pain in my ass.

"Obviously, you somewhat believed me, or else you wouldn't have let me try in the first place," he continued smugly. I gave him the finger behind my back.

"Shut up. I want to hear this."

I plucked the string, sound reverberating through my small bedroom. I heard a muffled voice, but the words remained indistinct. Before I could pluck it again, Dorian grabbed my wrist.

"Do you know what these are?" he asked. His face had gone deathly pale.

"Strings? Creepy-looking spider webs?"

"Those are life threads." His voice was a mere breath, so low, I had to strain to hear him.

"What?" I asked.

"Life threads." He cleared his throat, releasing my hand as if it were toxic. "Each one belongs to a soul that has died in this house. When you play it, you can follow the person's life from beginning to end."

I stared at the thrumming, black string in bemusement. A life thread? How could something that appeared so insignificant hold so much power?

"Now that I'm here again, I can remember what I saw in my previous dreams. The life threads I plucked." My voice was soft. Contemplative. Despite how crazy it sounded, I couldn't deny the rightness of Dorian's words. Maybe it was only a dream. Maybe it wasn't.

But I would finally receive some answers.

"I saw a church. There were these people in the church. A young girl." As I talked, my fingers tentatively plucked at the closest string. "It was so vivid. I could see everything like I was watching a movie, yet I had no identity. I wasn't actually there. I was just an observer."

I remembered the horrific screams. The blood. The bugs.

The people chanting ominous words just before the fire ripped them apart.

I moved to another string, a familiar one, and plucked it lightly. I noticed Dorian jump out of my peripheral vision.

"This one leads to the bathtub. I watched parents drown their own kid. They said he was the devil."

My voice shook.

Turning towards Dorian, I raised an eyebrow.

"Is it because of the house? Is that why there are so many deaths?"

Dorian's face was ashen, cheekbones sunken. He looked awfully ill.

"As I said before, this is a gateway to Hell. We call this particular area the Shadowland. It's a place between the living and the dead, where souls are kept."

"How do you know all this?" I asked.

His eyes were bleak when they met mine.

"I told you. I used to live in this house."

~

THIS TIME WHEN I WOKE UP, IT WAS A GRADUAL PROCESS. My eyelids fluttered against my cheekbones as my mind struggled to piece together what had just transpired. Unlike the last few times I'd fallen asleep, I remembered every detail of this dream vividly.

Including the tagalong.

Bolting upright, I glanced wide-eyed at Dorian. He was standing beside my bed, staring down at me with an indecipherable expression.

Surely I had imagined it. Surely Dorian hadn't actually entered my dream.

His next words crumbled any hope I had that my imagination had somehow improved in the last few hours.

"The life threads. How many of them have you touched?"

*No. No. No.*

*I'm not crazy.*

*I'm not crazy.*

*I'm not crazy.*

"That was real?" I asked shakily.

"Cami, it's important. You have to answer me." He knelt beside my bed, expression earnest, but that only caused tears to spring into my eyes. How could this be happening? This wasn't some B-horror film with bad special effects and stereotypical characters. This was my life, and my life wasn't supposed to include ghosts or gangs or dreamwalkers. And it most definitely wasn't supposed to include a doorway to Hell.

Yup. Nope. I was completely removing myself from the crazy train. Maybe if I plugged my ears, Dorian's words would become lost to me.

"Cami!" Dorian snapped, and I turned to face him. He must've seen the anguish in my expression, because his own considerably softened. "I know this is hard for you..."

"So it was real? You actually went inside my dreams?" The final words came out as a choked cry. I pressed my palm to my forehead, as if I could somehow will the tears to stay locked behind my eyes.

"I will explain everything," Dorian said. "But not now. Not here. It has already progressed if you can see the threads."

"So, what do I do? Do I leave?" His words weren't making sense to me.

A small, rational voice inside of my mind told me it had only been a dream. People couldn't see inside of dreams, despite Dorian's claim otherwise. Perhaps I'd been talking in my sleep, which was how he knew about the life threads. Anything was more plausible than what he was saying.

Dreamwalking.

Life threads.

The words echoed in my head.

"Oh god," I moaned before Dorian could respond. "I'm losing my mind, is that it? I'm officially losing it."

I began to laugh hysterically, ignoring the way Dorian eyed me with concern.

"Humans shouldn't be able to see the threads," he insisted at last, but I could barely hear him over my giggles. After my laughter finally subsided, I thought the words "life threads" once again and fell into another round of hysterics.

Brushing tears from my eyes, I turned my gaze towards Dorian. I was looking at him, but I wasn't seeing him. I had trouble focusing on just one thing.

"Human? You're talking as if you're something other."

Of course, that only made me laugh again. Me and my crazy mind.

Dorian offered me a sad smile. I noticed that his face appeared paler than usual, and tiny droplets of water cascaded from his forehead. Was he getting sick?

"I promise I'll explain everything later. I can't stay any longer."

"Oh no!" I lunged for him, but he stealthily sidestepped my hand. It wasn't an entirely hard feat, considering my head still throbbed from the alcohol and my stomach churned angrily at the sudden movement. I was totally going to vomit. If I just so happened to get it on his shoes? I would be pretty proud of myself.

Glaring up at him, I said, "You need to tell me everything now."

"I would if I could," Dorian promised. "But I need to leave. I'll be back as soon as I can."

Before I could scream or cry, he ran out my bedroom door.

The silence that followed his departure made goosebumps erupt on my skin. It felt almost as if I'd imagined the entire interaction.

But that was impossible, wasn't it? He had been here. With me.

Right?

I couldn't answer that question.

## 15

The next week was a repetitive cycle of the same thing.

To compensate for my lack of clothes, I stopped at the store and bought two pairs of jeans and a couple of shirts, all on clearance, with money I had saved up. They didn't fit perfectly, but they would have to do. I couldn't just tell my dads that a ghost had destroyed my wardrobe.

My blonde wig continued to taunt me. I would come out of the shower, only to see the leather outfit and blonde hair lying on the toilet seat.

I threw it in the garbage.

I burned it.

I sold it.

The outfit and wig always returned.

Nightmares plagued my sleep. Unlike with Dorian, I couldn't remember what they had been about, only that they'd terrified me.

After that, I didn't sleep. I didn't eat. I tried to plaster a smile on my face to get through the day, but everybody could see through my front. The twins questioned me repeatedly, and Leroy went so far as to buy me a brownie from the lunch line and offer it to me. Knowing Leroy, that was a pretty big deal. I hadn't talked to Kieran about the project, and he hadn't brought it up. Ty continued to bother me in the halls, but even he seemed more subdued as my behavior changed.

I hadn't seen Dorian since he left.

And when I asked around? No one had heard of him.

I really was losing my mind.

That Friday, I sauntered into the kitchen, rubbing sleep out of my eyes. Dad and Papa had already left for the day, and Colt was still sleeping. Surprisingly, Karissa was already up and was doodling at the kitchen table.

"What are you doing up?" I mumbled drowsily. She still had an hour until she had to get ready for school.

"Just drawing," Karissa responded with a shrug. She had been doing that a lot more lately—drawing. A part of me hoped that she would keep it up. I'd never found anything to bond with my sister with, and I hoped that a mutual love of art would draw us together. Music was that thread between Colt and me. But Karissa? She was an enigma. I didn't have the same relationship with her as I had with the others.

"What are you drawing?" I asked, fumbling through the cupboards in search of a mug for coffee. I hadn't drunk a lot of coffee before I moved here, maybe one or two cups a week. Now, I averaged a solid three cups each morning and one more in the afternoon. Anything to save me from sleep.

And my dreams.

"Stuff," Karissa evaded, always the eloquent one. Rolling my eyes, I quickly made an individual cup of coffee.

We were silent for a moment. Me, sipping my coffee.

Her, drawing in her notebook. I had just turned towards the cupboards to grab a bowl for cereal when her voice made me freeze.

"The Shadow Man is mad at you."

The coffee cup shattered on the ground. Hot liquid burned my arms, turning the skin a bright red.

"Crap!" Karissa screamed, jumping from the stool. She ran towards the faucet and put a rag beneath the flow of water. She gently pressed it against my arm.

I couldn't focus on the pain or the broken ceramic on my bare feet. My eyes stayed solely on my little sister.

"What did you say?" I whispered.

"What the heck was that?" Karissa continued. "A muscle spasm? Are you all right? Do you need a doctor? Those burns look pretty bad."

"Karissa." Grabbing her arm, I forced her to look at me. "What did you say? Who's mad at me?"

I knew I sounded crazy, feral, but my entire body was shaking uncontrollably. My brain was a whirlwind of emotions, fear being the most dominant one.

Karissa seemed confused by my question, and her eyes flicked to where I held her arm. I looked down with dawning horror to see my fingers leaving tiny, red indents on her skin. I released her immediately, and her other hand rubbed at the spot.

"I said that Papa is still mad at you for getting drunk. You're probably going to be grounded for a week."

She sounded scared.

Scared of me.

Because I had hurt her and myself.

Oh god. What was happening to me?

I was falling down the rabbit hole, down and down until

I could see nothing but a black abyss. But unlike in the movies, people couldn't survive such a fall.

∼

"You look like shit," Leroy announced, dropping his tray across from me on the table. Luke also gave me a worried once-over.

The cafeteria was festive today. The football team was playing its rival, and the entire school was decorated in the team's colors. Music blared from the speakers up above, making conversation difficult. You would think that the students would grieve the death of one of their fellow classmates. However, not one word was said about the dead gang member. There were no flowers, no memorial, no assemblies honoring his death.

I remembered, back in Chicago, one of my classmates got hit by a drunk driver. We'd had two days of school off, and when we returned, there had been mandatory counseling. The school didn't seem to care that we'd all barely known her—she had only arrived at the school a few weeks prior—let alone grieved her. However, there was an unspoken consensus that you were supposed to be sad when someone you knew died.

This school didn't seem to hold the same sentiment.

The police had asked their questions to everybody at the party. Everybody, that was, except for me. I imagined Papa had played a hand in that turn of events. How could it be me? His perfect, sweet Camila. Dad had seen me come home, passed out drunk, and I had been locked away in my room until the following afternoon.

A lot could've happened during that time frame.

Sunlight filtered through the various windows, and I

blinked my eyes against the bright intrusion. My sleep patterns had been irregular, to say the least, and my body was feeling the effects. It took considerable effort to focus on the twins before me when every part of myself wanted to burrow into the ground and sleep for hundreds of years.

"What are you doing tomorrow night?" I asked, changing the subject off of my less than stellar appearance. The twins simultaneously blinked at my abrupt topic change.

"Uh...nothing much. Why?" Leroy silently passed me his brownie, and I grabbed it eagerly. I'd been having difficulty eating and keeping food down. My body displayed the lack of nourishment I was receiving—skin pale, bones accentuated clearly through my skin, eyes glazed.

"You guys are coming over to my house tomorrow night," I said. My tone left no room for argument.

"Um..."

"And bring your ghost hunting gear," I added. The twins straightened in their seats, identical expressions of bemusement contorting their handsome faces.

"Cami, are you sure you're okay?" Luke asked. His eyes were somber as he gripped my hand in both of his. I flashed him a smile.

Fake.

A *fake* smile.

"I'm fine. Just make sure you guys come to my house tomorrow night. Does six work?"

"Why not tonight?" Leroy asked. He didn't sound as eager as I would've expected him to be. After all, they had practically begged me to allow them entrance into my home. He sounded almost...worried. Worried for me? Himself?

Stabbing at a piece of lettuce, despite knowing I was never going to eat it, I offered them another unhinged smile.

"I have plans tonight."

∼

Phoebe seemed momentarily surprised by my request.

"Really?" she asked, eyes wary.

We sat on the bleachers wrapped in a thick blanket. The night air was cool against my skin, and the wind ravaged the stands. Despite the weather, the football game was packed.

Colt and Ty had left earlier to grab some snacks, leaving Phoebe and me alone. I didn't know where my parents and Karissa were sitting, but I didn't care. They weren't my focus today. Oddly enough, both Phoebe and Ty didn't seem all that upset by the death of their friend. They both refused to even acknowledge him. When I asked how they were doing, Ty merely responded, "He deserved it."

I chose not to question them. Everybody grieved in their own way, right? Maybe ignoring the problem was their way of coping. Maybe they believed that they could bury their feelings so far down that they would be impossible to uncover.

"I don't know if it's a good idea," Phoebe continued anxiously. She brushed a strand of lilac hair behind her ear. Her teeth nibbled on her lower lip—the only indication that she was distressed.

"Please, Phe. I'm begging you."

"My parents are out," she murmured, and I could tell she was talking more to herself than to me. "They wouldn't know, but Ty would be mad."

"Please."

There must've been something in my voice, a hiccup or an intake of breath, because her eyes snapped to my face.

"Is there something happening at home?" she asked, lowering her voice to a whisper. "Is there something you want to talk about?"

I knew what she was thinking. Hell, it was the same thing I would have thought if the situations were reversed. Why else would I ask a virtual stranger if I could spend the night at her house? Of course, I couldn't tell her the real reasons.

That I was terrified of going back to my house.

That I couldn't sleep when I was there.

That my mind was being ripped apart each and every time I closed my eyes.

"Just stress," I clarified at last, offering her a feeble smile. I wondered if I could use Jaron as my excuse. I had only talked to him once since our fight, and that conversation had lasted approximately fifteen minutes before he had to leave. I didn't know what that meant for us as a couple. Were we even still together?

After a moment of consideration, I told her just that.

As I suspected, Phoebe agreed immediately.

"Boys are such assholes. I completely understand wanting to get away for a night. Besides, what they don't know won't hurt them, right?" She nudged my side with her elbow, flashing me a conspiratorial wink. I shakily smiled back at her, turning my attention towards the game just as Ty and Colt returned.

Colt immediately moved to snuggle alongside Phoebe, and Ty moved to sit beside me. I didn't know where his fan club was, but I didn't bother to ask.

"Mom and Dad are gone tonight, correct?" Phoebe asked Ty. Ty glanced towards his sister in surprise.

"Yeah. Why?"

"Camila is going to spend the night."

At that, both Colt's and Ty's eyes flashed to my face. It was Colt that I focused on though.

"Did you ask our parents?" he demanded, and I barely resisted the urge to roll my eyes. Why did he all of a sudden feel the need to act like my big brother? It was irritating.

"They won't care," I snapped. I had slept over at Fiona's house—and Jaron's—numerous times without asking permission. Granted, they weren't aware of my late-night activities with my boyfriend, but they had always trusted me to make the right decisions.

Stupidly, I was beginning to realize. I had yet to actually be worthy of their trust. My decisions ranged from bad to very bad.

"Cami..." Colt trailed off at whatever expression he saw on my face. I was in no mood for an argument.

"So a sleepover?" Ty murmured once the game resumed, but my attention was fixated firmly on Kieran. I yearned to map out his broad shoulders through touch alone. To feel his light, blond scruff against my cheek. To see his—

Apparently, sleep deprivation was making me a raving horn dog.

"Suck a dick, Tyson," I snapped.

"I'll suck yours if you suck mine."

Heat rushed to my cheeks at the implication of his words.

Definitely a raving horn dog.

"How about you suck your own dick?"

"While you watch? Kinky."

He was insufferable.

"You know, I don't think Phoebe has ever had a sleepover with another female. Me?" He leaned closer until his breath was caressing my earlobe. I shivered involuntarily. "I love sleepovers."

Snorting, I turned to face him. He was so close that our noses touched with that minuscule movement.

"Do you think I care about how many girls you slept with? Do you think that impresses me? It seems to me as if you're compensating for something. Lack of love in your life, perhaps? Mommy and Daddy issues? Leading girls along doesn't make you attractive, Ty. It just makes you a dick. And I, for one, want nothing to do with you."

I didn't know what possessed me to say that. My mind had been foggy, unable to fully comprehend everything I was seeing, but just then, it was extremely coherent. The words fell from my mouth like acid before I could stop them.

I wasn't even sure if I wanted to.

Ty blinked, stunned, but I turned away before he could respond. I continued to feel his eyes on me as the game played on.

## 16

The building Phoebe drove us to was a surprisingly nice apartment complex. I didn't know where I expected the gang princess and prince to live, but a well furnished building bustling with people? That wasn't high on my list of guesses.

Ty had driven back separately. On a motorcycle, of course. I was beginning to believe that Tyson was the stereotypical bad boy.

Gang related activities? Check.

Brooding personality? Check.

Motorcycle? Check.

The sleek machine was already in the parking lot when we arrived.

"We're on the top floor," Phoebe stated. She waved at the receptionist before leading us towards the staircase. "Unfortunately, the elevator is out of commission. You can blame Ty and his love of pranks for that." She chuckled at the memory, but I chose not to ask.

The hallway had red carpeting, and the walls were

painted a rich, mahogany brown. Numerous paintings hung on the walls, depicting everything from a farmhouse to a ballerina.

Phoebe led us into the apartment farthest down the hall.

"Sorry if it's a little messy," she said immediately with an embarrassed shrug. "I wasn't expecting guests."

She held her breath as she pushed open the door, gauging my reaction with wide eyes. The apartment was cute. It wasn't a word I'd ever thought I would use to describe the living space of Phoebe and Tyson. It had a simple layout that included a kitchen, living room, and a hallway that no doubt led to the bedrooms. The dining room table was in that brief bit of space between the kitchen and living room.

Tyson was already lounging in the living room, shirtless, with a cigarette dangling from his lips.

When we entered, his eyes immediately zeroed in on my face, and he offered me a sultry smirk and wink.

I rolled my eyes.

He was infuriating. Handsome, sexy, but infuriating. Punch-him-in-the-face type of infuriating.

Of course he had to be shirtless. Because he was an asshole, and assholes liked to walk around shirtless.

Stellar logic.

"Ty! Put a shirt on!" Phoebe snapped once she noticed her brother. She sounded as if she was on the verge of laughter.

"I'm relaxing," he protested. "I'm allowed to relax the way I want to in my own home." His eyes continued to penetrate my skin, and my body burned from the heat in his gaze.

"When have you ever walked around shirtless? You

know what? Whatever. We're going to be in my room." Linking her arm with mine, Phoebe led us down a small hallway.

Her bedroom was exactly what I'd pictured of the petite, lilac-haired girl. It was a combination of black and pink. Black bedding with fuzzy, pink throw pillows. Pink carpeting. Black walls. Even her clothing was an assortment of those two colors. Eyeing me cautiously, she quickly moved around the room, picking up dirty clothes and throwing them into a bin.

"Again, sorry for the mess. Ugh. I don't usually have people over."

"That's fine. I sort of invited myself over anyway." I pursued the photos hanging on the wall while she cleaned. There were, surprisingly, a few of her and Colt together. In each one, they were smiling happily at the camera. I noted a photograph of Tyson. He looked younger, maybe ten, but his shock of brown, disheveled hair was unmistakable. There was a certain innocence in his expression that was absent in the man I knew today. What had happened to harden him so? Where did the young boy go?

"So, tell me about the asshole ex," said Phoebe, diverting my attention away from the photographs.

"He's not technically my ex," I pointed out. I didn't know what Jaron and I were, and I didn't care to ask. I was growing tired of always being the one to initiate conversation. If he wanted the relationship to work, he had to put in the effort.

"Semantics." She waved her hand dismissively and sprawled herself on the bed. "From what I hear, he sounds like a douchebag."

Sighing, I moved to lie beside her.

"I don't know. Maybe? He hasn't always been an asshole.

He used to be sweet and attentive and..." I trailed off. There had been a time, when we had first started dating, when Jaron had treated me as if I were his entire world. I was his world, and he was mine. Life had a way of knocking you down repeatedly, destroying the good in your life while keeping the bad. What Jaron and I had used to be good. Amazing, even. Now? We were toxic, both for each other and the people around us. Dysfunctional.

"I think he's cheating on me," I admitted at last. The words made my stomach clench painfully. "With my best friend."

I supposed that the thought hurt me more than the action itself. The lack of trust and respect.

Trust, for my best friend and boyfriend.

Respect, for the relationship we'd had for years.

I hadn't imagined I would be forgotten and replaced so quickly after I'd left.

Phoebe grimaced in sympathy.

"I know the feeling. My ex-boyfriend slept with one of my closest friends. You remember that girl hanging all over Tyson?"

I squeezed her shoulder.

It was official. Boys were assholes.

"I'm also sorry about Johnny. I know it must be rough for you," I lamented, realizing that I hadn't yet offered my condolences.

Phoebe glanced at me, startled.

"There's a lot you don't know about us," she answered at last, her tone almost dismissive. "We have a...rivalry going on with the next town over. Johnny always stuck his nose where it didn't belong."

I wondered if she knew about the ritualistic style of the

killing. I knew that the details hadn't been made public yet, but I just assumed that she had been told.

I debated whether or not to tell her. Just as quickly as the thought occurred to me, I dismissed it. I remembered vividly my bruised and bloodied knuckles and the blood staining my blonde wig.

*A coincidence*, my mind said, but I kept my mouth shut all the same.

"Besides, Johnny was kind of an asshole." Her eyes flickered with something dangerous. Something dark. As quickly as it was there, it disappeared. She was back to her bubbly, happy self.

"Now, let's watch Netflix and eat ice cream until our minds turn numb!"

After a long *Gossip Girl* marathon, I finally gained the nerve to ask her where the bathroom was.

"Two doors down," she answered dismissively. She was utterly entranced with the relationship between Blair and Serena.

Grabbing my toothbrush and pajamas out of my bag—I'd come prepared when I went to the football game—I tentatively ventured down the hallway while reflecting on what I'd heard from Phoebe.

She spoke as if Johnny had been a bad guy, a bad person. She spoke as if he almost deserved death.

Did anyone deserve death, let alone a teenage boy? Weren't they friends? The mystery surrounding Johnny and the Creepers increased. Intensified. The more answers I received, the more questions I gained.

Still lost in my thoughts, I pushed open the bathroom door.

And screamed.

Muscular.

Butts.
One butt.
With dimples.
Brain malfunctioned.
Water.
Toned back.
Legs.
Butt.

"What the hell are you doing, Ian?" Tyson demanded, pushing me behind him. I barely processed the movement. My brain was still short-circuiting. It only got moderately better when Ian grabbed a towel and wrapped it around his waist. Moderately, because it gifted me a view of his delicious eight-pack and the light spatter of hair low on his stomach.

Me no human. Me not know how thoughts work.

"I was showering," Ian replied easily, flashing me a smile.

Was it getting hot in there?

"What the—Stop looking!" This last statement from Tyson was directed at me. Was I looking? I honestly couldn't tell you.

Ty angrily stormed farther into the bathroom, placing himself between Ian and me. His eyes flashed with an almost incandescent fury.

"Wait? Ian?" I said as something occurred to me. "The Ian that drove me home the other night?"

The night Johnny died.

The night I officially lost my mind.

The night my life forever, irrevocably changed, though I barely understood the extent of it at the time.

"The one and only." He smiled yet again, and I noticed a dimple appear on his cheek.

Both ass and face dimples?

Swoon.

"Sorry I got you arrested," I muttered.

"Nah. It's all good. Crossed something off my bucket list."

"Happy to help."

Was I smiling? Drooling? Standing there awkwardly?

The world may never know.

Tyson, seemingly fed up with my behavior, grabbed my hand and pulled me into the hall. His touch was surprisingly gentle, despite the anger evident on his face. I heard Ian's laugh as the bathroom door slammed closed.

Finally coming to my senses, I wrenched my arm away from Tyson's iron grip.

"What the hell, Ty?" I screeched. "You can't just manhandle me whenever you feel like it!"

"What the hell are you doing to me?" Ty snapped right back. He thrusted a hand through his hair, his agitation physically manifesting itself.

"What do you even mean?" I was screaming at him, overcome by this elemental fury I didn't completely understand. Ty just irritated me so freaking much.

"I mean that I can't get you out of my fucking head! I haven't been able to even kiss another girl since you told me to fuck off!"

Planting a hand on my hip, I leveled him with my best glare.

"So you're saying because I told you to stay away from me, your dick has been flaccid?"

His eyes flared. "You...!"

"I'm not just a toy you can covet, Tyson! I'm not like those other girls that you can walk all over!"

We were nose to nose, my hands clenched into fists

beside me. I was breathing hard, panting almost, but I refused to look away. His eyes captivated me, held me hostage. They were both haunting and beautiful, aged by horrors I had yet to understand.

"You annoy the hell out of me, woman," he hissed at last.

And then he kissed me.

It was rough and angry. A clash of lips and teeth. A competition for dominance. His tongue tangled with mine, and my fisted hand slowly unclenched to grip his hair. I pulled his head, hard, and he lifted his head eagerly to give me access to his neck.

I hated him so freaking much.

Planting kisses across his collarbone, I smiled internally when his breathing stuttered. It felt powerful to have a guy like Tyson writhing under my hands.

Jaron had never...

The thought made me gasp, and I pushed Tyson away as if he were on fire. He pulled back immediately, eyes hooded with desire. When he saw my horrified expression, his own changed and tightened, lust giving way to impassivity. I still noticed the hurt in his eyes, there and gone in less than a second.

"Save me the whole 'it was a mistake' bullshit." He crossed his arms over his chest.

I knew he was right. I knew it was a mistake.

But not for the way he was thinking.

It was a mistake because I still had a boyfriend, and the last thing I wanted to be was a cheater. It was a mistake because I was screwed up in the head, and I struggled to differentiate between right and wrong, white and black.

At the same time, tiny licks of fire danced across my skin. I had never felt such an intense reaction before with Jaron.

Before I could say all of that, before I could salvage our deteriorating relationship, Ty had turned away. He was walking away, and I was helpless to do anything but watch him go.

"Ty..."

My phone rang, interrupting whatever I was going to say. Maybe that was a blessing in disguise.

Sighing, I held the phone to my ear.

"Hello?"

"Cami? Are you still at Phoebe's house?" Papa's frantic voice came over the speaker.

"Yes. Why? What's wrong?"

Tyson paused at my panicked words, turning back towards me with furrowed brows.

"There's been an accident," Papa said. His voice sounded as if he was on the verge of tears. That, by itself, was wrong. Papa didn't cry. He didn't show emotion. It just wasn't in his character to display such weakness. "It's Colt."

My body turned to ice. I was dimly aware of Ty saying my name, shaking my shoulders. I heard him yell for Phoebe before taking the phone still grasped tightly in my hand.

Colt. Colt. Colt.

I only had a second to focus on my brother's name before my vision darkened.

∽

THEY TOLD ME A KNIFE HAD FELL ONTO HIS HAND. THE ANGLE of the blade, they said, cut it clean off. They said that it was just bad luck.

They said...

They said...

They said...

I didn't believe one word of it. A knife, tucked safely away inside the kitchen drawer, happened to mysteriously appear out of thin air and fall? It just happened to hit his wrist, disconnecting his hand?

I didn't believe in coincidences, and I didn't believe it was an accident.

Papa had insisted I head home. He'd told me that there was no point in going to the hospital. I would just worry, and my depression and anxiety would get the best of me.

I knew he was right, but I wanted nothing more than to run to my brother's side.

The ride to my house was tense. Ian drove, and Ty sat in the front seat. His lips were pursed, and his hand was white from where it gripped the seat handle. Phoebe, beside me, was sobbing silently.

Everything was a blur. The faces, their soothing words, the roads streaking by. I barely remembered pulling into my house, helped out of the car by Ian. Ty helped his sister.

Vaguely, I recalled telling them to go home. I didn't need their pity.

But they stubbornly stayed. Ian and Tyson made themselves comfortable on the couch. Phoebe expertly made her way downstairs into Colt's room and curled into a ball on his bed.

I was annoyed by her behavior. She didn't know him. Not like I did. What right did she have to cry? To grieve? He was my brother, and she'd only known him for two weeks. I was just so angry.

At her.

At the world.

My anger only intensified when I threw open my bedroom door.

The stupid black leather outfit was once again draped over the side of my bed, the blonde wig resting beside it.

Hysteria and anger warred for dominance when I caught sight of my bedroom wall. The ominous writing in red, bright against the beige walls, made me vomit.

DON'T LEAVE ME AGAIN

## 17

I slept on and off that night.

My dreams, my nightmares, threatened to consume me like a dark, sticky tar. Once my head went under, it was impossible to escape.

I thought about Colt. A lot. Anger and guilt were the dominant emotions. Anger at whoever did this to my brother, and guilt for being the cause. He'd been punished because I had left. I'd been selfish, driven by this need to save myself, and my family had been forced to pay for this decision. The guilt drowned me.

The nightmares may have been the shove into the water, but the guilt was the chains keeping me tethered to the ground, drowning me. Killing me.

I didn't leave my bed.

All I could do was stare blindly at my now paint free wall as if it held all the answers. I could still see a smear of pink across the light surface. It was a reminder of my failure.

Dorian was right—my house was haunted.

The realization should've taken me by surprise. I should've screamed and cried and pounded my fist against the walls. Instead, all I felt was numb. Something innate within me had suspected as much.

At one point, Ian came into my bedroom with a plate of food.

"How are you feeling?" he asked, setting it down on my bedside table. I stared at something over his shoulder. I didn't know what I was looking at, only that it couldn't be him.

My voice quiet, I said, "There's this darkness inside of me. This darkness that is trying so desperately to escape." Trembling, I finally dared to meet Ian's eyes with my own tear filled ones. "We can't let this darkness escape."

He didn't call me an idiot.

He didn't say I was insane and threaten to have me committed.

Instead, he merely looked at me with large, kind eyes.

"Why not?" he asked.

"Because everyone will die."

∼

"Cami," Tyson said, poking his head into my room. "There's someone here to see you."

It was Saturday night, and I still had yet to leave the bedroom, outside of occasional bathroom trips. If I'd decided not to leave the bedroom, the Twisted Trio had decided not to leave my house. I could hear Phoebe inside of Colt's bedroom, and Ty and Ian were watching a football game in the living room.

It should've bothered me that they were in my house, uninvited, but it didn't. If anything, I was incapable of feeling any emotion besides an icy numbness.

"What?" I asked, barely processing his words. Who would come to see me?

Who would—

Crap.

The twins.

I'd completely forgotten I had invited them over.

Scurrying towards my closet, I grabbed a sweatshirt and quickly threw it on over my pajamas.

"I can just send him away," Tyson offered. He sounded almost angry at the intrusion.

"No. I invited them." I padded barefoot down the hallway, Ty trailing behind me like a shadow. Ian was sitting in the living room, watching the game. He paused it when he saw me.

"Finally decided to join the living," he jested, eyes twinkling. I barely managed to give him a smile. But I *did* manage it.

The door was cracked open, evidence that Ty had already answered it. I pulled it open the rest of the way, expecting to see my ginger twins, only to be shocked by a familiar set of broad shoulders and buzzed blond hair.

"Kieran?" I asked, stunned. The giant of a man had his backpack slung over his shoulder. His face was set into a scowl as he took in Ty behind me.

"I thought we could finish our project today. It's due Tuesday."

Crap. I'd completely forgotten about that.

"I don't think now's a good time," Ty coldly replied for me. I noticed that he was abnormally close to me in the entryway, his chest brushing my back with each breath he took. Kieran's eyes were fixated on the space, or lack thereof, between my body and Ty's.

"And I don't think you have the right to tell me what to

do," I snapped, moving my body away from Ty's. I noticed Kieran's lips twitch upwards.

To Kieran I said, "Maybe Monday after school? My brother got into an accident."

Kieran's eyes finally zeroed in on my face, dismissing Ty as if the brooding, imposing figure weren't even there.

"Is he okay? Are you okay? What happened?"

Ty made a nonsensical noise in the back of his throat, and I elbowed him in the stomach. Hard.

Did he really have to act like a dick when my brother was in the hospital?

I knew that his attitude wasn't intentional. That was just Ty, the good and the bad. I couldn't fault him for being himself, though I sometimes did wish that it didn't include an alpha personality.

The sound of a car door slamming shut had my eyes flicking over Kieran's shoulder.

My ginger twins had arrived. They looked slightly anxious as they stared at Kieran's muscular form in the entryway and Ty's imposingly large figure behind me.

Leroy was wearing rainbow pants today and a green tank top. Luke was wearing his standard superhero T-shirt and jeans ensemble.

And yes, they both made my mouth water.

Shut up.

It was a fleeting thought that broke through my customary numbness. I scoffed at how ridiculous I was for even *having* such a thought, given the horrid situation.

"I didn't know you were having a party," Leroy, oblivious to the mounting tension, said, skipping up the stairs. He grabbed my waist and gave me a quick kiss on the cheek. Of course, I began to blush an embarrassing shade of red.

"Okay!" I clapped my hands together with mock cheerfulness. "Everybody but the twins need to leave. Now."

Kieran and Ty both turned to stare at me as if I were insane. Ian, finally gracing us with his presence, began to snicker.

"What?" Ty asked incredulously. Was it really so strange that I wanted him gone? Ty and his stupidly inflated ego.

"You. Leave. Now."

I nodded towards Ian.

"Can you grab your sister, please? Tell her I'll text her later."

Ian, still looking too amused for his own good, saluted me before heading down the hall. Now, it just left me with two very bemused twins, one glowering asshole, and one stoic giant.

"The project..." Kieran mumbled. He ducked his head down, but not before I saw a splatter of red on his cheeks. Was Kieran embarrassed?

That I was sending him away?

Or that he had come in the first place?

"I'll stop by your house later on," I promised him hurriedly. I needed to get the twins inside. I needed to get to the bottom of this hole I had unintentionally dug myself. "Text me the address."

"Your parents aren't home," Ty bit out scathingly. He grabbed my shoulder and spun me around. "It isn't a good idea for you to have two males in your house that you don't know well."

I couldn't help it. I began to laugh at the irony of the situation. Had he not realized that he was a stranger as well? Did he think because we shared one ill-advised kiss that he was now privy to the workings of my entire life? He winced, as if he only now realized what he'd said.

"I don't..." Running a hand through his hair in agitation, he clamped his mouth shut. He alternated between glaring at Luke and Leroy and pleading with me. I could tell he didn't want to leave me alone with them.

What I couldn't tell, however, was why.

It wasn't just jealousy darkening his features, though there was plenty of that too, but something deeper. Darker. Something akin to fear.

I wanted to look further into it—what could cause such an intense emotion to break through his apathetic front?—but he was hurrying away before I could enquire. Ian was behind him, an arm wrapped around Phoebe.

She looked better. Face brighter, eyes sparkling, hair combed. I wondered if it was because she realized how silly she had been, crying over a guy she barely knew. I didn't believe in insta-love.

Oblivious to my thoughts, she pulled me in for a quick hug.

"Text me as soon as you get an update," she whispered. I patted her back in reassurance. "Seriously, Camz, text me."

My body froze at the nickname. Before I realized what I was doing, I pushed her away and took a fearful step away. Luke placed a steadying hand on my shoulder, eyebrow raised.

"Don't call me that," I said. My voice sounded shaky to my own ears.

Phoebe's eyes widened.

"I didn't know..."

"Don't say that name to me ever again." I took a breath to calm myself. Calm. I had to remain calm. The darkness only took control of me when I allowed my emotions to run rampant.

My mind flashed back to a year ago.

*Roaring crowd.*
*Bright stage lights.*
*Black miniskirt and dark corset.*
*Blonde wig.*

*"Camz!" the audience chanted. It was a character I'd created, a girl of my own making that didn't feel insignificant when compared to Fiona and others like her.*

*The darkness inside of me purred.*

## 18

"What is that?"

I surveyed the object in Luke's hand. It was small and silver, with blue and red lights that flickered sporadically at the top.

"This?" Luke held up the object. "It's an EMF. It begins to beep when there is a strong electromagnetic disturbance."

"Or a ghost?" I whispered quietly. He glanced at me out of the corner of his eye.

"Or a ghost," he agreed after a moment. "Spirits tend to leave behind an energy. An EMF allows you to locate particularly strong hotspots."

"How did you learn all of this?" I asked, watching his long fingers fiddle with a dial. When he didn't answer right away, I hurried on doggedly. "I mean, I know you said that you are a part of a ghost hunting club..."

He smirked. It was the first real smile I had ever seen on his face. He wore his mask so often, so effortlessly, that it was difficult for me to discern which of his faces was a lie.

I liked his smile.

"It's just me and my brother," he admitted, his voice rough with amusement.

"Huh?"

"The club. Nobody wanted to join. So it's just me and my brother."

I felt a twinge of sadness for the twins. From what I could see, they were isolated from the other students. Leroy because of his eccentric behavior, and Luke because of his timid, quiet one. Some of the kids referred to them as "weird" or "strange." At least they had each other.

That couldn't be said for all those other kids who had fallen victim to bullying.

"Well, you have a third member," I declared, smiling up at him. He smiled back at me, and it was like bloated, gray storm clouds moving away from the sun. He really did have a glorious smile. It was a shame it was always hidden away. As if he were privy to my thoughts, that smile disappeared immediately just as the thunder of footsteps echoed from down the hall.

"I set up the cameras," Leroy stated, entering the room. He wiggled his hips in excitement. "I was thinking we could have the base in your bedroom, Cami, if that's all right with you."

"That's fine."

My room. Colt's room. The living room. Hell, I would even stand in a dumpster if that was necessary to rid the house of such evil.

Such...darkness.

I didn't like to correlate evil and darkness, though some considered the terms one and the same. You could have darkness and not be evil, just like you could have light inside of you and still be evil.

At least, that was what I thought.

Hoped.

Believed.

How else could I explain the darkness brewing inside of me, percolating in the pit of my stomach like a nest of slithering, hissing snakes? The steady presence growing stronger and stronger each day?

I didn't want to believe that it was evil, despite its macabre fascination with death. I had to believe it wasn't malevolent.

I *had* to. The alternative was too much for me to compute.

Shaking my head, I gifted Leroy with a small smile.

"Explain the operation, good sir." I gave a dramatic curtsy. Leroy chuckled, but made a sweeping motion down the hallway.

"Right this way, madame."

I couldn't help but laugh when I noticed the way Leroy was walking—legs perfectly straight and arms swinging mechanically by his sides as if he was attempting to impersonate a stereotypical, old-fashioned, stick-up-the-ass, movie butler.

"You are such a weirdo," I said once the giggles had subsided. Leroy ruffled my hair affectionately.

"Takes one to know one."

He quickly explained all of the equipment. Half of them I forgot immediately after he said the name. There were infrared cameras in each of the main rooms. The only rooms excluded were the bathrooms and the garage. The cameras sent the video feed back to monitors inside of my bedroom.

"Where did you get all of this equipment?" I queried. This was some heavy-duty *Supernatural* shit. All we needed was the *Ghostbusters* theme song to begin playing and we would be gold.

Leroy and Luke exchanged anxious glances, and my pulse spiked at the telling gesture.

"Did you steal it? Please don't tell me you stole it."

"We didn't steal it, sugar bop," Leroy said with an exaggerated eye roll.

Well, thank the—

Sugar bop?

Before I could ask about the new endearment, Luke was already talking, his quiet voice able to innately command my attention.

"Tell us about the house. The things going on."

Leroy sprawled himself out on my bed, but Luke remained standing. His muscular arms bunched beneath his thin shirt when he crossed his arms.

I debated how much I should tell them.

On one hand, they might think I was completely insane.

On the other…

I thought of my older brother. He was in the hospital now because of me. Because of whatever was wrong with this house. Of that, I was certain.

My resolve settling, I moved to sit beside Leroy on my bed. He propped himself onto an elbow to see me better.

"Before I tell you about my house, I should tell you about my childhood." I saw them exchange another twin glance, but I hurried to continue before they could interrupt. "I'm adopted, as you can probably tell. My parents got me when I was about three, maybe four.

"I don't remember anything about the early days of my life. A stupid accident caused me to lose those memories. Everything I tell you is what I have been told, okay? I don't know how true all of this is."

My hands absently grabbed at the hem of my shirt. It was a lot harder than I'd expected to begin such a conversation. I might have had lunch with the twins every day for the past two weeks, but I didn't know them. Not really. It was difficult for me to tell them such personal information when I didn't even know their last name. For Colt, I would tell my story.

Even if that led to me being locked up in an insane asylum.

"I was found in the woods, alone and seemingly feral. My dads were very open about that. They didn't want to have secrets between us. Apparently, I'd lived in an abandoned cabin for years.

"When asked how I survived, I would only say one name. Over and over, I would repeat this name—the Shadow Man."

I watched Leroy's and Luke's expressions carefully. As expected, their eyes widened in shock, and their lips parted. It would've been almost comical to see such an eerily similar expression on both of their faces if the topic had been anything other than my macabre, demented childhood. It was wreathed in shadows and darkness, in spiders and despair.

"I was a troubled child, at least according to my parents. I would steal, lie, hit, and scream. There was nothing I didn't do. Every time I was asked about my actions, I would say that the Shadow Man made me. My therapist said that it was an imaginary friend I had created to help me while living alone. She said, and the cops agreed, that it would be impossible for me to have survived by myself for as long as I had at my age. They think my parents must've abandoned me in the woods only days before I was found.

"But I would say differently. I claimed that I had been in

the woods since I was a baby. I said that I remembered every detail of my birth. I was three years old, and I was able to speak with such eloquence and intelligence. Nobody could figure me out."

I took a deep breath. My fingernails dug into the palm of my hand, and I knew they were going to leave crescent-shaped indents.

"I fell on the playground a few years later. Hit my head. Lost a bunch of memories." I shrugged as if it were no big deal to lose a very important piece of myself. It was my childhood, the days and moments that shaped me into the person I was today. It was torture, agonizing torture, not to remember.

"My behavior changed soon after. I stopped acting up, and I stopped talking to and about the Shadow Man. But then I came here..."

I explained everything that had happened in the house so far. I grazed over Johnny's death, not wanting to confess that I believed myself to be involved. That was something I would figure out by myself.

I told them about Camz. About the darkness. About the side of me I kept hidden behind lock and key.

I had never felt freer than I did right then. Maybe I'd felt it before, when I was singing to Tyson, but that had been the darkness's contentment, not mine. The darkness craved attention, but I just wanted acceptance.

My heart juddered loudly at every word I said, every confession I made, until I thought it was going to burst from my ribcage. I needed to end this conversation before I inevitably exploded, losing even more of myself than I thought possible.

"Enough about me," I exclaimed hurriedly, turning on my side to face Leroy fully. My eccentric twin's eyelashes fluttered against his protruding cheekbones like twigs of ebony. The final result was a hooded expression that made my face erupt into flames. Schooling my features, I continued, "You still have yet to tell me where you got this equipment and how you got into the ghost hunting business."

It was Luke who answered, surprisingly. He had perched himself on my desk chair, his back towards us as he carefully watched the monitors. To me, the screens appeared to show nothing but darkness.

"Our parents believed in this type of stuff," he admitted softly. He still didn't look back at me. "They would often go on hunts with this equipment."

Tentatively, unsure if this was appropriate to bring up, I questioned, "You're using a lot of past tense words. Do they not do it anymore? Ghost hunting, I mean."

Again, there was a long, pregnant silence. All I could hear was the whir of the fan above our heads.

"They disappeared," Leroy said. For once, he wasn't smiling. His face was uncharacteristically solemn as he reflected on what must've been a difficult topic. "They went on a job, and they never came back."

"What was the job?"

"A teenage boy went missing. The parents believed that a ghost had something to do with his disappearance," Luke added, attention still fixated on the screens as if he found something on them riveting. He gave a small, nonchalant shrug. "They never returned home."

"Police ruled it as a missing persons case. That was a couple of years ago."

"And you haven't heard from them since?" I asked, struggling to wrap my head around this onslaught of information. My heart ached for the twins. I couldn't even imagine losing my family, the people I loved more than anything in this world. The fact that they—at least Leroy, though sometimes Luke—were able to smile every day was a testament to their characters.

Reaching out a hand, I gave Leroy's a squeeze. He flashed me a weary smile, but I suspected there was more he had to say.

"Cami, we need to be honest with you." His voice was hoarse with a suppressed emotion. Before he had even spoken, I knew what he was going to say. His next words confirmed as much. "The house they were investigating was your home."

I nodded gravely.

I had suspected as much. Fate had a funny way of working. The people we met, the people we brought into our lives, were not coincidences. I was just beginning to realize that everything happened for a reason, for a grand and elaborate plan outside of our control and even our understanding. We were forced onto a roller-coaster, enduring hill after hill, with no chance of stopping. We could crash, we could fall, but the ride would continue.

All we could do was hold on.

"That's why we're in this town to begin with," Luke added. "Sometimes, it takes months to complete a job. We moved here two weeks before they disappeared."

"And then we became stuck." That was Leroy who spoke, voice curt.

"Stuck," his twin agreed. "Bounced from home to home."

"Unloved..."

"Unwanted..."

Tears sprang to my eyes, and I squeezed Leroy's hand even tighter. I was sure my grip would leave bruises, but I didn't care. I wanted him to know that he wasn't alone. Just as quickly, pseudo cheerfulness replaced the sadness darkening his eyes. His smile was forced, the barest twitch of lips, but it was able to hide a grief and sadness so prominent that it seemed to perfume the air.

But they didn't ask me to elaborate on my past, so I didn't ask any questions about theirs.

"Let's get this party started." He rolled himself off of the bed, rubbing his hands together. Despite his words and smile, there was no excitement in his eyes. Why had I never noticed how haunted he was before? How broken? He could try to mask his pain behind smiles and laughs and corny jokes, but I was just beginning to realize that he was merely held together by tape and poorly placed bandages. I wondered if he'd ever had the chance to grieve for his parents. To heal.

Clearing my throat, I stood up as well.

"So we're going to use the ghost machine thingy thing?" I nodded towards the object still held in Luke's hand. Luke smiled slightly at my, admittedly, poor attempt at humor. I never said I was going to have a career in comedy.

"Let's turn this bad boy on."

Breath held in anticipation, I watched as Luke did just that.

Immediately once the machine was on, a loud beeping emitted from it and reverberated throughout my bedroom. It was loud and erratic, the noise screeching in tandem to my rapidly beating heart.

Luke and Leroy exchanged anxious glances.

"What does that sound mean?" I asked, my frown deepening when the twins didn't immediately answer me.

Body stiff, Luke took the machine out of my bedroom. The beeping immediately quieted. The second he stepped foot into my room, the noise began again, ear-shatteringly loud.

"That doesn't seem good. That's not good, right?" I flicked my gaze fearfully from Luke's impassive one to Leroy's stricken one.

"No," Luke said at last. He finally met my eyes. "It's not."

The noise from the machine seemed to get louder and louder the closer Luke came to the...

I gulped audibly.

To the closet.

Coming to the same conclusion I had, Luke hesitantly opened the wooden door. It squeaked on its hinges, the sound foreboding in the tension filled room. Absently, I reached for Leroy's hand, and he gripped it back encouragingly. This time, it wasn't him I was trying to comfort. I needed *him* to comfort *me*.

Eyes fixated on the new clothes hanging from the metal bar and the boxes on the ground, Luke brought the EMF against the wall of the closet, directly above the secret doorway.

"There's a secret room," I whispered shakily. "But it's smaller than the closet."

I watched, transfixed, as Luke removed the board covering the closet's hole. Leroy continued to hold my hand as I held my breath.

Luke crawled into the tiny room on his hands and knees. It would be a tight fit for someone like him, not impossible like it might've been for Kieran or even Ty, but insufferably small. I could only hope he wasn't claustrophobic.

"The wall is hollowed in here," Luke called after a moment of agonizing silence. I let out the breath I hadn't realized I'd been holding. I had been terrified in that minute he hadn't spoken. Terrified that the monster had gotten to him. Terrified of what he would see.

Terrified of a lot of things.

"Hollowed?" Leroy asked his brother. The hand that wasn't holding mine fiddled with the edge of his fedora.

"Yeah." Luke's voice sounded muffled. "I think there's something behind it."

"Can we tear it down?" I asked.

Recklessly.

Stupidly.

Fearfully.

Because wasn't that the reasons for all of my actions? Fear? Wasn't that the reason for everyone's behavior?

Luke's red hair appeared from the hole in the darkness. The flashlight on his phone accentuated his high cheekbones and the splatter of freckles on his nose.

"With tools, yeah." He hesitated, seeming to debate something internally. Finally, he sighed and met my gaze resolutely. "But are you sure it's something you want to do? Destroy a wall? Shouldn't you get your parents' permission?"

I knew that his words made sense. Perhaps this was something I should've discussed with my parents.

Perhaps.

Such a funny word. It seemed to hint at a multitude of outcomes. *Perhaps* if you did this instead of that. *Perhaps* if you said this instead of that.

Perhaps.

*Perhaps* I would be locked up in an insane asylum if I had expressed my fears to my fathers. I knew that their love was unconditional, but the darkness inside of me whispered words of doubts.

What if their love had limitations?

What if you finally proved to them that you were the monster they'd always suspected you to be?

Perhaps.

Before I could respond to Luke, the doorbell rang. The sound echoed through the immense house in a twinkle of bells.

I frowned.

My dads weren't expected back until tomorrow morning, while Colt was in another round of surgery. Karissa would be at our grandma's house until tomorrow as well.

Was it Kieran, coming back to work on the project?

Or Ty?

Maybe it was Dorian.

I secretly hoped it was the latter, not because I didn't want to see the other two, but I had the distinct feeling that Dorian knew more than he let on about the house and the spirits plaguing it.

The noise startled us all. Luke cussed as he jumped and banged his head against the low ceiling, and Leroy flinched.

"It's probably just my dad or something," I assured them placatingly.

I mean, I was almost one hundred percent sure it wasn't a ghost. Okay, maybe more like fifty percent.

"It'll be fine," I repeated, hoping that the false confidence in my voice became real. A part of me wanted to channel Camz, my inner darkness, but I pushed that feeling down. It had to remain buried for everybody's sake.

Tentatively, I ventured down the hallway. I could hear Leroy and Luke a few paces behind me, words nearly indistinct as they argued. Straightening my shoulders, I pushed open the door.

I didn't know what I'd expected to see on my doorstep. What I didn't expect, however, was an unfamiliar girl.

She had straight brown hair, a slightly tanned face, and wore the leather jacket I'd begun to associate with Ty and his gang.

"Cami?" Her voice was pure ice. It slithered down my spine, clawing its way through my skin like piercing nails. I shivered involuntarily at the blatant hatred in her eyes.

"Yes?"

Before I could say anything more, her palm connected with my cheek. My head swung wildly to the side, and I heard the twins run to me from behind. My hand immediately went to rub at the sensitive skin.

"Stay away from my boyfriend, you bitch," she hissed. Without another word, she turned on her heel and stormed down to an impressive silver car at the end of the driveway.

"Are you okay?" Leroy asked immediately, body thrumming with barely contained tension. His arm wrapped around my shoulder, pulling me into him. I was stunned and hurt. And also confused. Very, very confused.

"Here." Luke returned from the kitchen holding a frozen package of peas. When I continued to stare blankly at the retreating car, he brought it up to my face. I winced at the initial sting and attempted to move away. "No. We don't want it to swell."

"Who was she?" I whispered.

"That was Ali Blossom," Leroy supplied. He still had yet to release my shoulders, but I didn't mind. I enjoyed his hug.

"Who?"

"She goes to school with us," Luke added. He pulled the peas away from my face to inspect my face. "It's a little red, but I don't think it'll bruise."

"Who is her boyfriend?"

I was confused and angry. There always seemed to be this mentality that women had to put one another down to make themselves stronger. I didn't believe that any more than I believed that all women were backstabbing bitches and all men were jerks. Each person had numerous layers that I ached to uncover. I didn't understand her animosity towards me. It honestly made me sort of sad to know that someone hated me enough to physically harm me.

"Who knows?" Luke said, answering the question I had forgotten I'd asked. Frowning, I turned towards him. "But I'm pretty sure she had a thing with Ty."

Ty. And her.

I felt revulsion churn low in my stomach. He'd kissed me! He'd kissed me while he had been in a relationship! My anger made my blood boil, though I knew my reaction was slightly hypocritical. I'd kissed him back, if only for a moment, while I was still dating Jaron.

"What do you want to do?" Luke asked me softly. I knew he wasn't just talking about Ali.

"I think we should do some research. About the house. About the murders. About everything. How does Monday sound?"

Luke and Leroy looked at one another over my head. I was getting really annoyed with their twin speak. My agitation must've shown on my face, because Leroy smiled wryly. Luke, on the other hand, remained somber.

"Are you sure that's a good idea? For you to be in the house by yourself?"

I frowned. The house was big and imposing, and I felt evil seeping through every crack of the immense building like a poisonous gas. However, I didn't feel unsafe. I feared for my family and friends, but for myself?

"I'll be fine," I whispered. I didn't know who I was trying to convince—them or myself.

## 19

The branches snagged my clothes. Their wooded hands reached for me, called to me, claimed me. I pushed them away, a cry getting torn from my throat as a particularly sharp stick scratched my hand. Blood welled, and I cradled it against my chest.

The forest was dark and daunting. The moon provided little light in the oppressive darkness, as the boughs above assured as much.

Still, I ran.

My feet pounded against the ground. Leaves crackled, twigs snapped, and my legs ached with every step I took.

I didn't know where I was running to, only that I had to move faster.

Wind whipped my hair around my face, and the sharp chill of it caused goosebumps to erupt on my skin.

The forest was unexpectedly silent. I presumed I would hear crickets in the distance, the occasional hoot of an owl, the thundering of footsteps from a deer. Instead, I was greeted with nothing but toe-curling, eerie silence. It was one with the darkness, curling around my body like a dark, sticky tar.

Finally, after what felt like hours, I arrived in a small clearing. Candles were positioned in a circle, highlighting every detail of the grotesque scene.

There was a girl sobbing on the ground. Her dark hair, now matted with blood, and bruised face were unmistakable.

Ali—the girl who'd slapped me.

Standing above her, tall and imperious compared to her trembling form, was a figure. I couldn't decipher any distinguishable features, due to the dark cloak obscuring his face from view.

"Stop!" I screamed, charging forward. Ali looked towards me hopefully.

But every step I took towards them only brought me farther away. I ran and I ran and I ran, but I never reached my desired destination. It was almost as if I were stuck on an invisible treadmill with no way off.

I saw, in painstakingly clear detail, as the hooded figure cut off Ali's hand. The blood bubbled, the color almost black in the flickering candlelight.

My voice turned raw from screaming.

The knife came down again, this time on the opposite hand, and I watched it fall to the ground as well.

All I could do was watch.

She coughed up blood, her face turning white, before she collapsed.

*No. No. No.*

I fell to my knees, still crying, still pleading, still praying to a God I wasn't sure was listening. I barely processed the figure stepping towards me. A part of me knew that I was going to die...and a larger part of me thought I deserved it.

I was going to be dismembered just as Ali had. All I managed to do, though, was stare up at the murderer tearfully.

Hands appeared from under the long sleeves of the cloak and pulled down the hood.

I found myself staring at...me.

Camz.

Tan skin, blonde wig with a dark tendril escaping, and blood. So much blood. It coated her face and clothes like a layer of red paint.

"No..." I whispered pathetically. Camz took a step closer.

"I am you. You are me. We are one."

Before she had even finished speaking, I was shaking my head vehemently, my denial bleeding from my lips like a sickly poison.

"I'm not like you."

"I am you. You are me. We are one," she repeated. She was wearing the standard Camz attire—dark miniskirt, black stockings, and leather corset. She smiled, showcasing a row of bloodstained teeth.

"Wake up, little Cami. Wake up."

*"Wake up."*

I jolted upright in bed, heart pounding, which steadily decreased to a semi-normal rhythm when I realized I was in my bedroom.

*Just a dream. Just a dream.*

Groaning, I blindly walked towards the bathroom.

*Just a dream. Just a dream.*

It was only when I turned on the light that I noted the face staring back at me.

I was wearing Camz's outfit and her blonde wig. Unlike in my dreams, there was no blood staining the outfit. It allowed me to believe, for only a moment, that I had subconsciously put the outfit on during my nightmare. It would make sense.

I refused to believe the alternative.

I refused to believe that the darkness was winning.

∼

There was someone already in the kitchen when I went to grab a cup of coffee.

"Kar," I greeted, noting my sister's shock of ebony hair bent over the kitchen table. "I thought you weren't going to be home until later?"

She glanced up from the sheet of paper she was coloring on, not looking pleased with the intrusion.

"Grandma and Grandpa dropped me off earlier. They went to say hi to you, but they told me you were still sleeping."

I felt my body sag in relief at her words. If I was asleep when they went to check on me, then there was a good chance that I had been in my bed the entire night.

That I hadn't snuck out to meander through the woods.

The dark tendrils that remained from my dream made me shiver. I couldn't remember every detail now that I was fully awake, but I could clearly see Ali's terrified face highlighted in the ambient glow of the full moon.

"So I was thinking…" Karissa began conversationally.

"Well, that's scary."

Karissa gave me a scathing look that said she did not find my humor amusing.

"Anyway," she mumbled, turning her glare away from me and back towards her drawing. "I was thinking that we should hang out today."

My heart swelled. Never—and I mean that literally—

had Karissa instigated bonding time. I couldn't even remember the last time we had done anything more than watch the occasional movie together in the living room. She would always come up with an excuse why she couldn't spend time with me. I didn't take it personally. She was just coming into herself, and kids at that age had this idiotic mentality they were somehow better than everyone else. I'd been the exact same way when I was her age.

But...

"I would if I could," I began, already hating myself. "I just have to work on this huge chemistry project that's due on Tuesday."

I could tell she was drifting away from me. Her piercing eyes had narrowed before dropping down to the black crayon gripped tightly in her dainty fist.

"Whatever."

I hurried to explain. This was a huge stepping stone in our precarious relationship. While it may have seemed small to some, it was the equivalent of crossing the ocean for us. We never leapt. We were always too scared, too timid, to take that jump.

It devastated me that I had to say no. I wanted nothing more than to spend the entire day with my little sister, learning her secrets, gossiping like old times, watching movies.

"You know I totally would!" I hurried to explain. "I just made plans Monday after school, so now I need to work on the project today..."

She gathered up her papers and pencils, already shaking her head.

"Don't worry about it. It's fine."

From her tone, I gathered that it wasn't fine. It was the furthest thing from fine it could be.

"Kar..."

"Whatever."

Before I could suggest doing something later that night instead, she stomped upstairs. I heard the sound of a door opening and then slamming shut. I don't know if you knew this, but that was universal sister speak for "I'm pissed off."

Why couldn't I do one thing right?

First Colt, and now Karissa. I was a human wrecking ball, terrorizing and breaking everything in its path. So far, there hadn't been any casualties. How long would my luck hold?

Dragging a hand down my face with a heavy sigh, I hurried to finish my coffee and grab my backpack.

Kieran had texted me his address the day before, after I'd kicked him out. I figured if he thought it was acceptable to show up at my house unannounced, I could do the same to him.

I called up to Karissa to tell her that I was going to be gone for a couple of hours. She, of course, didn't respond. I also texted my parents, letting them know where I was going to be.

The address Kieran had given me was not a far walk. In the early morning, there was barely any traffic clogging the streets. The air was warm, but the breeze was surprisingly cool. I was grateful I'd remembered my jacket.

The house my phone led me to was enormous. Two twin pillars connected level after level of swooping arcades. The driveway looked as if it had been recently paved, a dark black contrasting with the perfectly manicured, almost artificial appearing grass. I noted a fountain near the side of the house, along with a garden.

"Holy shit," I muttered, taking in the extravagance and

opulence of it all. This building made my house look like an abandoned shack.

I walked up to a set of intricately carved doors, each with a golden knocker. I almost didn't dare touch something so ethereal in beauty, as if my darkness would somehow tarnish it.

After a moment of indecision, I hesitantly used my fist to knock on the door.

There was silence, quickly cut off by the swoosh of the door opening. A gray-haired man with a wrinkled face and a black suit greeted me.

"Hi," I muttered, suddenly feeling immensely awkward and unsure. Was this Kieran's father? Was I supposed to bow or something? How do normal people behave around the rich? "I'm looking for Kieran."

"Master Kieran is upstairs in his bedroom," the man drawled. His voice, like his appearance, was dignified and proper, reminding me distinctly of brittle paper. It made me feel utterly dull beside him.

And "master"? What the hell?

"Can I go up and speak with him? We need to work on a project together for school."

The man considered me with his beady, pinprick dark eyes. I had the feeling I'd just been seen more clearly than ever before in my life. The intensity of his scrutiny made me cower away. After one more long minute of careful observation, the man stepped back to allow me entry.

"Right this way."

The inside was just as gorgeous as the outside. Polished, wooden floors. Three-tiered chandeliers. Beautiful leather furniture. He gestured towards a spiral staircase.

"First door on your left."

He eyed me cynically before disappearing around the corner.

Okay then.

I followed his instructions, hesitating briefly when I heard loud music on the other side of the door. I did not want a repeat of the whole Ian incident.

Maybe I didn't.

Probably didn't.

Probably shouldn't.

I knocked quickly.

When there was no response, I knocked again.

Fuming with irritation, I knocked a third time. The music continued to blare on.

After only a brief hesitation, I threw open Kieran's bedroom door.

The first thing I noticed was how cluttered his room appeared to be. Football equipment was hanging out of an opened duffel bag. Books were strewn across the nightstand beside his bed, and clothes were scattered across the floor. The second thing I noticed was Kieran himself.

His profile was visible as he faced the mirror on the wall, his head nodding to the beat of the song. He was shirtless, his muscles defined and drool worthy. He appeared to have something in his hand. I noticed it glimmering in the bedroom lighting. As I watched, he brought the object to his wrist and began to slash at the skin. Blood welled, and it was only then that I realized what the object was.

A razor.

"Kieran!" I screamed, running towards him. He jumped, startled, and dropped the razorblade. On closer inspection, I could see row after row of bloody gashes marring his porcelain skin. Some were older, perhaps from a few days ago, and others looked brand-new. The blood was fresh and ran down his arm in red rivulets.

His eyes widened when he caught sight of me.

"Camila," he whispered softly, almost reverently. I grabbed his wrist gently, despite the anger thrumming through my body, and surveyed the mutilated skin.

"Okay. Let me grab you a bandage. Where do you keep them?"

His eyes were still large in his handsome, arresting face.

"In the bathroom across the hall."

After quickly grabbing a washcloth, a box of Band-Aids, and some generic cleansing alcohol, I hurried back towards Kieran. He hadn't moved from where I'd left him—arm held in front of him, eyes staring blindly ahead. Without a single word, I grabbed his hand yet again and began carefully pouring alcohol onto his wounds. He winced, but I shushed him with one eloquent look.

"How often do you do this to yourself?" I asked, applying the last bandage to one particularly deep cut.

His answer was gruff. "Enough."

"*Why* do you do this to yourself?"

I didn't understand it. Kieran was popular, the star quarterback, and the king of the school. He had people vying to become his friend. Girls threw themselves at him. And his house? It was a freaking mansion.

I knew that there was more to the story than what I could see. The superficial and materialistic stuff were not the only factors. You couldn't just decide whether or not you wanted to be depressed. It wasn't a conscious decision you could make, like choosing to wear green nail polish instead of red. Your mind became your enemy, and your thoughts became your destroyers.

When Kieran didn't answer, I nodded solemnly.

"You don't have to tell me. I don't expect you to. But is there anyone you *can* talk to?"

Again, Kieran didn't answer. He just continued to stare at me with an unreadable expression.

"You can't do this to yourself, okay? It's not safe. I understand that you might feel like you need an outlet…"

"You don't know shit about me," Kieran bit out, tone a guttural growl. It sliced at my heart as keenly as his blade had just cut at his skin. He wrenched his arm away from me, and I allowed him to go. Retreat. And that was what he was doing, I realized. He felt as if there was no other outlet in this incessant battle against himself. I knew because I had once been the same way.

Correction—I still was the same way.

"You're right—I don't." I had to venture carefully. I was treading in dangerous waters, and I refused to allow Kieran to be a passenger on my leaking ship. One wrong move, and we would both drown. I'd heard that when your head first went under, it was a struggle. You fought desperately to swim towards that pocket of fresh air taunting you from above. And when the water rushed your lungs, you felt nothing but blistering pain. Gradually, that pain receded, and you slipped easily into bliss. "Do you have any pets?" I blurted, desperate to divert his attention away from his own morose thoughts.

"Pets?" He stared at me incredulously.

"Yeah, do you have any?"

He absently reached for his shirt on the floor and pulled it over his head. The sleeves reached the tips of his fingers, effectively covering up any evidence of his previous activity.

"No," he answered at last. He moved to sit at the edge of his bed. "I don't have any."

"I don't either," I admitted. I dropped my backpack onto

his desk and sat beside him. "But I want a dog. Or a cat. Or a horse. Anything, really."

"Even a snake?" Kieran asked. He was silent for a moment, lost in his own thoughts, before he spoke again. "What are you doing, Cami?"

"What do you mean?"

"What are you doing?" The big man, even sitting, towered over me, yet I didn't have any fear or anxiety. There was so much tenderness in his face.

"What I'm doing is working on our chemistry project." I abruptly stood and walked to my backpack. Pulling out our lab notes, I retook my seat beside him. His expression was indecipherable as he watched me.

"Cami..."

I smiled up at him. "Let's get to work."

## 20

I'd always considered school my own personal purgatory. Not hell, necessarily, but a cage that I couldn't escape from. Back in Chicago, I was chained to my friendship with Fiona and my relationship with Jaron. They'd trapped me in a way I'd never realized before. Away from them, if only for a moment, was freeing and liberating.

I hated having those thoughts about my supposed best friend and boyfriend.

For the first time in months, I was excited to go to my new school—or any school in general—when I woke up that morning. I was excited to see the twins and even Kieran again. I was excited to bitch-slap Ty for kissing me while he apparently had a girlfriend. I was unfamiliar with this elation.

"Cami! There's a car out here for you," Dad called.

"Huh?" I quickly placed my hair into a disheveled bun before prancing downstairs. Dad stood in the foyer, my backpack in one hand, a to-go cup of coffee in the other. My dad was seriously the most amazing person ever. "Where's

Papa?" I took the coffee from him and shrugged on the backpack. "And how's Colt?"

His eyes darkened, though I didn't know if it was because of my question concerning my father or my brother.

"Colt has a long road of recovery," Dad admitted after a moment. "But he should regain function in his hand."

"And Papa?"

I turned towards the doorway, surprised to see Luke leaning against the wooden frame. He lifted his hand by way of greeting.

"Papa got called into work earlier this morning." His expression darkened even further before quickly smoothing over. "Have fun at school!"

I kissed his prickly cheek.

"Love you!"

I waited until Luke and I were outside before speaking.

"What are you doing here?" I wasn't upset, just confused.

"We thought you could use a ride to school today," Luke said with a shrug.

"We?"

An identical face to the one I was standing next to popped out of the passenger window of the car. He wore his signature fedora and a golden suit jacket.

"Hey, beautiful butterfly!" He glanced down at the tire of the car. "It has been *tiring* waiting for you."

"Hey, handsome man!" I called back, my lips curving into a tentative smile. There was something about Leroy's energy that was almost contagious. If I was the dark, then he was the light chasing away my shadows.

I threw myself into the backseat, purposely hitting Leroy in the back of the head in the process. He pinched my arm in retaliation.

"You guys are going to be the death of me," Luke muttered as he buckled himself in.

"Death is only the beginning," I stated ominously, flashing the serious twin a wicked grin.

"The beginning of the end. Where an end leads to the beginning, but it doesn't actually end," Leroy added, and I began to laugh at Luke's irritated expression. Leroy was definitely a lot to handle.

My laughter subsided with Luke's next words.

"Anything happen after we left?" His eyes flicked to mine in the rearview mirror, and my lips tugged downwards into a frown.

Did anything happen?

I'd had a strange, vivid dream that constantly eluded me. It was like trying to grasp air—impossible. Despite this, I could still feel the blood slithering down my skin like a living entity—a nest of rats, perhaps, or a den of hissing, slithering vipers. I could still hear Ali's pathetic gasp as the life was drained from her, though the rest of the dream remained an elusive mystery.

It terrified me. There were so many things that were unknown. There were so many things that were not *meant* to be known. My head was spinning in tandem with the world itself, around and around and around, like a carousel you couldn't get off of no matter how hard you tried. All you could do was hold on for dear life and pray you didn't vomit.

"Dreams," I answered at last. "Just bad dreams."

Leroy reached behind to squeeze my hand, and I gave him a timid smile. The remnants of my dreams continued to haunt me, even now that I was awake.

We pulled into the school parking lot, and Luke parked the car a few spaces away from a familiar motorcycle. My vision turned red when I spotted his brown hair peeking out of a dark helmet. Tyson was leaning casually against his bike, one hand in his pocket and the other scrolling through something on his phone.

"I'll be back," I muttered to the twins darkly. They followed my line of vision, and Leroy grinned.

"Shit is going down! Kick some ass, baby girl," he squealed happily, and I pecked him on the cheek.

"You're such a psychopath," I murmured. I noticed that Luke, unlike his eccentric twin, was *not* smiling. He actually appeared nervous, bordering on fearful, as he tapped his fingers against the steering wheel. When he noticed my probing gaze, he smiled slightly.

"Just be careful. Ty's group is...dangerous. I don't want you getting on the wrong side of things."

On reflex, I leaned over the console to squeeze his shoulder. The sincerity in his voice caused fluttery butterflies to spread throughout my chest, their wings battering in tandem to my rapidly beating heart.

"I'm always careful. Besides, Ty is actually a big softie."

Leroy snorted, but Luke still appeared wary.

"Seriously, Cami. Be careful."

I knew he was right. My feelings for Ty were a toxic cocktail of mixed emotions. The cocky gang member was made of spun glass that seemed seconds away from tumbling to the ground and shattering. I was under no illusion that when he inevitably broke, he wouldn't take one of those shards of broken glass and...

And what? Slash my neck? The analogy was, admittedly, ridiculous, but there was no denying that darkness lingered beneath Ty's beautiful face. Just as it did mine.

Nodding solemnly at Luke, I strode towards where Ty was standing. There was no fan club this time. No Phoebe.

No Johnny.

No...Ali.

I chose not to look too closely at that.

"Tyson," I greeted stiffly. He glanced up, surprised, and a glorious smile lit up his face. He looked as if he was genuinely happy to see me. As if we were best friends or lovers that had been parted for more than a day.

It made my stomach tighten almost painfully.

"Cami." He extended his arms as if he meant to give me a hug, but I quickly sidestepped him.

"No, Ty. I need to talk, and I need you to listen."

He opened his mouth, to no doubt talk, but I quickly placed my hand over it. His eyes widened in surprise.

"That kiss? It was a mistake."

The light in his eyes flickered once before dying out. It was such a drastic change, like a bloated storm cloud moving in front of the sun.

"*Listen*," I stressed again when his lips parted beneath my hand. "I'm not saying it didn't mean anything. I'm not sure what it meant, to be completely honest. But I have a boyfriend, and you apparently have a girlfriend. I broke off the kiss because I felt ashamed. It wasn't fair to you or to Jaron. It also wasn't fair to Ali."

"Ali?" he mumbled around my hand. Or at least I think that was what he'd mumbled. His words were nearly inarticulate.

"She came to my house the other day," I admitted. "Confronted me."

I left out the part where she'd physically assaulted me. It didn't seem important.

His eyes narrowed, and his lips parted yet again. I could feel his warm breath against the palm of my hand and the flick of his tongue. I didn't know if the tongue licking was intentional or not, but licks of fire burned my skin.

His hand grabbed my wrist, and he gently pried it away from his mouth.

"I'm not dating Ali," he said at last. "I'm not dating anyone. I would never cheat. Ever."

He spoke with such conviction, such heat, that it was impossible not to believe him. It only proceeded to make me feel crappier.

He may not be a cheater, but I was. I'd kissed him back, and worst of all, I had enjoyed it. He must've seen something on my face, guilt and self-loathing no doubt, because his expression softened considerably.

"*I* kissed *you*."

"But I kissed you back." My voice was pathetically soft.

"I kissed you," he continued, ignoring my outburst, "when I knew you were vulnerable. I knew you were fighting with your boyfriend, and I used it to my advantage. And...I'm sorry." The last words sounded foreign coming from his mouth, as if they weren't spoken often.

"I'm sorry too." I paused. "But I don't think it should happen again."

"Because of your boyfriend?" he asked in obvious disbelief. "He's a dick."

"It's not just because of Jaron..." I trailed off, picturing my boyfriend's face. I'd once believed him to be the handsomest man alive, the epitome of perfection. Now? I was beginning to realize that perfection was subjective. What was perfect to some was annoying to others. Jaron was now just annoying. He didn't treat me like a queen, despite my repeated attempts to treat him like a king.

"It's because of you," I finished at last. His brows furrowed together.

"Me?"

"Do you think I've forgotten the way you treated me

when we first met? At the restaurant?" His frown deepened. "You teased me...and I don't believe you were entirely joking." He opened his mouth yet again, but I hurried on doggedly. "I know you may be sorry now, but I'm someone you need to earn. I'm not a one-night stand type of girl. I'm the woo with flowers kind."

He appeared honestly confused.

"Are you saying that I have to...woo you?"

"I'm saying that if you're not willing to put in the effort, you don't deserve me." I was feeling confident and beautiful. My fight with Jaron had left me invigorated. I finally knew my worth, and a little voice inside of me demanded nothing less. I questioned, briefly, if that voice was my darkness gaining purchase, but I dismissed that claim. It was confidence, nothing else. Confidence that I had finally gained after years of living in my friends' shadows. "I don't think that I'm what you need."

He spoke through gritted teeth. "You don't know what I need."

"And I don't think you do either," I pointed out. "But when you figure it out, let me know."

I left before he could say anything else. This was for the best, for both of us. We were two tortured souls drawn to each other. Until we could rid ourselves of our toxic influences, we could never have a legitimate, loving relationship. It just wasn't possible.

Head reeling, I stopped in front of the twins. They were watching me with matching, curious expressions.

"You okay?" Leroy asked immediately.

"What happened?" Luke added.

"We just talked," I said softly. I could feel Ty's eyes penetrating the back of my head. Forcing myself to smile, I linked my arm through Leroy's. "Let's get to class, sexy. It looks like it's going to rain."

∼

THE FIRST HALF OF THE DAY WENT AS IT NORMALLY DID. I HAD lunch with the twins, as per usual, before heading to my next class. I couldn't help but reflect on chemistry that morning.

We'd turned in our completed project a day early. Kieran had been subdued, silent almost, which wasn't anything new or unusual. What was new, however, was his attempt to make a joke.

One of the stoner girls had made a comment about Christmas. She'd joked that the only thing on her Christmas list was weed.

Kieran had leaned over to say, "Marij-want-a for Christmas?"

It was so unexpected, so unlike the solemn, brooding male and more like my fedora wearing twin, that I snorted in disbelief. And then I began laughing hysterically.

My lips turned upwards at the memory. I was grateful that Kieran was finally breaking out of his oppressive shell. I was even more grateful that there hadn't been any new cuts on his wrists. I'd checked, and the bandage was still firmly in place beneath his sweatshirt.

After lunch, the principal surprised me by calling me down into her office. She sat behind her desk, hands folded and hair placed into an elaborate bun at the top of her head. For a moment, she merely stared at me. I, of course, stared back. I wasn't the most expressive student to begin with, and she was not helping matters. After a moment of awkwardly staring at one another—a battle, in my mind, for dominance—she finally glanced down at her computer.

"How has school been?" she asked. "Making friends?"

I nodded mutely. Had my parents made her do this? I didn't understand if this was normal for small-town principals. How much of an interest did they invest in each kid?

"I just want to make sure that you have a positive experience here. I know how difficult it can be for students to switch to a new school during their senior year."

Her expression was so earnest, so sincere, that I felt compelled to answer.

"It's going great," I admitted at last.

She was silent for another long moment. The only sound was the clank of her nails against the keyboard as she typed vigorously away. Her eyes were misty when she finally looked up.

"You remind me a lot of my son. He would've been only a couple of years older than you." She sounded lost just then. Despite her statement being directed at me, I had the distinct feeling that she did not want a response. Her haunted eyes were staring at something above my shoulder. Shaking her head vehemently, she finally turned to stare at me, expression closed off and impassive. "I just thought I would check in."

I thanked her before hurrying out of the office. Despite her kindness, the uneasy feeling in the pit of my stomach continued to churn restlessly. There was something about her that made my hackles rise.

My phone dinged as I walked into my final class of the day.

**Papa:** Go straight home after school.

. . .

Frowning, I texted back.

Me: Why?

Papa: There's been another death. Go home.

I stared at the phone. I saw the words, but I couldn't process them.

Death. Death. Death.

My hands began to tremble, and I all but collapsed into my seat.

Death. Death. Death.

He didn't have to say the name of the person who'd died. I already knew.

And I also had the suspicion that she'd died of blood loss.

I dimly heard somebody calling my name, but it was barely audible over the roaring in my ears. The crude word replayed in my head.

Death. Death. Death.

I was aware of the floor rushing towards my face as my body tilted precariously to the side.

And then, I was aware of nothing.

∽

The distinct sound of laughter woke me up.

I peeled open one eyelid at a time, blinking against the

blinding synthetic lighting above me. I appeared to be in the school's medical center with white painted walls, a single sink, and three cots positioned side by side. None of the beds, besides mine, were occupied.

"Hello?" I whispered, swallowing around the acorn-sized lump lodged in my throat. The only sound that greeted me was the tinkling of laughter. I tried to recall the nurse's name, but I came up blank. Needless to say, I had yet to visit this particular section of the school in my two weeks as a student.

I heard the laughter yet again, right outside of the door, and I made an immediate beeline in that direction.

The hallway was dark. There were no windows down this particular stretch, and the only light was from an opened doorway near the very end of it.

"Hello?"

Okay, so here I was, faced with a dilemma.

I had seen horror movies before. I had even been the type to scream at the screen because the main character made a stupid decision that led to her eventual demise.

Did I want to walk down the creepy, dark, abandoned hallway?

No way in hell.

Did I feel a force propelling me forward?

Yes, most definitely.

The farther I walked away from the nurse's station, the scarcer and dimmer the light became. It was quite literally like seeing a light at the end of the tunnel.

The hairs on the back of my neck stood on end.

"Hello?"

My stupid, traitorous feet continued to drag me forward. I was nothing more than a puppet just then, and the lack of control terrified me.

Somebody up ahead began to laugh, and I finally caught a glimpse of dark hair.

"Karissa?"

I inspected my sister's profile. Dark, chiseled cheekbones. Amber eyes. Full lips curved into a smile.

Suddenly, I was running. From the darkness? To my sister? I couldn't tell you.

I could hear my little sister's laughter, reverberating through the hallway like wind chimes. "What are you doing here?" I demanded.

I finally reached the blinding light, nearly stumbling over my own two feet in my desperate haste to stop. My sister stood silhouetted in the open doorway.

"Karissa?" I asked, suddenly hesitant. Her back was towards me, long hair cascading down her shoulders in two identical braids.

"He wants you to come home." The voice that came out of her tiny, elfin body was not my sister's voice. It was two octaves lower than usual, and it seemed to be numerous voices overlapping. I staggered back a step.

"He's coming for you." She lurched forward, and I immediately moved to follow her. The momentum led us out of the school and into an unfamiliar forest.

Of course, it could've been familiar. All forests looked the same to me—weeds, trunks, leaves, and the occasional critter scurrying about.

"Karissa?" I whispered, spinning in a circle. I could no longer see my little sister. It was as if she'd suddenly dematerialized. One second, she was there, and the next, she was gone like smoke emitting from a blazing fire. "Kar?"

My body was so tired, my eyelids unbearably heavy, like weights had been applied to the thin skin. I just wanted to sleep.

Sleep...

Curling up on the ground, I wrapped my arms around my legs.

Sleep. I just wanted to sleep.

So I did.

## 21

If this was death, it was a welcome relief. The previous throbs and aches had completely diminished. The darkness surrounded me like waves from the sea, and I knew that we were one and the same. I was made to live in this darkness.

And then suddenly, I awoke.

My body was cold, as if I'd been plunged headfirst into the Arctic Ocean in the middle of winter. Hands trembling, I became aware of someone saying my name. Shaking my shoulder.

"Her lips are turning blue," he said harshly, but his voice sounded as if it were spoken through a filter. I wanted to respond, wanted to tell him that I was freezing, but the words wouldn't leave my parted lips.

Something was draped over my shoulders, and then I felt hands beneath my knees. My body was hoisted up as if I weighed nothing at all. My head lolled against his shoulder, and I muttered something indistinct.

There were more voices, each getting louder and louder as the seconds dragged on. I recognized them, yet I was unable to put a name to the face or a face to the voice. My mind was muddled, hazy almost, like looking through a fun house mirror. I barely processed the dark forest towering malevolently over me or the moonlight slashing through the darkness.

Where was I?

I tried to recall what had happened, but my brain was unable to form any coherent thought.

"We found her!" the person holding me announced. There was a shuffle, and then I was placed into a different set of arms.

"Thank you, Ian," a familiar voice whispered gruffly. I felt lips press against my forehead, and I burrowed myself further into his comforting embrace.

Papa.

"Is she going to be okay?" The man—Ian, apparently—asked anxiously.

"Thanks to you, she will be." Papa's voice sounded strange. It was husky, almost, as if he was speaking through gritted teeth. As if he was attempting to hold back an emotion that wanted to erupt out of him. "I put a call into the station to stop the search, but you should probably let those boys know. They seemed really worried."

Ian said something else, but I couldn't hear his words. I shivered further into the leather jacket, inhaling the cinnamon scent that was uniquely Ian's.

I don't remember how I arrived back at the police station. One second, I was outside, in my father's arms, and the next, a paramedic was looking me over. After declaring that I was going to be fine, Papa moved me to a seat in front of a heater inside of his office and handed me a cup of hot chocolate.

And then he watched me.

I couldn't help but glance at everything besides my father's sharp eyes. His desk cluttered with papers and files. A coat rack in the corner of the tiny office. An archaic desktop computer. I'd thought, based on my extensive television research, that Papa would have a cubicle, not an office. I didn't know a lot about police work, but I'd assumed they spent more time in the field than behind a desk.

If the paperwork and books were any indication, I was wrong.

After another long moment of silence, I let out a puff of annoyance. I hated the silence that currently engulfed us both.

"What, Papa?"

His hand was white where it clenched his own mug.

"You went missing. From school. The nurse went to check on you, and you were no longer there. With all the murders and deaths..." He trailed off. He looked terrified at that moment, and very young. Behind his bushy beard, his lips were tilted downward. "Why the hell did you just take off? Why did you go into the woods by yourself? What the hell were you thinking?" he asked, voice rising with each word until he was practically screaming. He continued to speak before I could get a word out. "Do you know how it felt to discover that your daughter disappeared from school after you had just returned from a gruesome case? And then I had to call your father and brother and tell them as well?"

His body suddenly deflated as the anger transformed into fear and hurt. I felt tears well in my own eyes.

I couldn't remember why I'd entered the forest in the first place. The last thing I remembered was receiving his text about the recent death. After that? Everything was a mystery. The fog in my brain had yet to recede.

"I am so sorry, Papa," I said, wiping away a stray tear. "I

must've been sleepwalking again or something. I honestly don't know how it happened."

He took a deep breath and dropped his head into his hands. His body shook with silent sobs.

"What exactly happened?" I asked after a moment. While he didn't look up, his body had stopped shaking. He looked so vulnerable just then, so despondent, like a defenseless child.

"We couldn't find you. No one could. We called your friends, searched the school, checked the cameras. There was nothing. One second, you were in the nurse's station, and the next, you were gone. You don't know how fucking worried we've been." He took a shuddering breath, and I leaned forward to squeeze his hand. I could tell he needed the comfort.

"We organized search parties to search the woods, and we..." He trailed off as his phone began to beep. Letting out a soft curse, he stood abruptly. "I need to take this. Don't move, okay?"

I gave him a cheeky smile and saluted.

"Yes, sir."

He watched me, eyes unreadable, before leaning down to kiss my cheek again. He didn't want to leave me, but he didn't have a choice. Releasing a heavy sigh, he quickly exited his office.

Alone at last, I sagged into the chair. The heat emitting from the heater warmed my frozen body. My hand itched to touch the flames I knew lurked beneath the machine, ached to feel them lick at my skin. For some reason, I thought that the fire, and the accompanying burn, would feel comforting. Relaxing.

Familiar.

I pulled my hand back a second before it would've touched the heater.

What was wrong with me?

Pulling Ian's jacket tighter around my shoulders, I inspected Papa's profile through the blinds in his office. The hand not holding the phone moved erratically, as it always did when he was agitated, and his face turned redder the longer he talked. I wondered who was on the other end of the phone. Was it Dad? Or was he talking to someone about the case?

Speaking of the case...

My eyes flicked to my father's desk. There were numerous manilla folders, all closed, and a stack of stapled papers. I glanced once more towards my father before moving stealthily from my seat to the desk.

I held my breath, afraid of what I might see but also afraid of what I wouldn't. I needed there to be answers in these folders. For my own sanity.

The first file was not relevant to the murders. It merely detailed a suspected robber and gang member. It wasn't the Creepers, Ty's gang, but another one. The Black Hawks.

The next file was just as useless. After a quick scan of the pages, I concluded that it was a home invasion case. Again, interesting, but not helpful.

It was the third file that caused the blood to leave my face. My hands, already trembling from the cold, dropped the papers through frozen fingers. Despite this, the images were already imprinted into my brain, etched into my eyelids like a demented tattoo.

There were two pictures paperclipped to the inside cover of the file. The first one was of Johnny. He was shirtless, strange symbols carved into his chest. Around him, made out of sticks, blood, and candles, was what appeared to be a star.

I vaguely remembered what Dad had said, something about ritualistic killings.

The second picture was of a familiar girl. My heart hammered against my chest, threatening to tear apart my ribcage. Ali.

She, too, had symbols slashed into her breasts. Her body had been found in the center of a star. Unlike with Johnny, her hands were cut off.

I became violently ill, barely making it to the trashcan in time. I didn't have a lot to offer up, but by the time I was finished, I'd thoroughly emptied my stomach's contents. Wiping my hand against my mouth, I glanced once more at the fallen file.

I knew there were more pages that I could've seen, I knew that, but I also knew I wasn't physically able to see anymore.

Johnny was dead. After he'd kissed me.

Ali was dead. After she'd slapped me.

Oh god.

Tyson.

He'd kissed me.

Did that mean...?

I refused to believe that he was next. I was not an optimist by any means, but I sure as hell wasn't demented enough to believe he was dead or would be. I tried to tell myself that it was only a coincidence. That their deaths had nothing to do with me, my dreams, or the strange entity haunting my house.

Coincidence.

It had to be. I didn't believe in a lot, but I believed in that.

The alternative, that the darkness's malicious hold on me was gaining traction, was too horrible to consider.

I felt like I was dying. It wasn't fast and painless, like a gunshot to the head would've been. It was slow and churning, the rumbling of a volcano before it eventually erupted. It was the feeling you got when you were underwater, desperate for air. Your vision went dark, and you began to panic. Panic.

Yes, I was panicking.

Because two people were dead, and I was somehow connected to it. Their deaths were my fault.

My fault.

Movements mechanical, I crouched down to pick up the fallen folder and pages, placing them back on the desk where I'd found them. I didn't dare glance at any of the papers. I didn't want to risk seeing the pictures again.

My father found me a few minutes later, curled up in the chair with my face pressed against the collar of Ian's jacket. His expression softened when he saw me.

"Are you ready to head home?" he asked.

"Yes, please."

He nodded solemnly and pressed a palm against my back to lead me to his car. The wind was sharp against my skin, but I found the pain welcoming.

"Shit," he cursed, patting down his pockets. "Forgot the keys."

"Careful, Pops," I joked with a small smile that didn't quite reach my eyes. "You're turning into Dad."

"Oh ha ha. Wait here. I'll be back in a second."

Before I could protest—I really didn't want to be left alone—Papa raced back towards the police station's glass doors. I instantly felt silly for my irrational fear. I was inches away from a police station, for Pete's sake. I could still see the officers moving about through the window that took up an entire wall.

Movement across the street caught my attention. I whipped my head in the direction of the noise, surprised to see a head turned towards me. I couldn't see any distinct features, but the streetlight did illuminate a dark jacket with a red patch on the left shoulder. My frown deepened when the figure continued to stare in my direction.

The feeling was unnerving, and I resisted the urge to run back inside the safety of the building. My skin pebbled with goosebumps. It was almost as if his eyes were penetrating my skin. Slicing through my barrier of clothes. Seeing me...

"You ready?"

I jumped at Papa's voice.

"Cami?"

Breaking my gaze away from the mysterious figure, I offered my dad a small, albeit fake, smile.

"Sorry. Just zoned out. Yeah, I'm ready."

I glanced back towards the streetlight.

The person was gone.

∾

Dad and Karissa were both still up when we arrived home.

Before I'd even made it all the way into the house, Dad wrapped his thick arms around me, sobbing into my neck.

"Cami..." he moaned. I patted his back, whispering soothing words meant to calm. I couldn't even begin to imagine the pain and fear I'd unintentionally put them through. All I could do was hold him a little tighter, a little closer, as if that psychical movement could somehow placate his mental anguish.

"I'm so sorry, Daddy," I whispered. I felt another body wrap around me from behind.

Karissa.

"We were so freaking worried," she mumbled, voice choked with tears. I released one arm from around my father to wrap it around my little sister. The position was awkward, but it allowed me to hold them both close.

After what felt like hours, Dad and Karissa both detangled themselves from me. Dad turned to Papa over my shoulder.

"When do you want to leave?" he asked.

"Where are you going?" My gaze flicked back and forth from Papa's grim expression to Dad's anxious one.

It was Papa who answered, voice grave.

"It's Colt."

"Is he okay?" I could feel the familiar tendrils of panic clawing up my body, suffocating me. Had the surgery not worked? Did he lose his hand?

"Colt's fine," Dad assured me, placing an arm around my shoulders. "He was just being an idiot."

"When he discovered that you were missing, he decided that he was going to search for you," Papa added. A tiny smile betrayed his amusement at my older brother's antics. "Accidentally tripped and sprained his ankle."

"How's his hand? Did he hurt it in the fall?" I bit my fingernail, a nervous habit I was determined to break.

"He's fine. He'll be in the hospital for a while, and he'll need a lot of physical therapy. But he's fine."

I let out the breath I hadn't even realized I'd been holding.

"So will you two be okay tonight by yourself? I want to check on Colt, and Papa has to go back to the station," Dad said, glancing between Karissa and me. "One of us could stay back if that's what you would prefer, but Papa set up an alarm that notifies both us and the police station if there are any intruders."

"We'll be fine," I hurried to assure him. They needed to be with Colt right now. "All I'm going to do is sleep anyways."

I debated whether or not to ask if I could go with them. I yearned to see my brother, to see with my own eyes that he was whole.

Yet I had my little sister to think about. She had school tomorrow, and I knew she already would only get a few hours of sleep.

"Text me with updates?" I added, my words turning into a question. Papa and Dad both smiled at me, pleased with my response.

"Of course, sweetheart," Dad promised. They each kissed my cheek before leaving, with Papa warning us to keep the doors locked all night and to not answer the door for anyone.

Soon, it was just Karissa and me.

"I'm going to bed," she said before I could say anything to her. She eyed me with distaste. Apparently, now that she knew I was alive and well, she could go back to being a brat. I couldn't entirely blame her. She was tired and hormonal and cranky. Hopefully, sleep would tame the beast.

"Yeah, that's probably a good idea," I said to her retreating back. She paused on the staircase, one hand resting on the rail. She turned her head to face me marginally.

"I'm really glad you're okay."

"Me too."

Without another word, though I didn't expect anything

else from my younger sister, she stomped upstairs. I heard the telltale sound of her door being slammed shut.

Releasing a breath, I quickly locked the front door. I was completely and utterly unnerved. Between the murders, the mysterious figure watching me under the waning glow of the street lamp, and the supposed hauntings, I was unhinged. I wouldn't necessarily say terrified just then. Numb would've been a more adequate description. I'd dealt with too much for my mind to fully comprehend. This was something you would see in a movie, not something you would experience in real life. I kept expecting to open my eyes and escape this horrible nightmare. Maybe someone would admit to playing an intense, practical joke on me.

I'd just opened my bedroom door, eyelids heavy, when I noted the figure fiddling with my stereo. I screamed, the noise muffled by the steady bass from the radio, and scrambled for the knob on my now closed door.

"Woah. Easy there," a familiar, amused voice said. This was followed immediately by, "You have shit music."

"Dorian?" I whispered, flicking the light switch on. The dark, indecipherable silhouette was chased away by the light to reveal his tousled blond hair and sturdy shoulders, clearly defined beneath his white shirt.

"Total shit. What the hell do kids these days listen to?" He held up a CD, frowned, then put it back down. Despite recognizing the man in my room, I did not relax my defensive stance, courtesy of my overprotective parents.

"What the hell are you doing in my room?" I whispered harshly. It didn't escape my notice that we were alone in the house, minus my defenseless sister. I didn't know him.

I didn't trust him.

My right hand instinctively reached for the softball bat near my doorframe. I hadn't played softball in years, not since Fiona had called me an awkward runner and Jaron had insisted that volleyball was the sport to participate in. Truthfully, I hadn't even been that good at the sport.

But a head? That I could hit.

I was actually the World Series home run champion...in *Wii Sports*.

It was a real thing.

"You shouldn't be in here," I hissed. Dorian's smile only grew when he saw my hand gripping the baseball bat.

"I was worried," he admitted after a second.

"So you decided to break into my house?! Into my room?" I was furious. Still, my sixth sense did not send out any red flags. Sure, I was agitated, but I wasn't scared. Not anymore. Taking a breath meant to calm myself, I added, "You have five seconds before I call the cops."

He chuckled. Actually chuckled.

"I don't think the cops will do much, sunshine." He smirked, and I bristled at the endearment. Sunshine. If only he knew how little light I actually had.

I was suddenly extremely tired. The day had been long and overwhelming. I wanted nothing more than to curl up in my bed.

"What do you want, Dorian?" I whispered at last. He finally turned to face me fully, my bad taste in music apparently forgotten.

"You need to be careful, Cami," he said. When I blinked at him like an imbecile, he took another step closer and grabbed my arms. His touch was surprisingly gentle, despite the urgency in his voice. "I can't tell you everything—I'm not allowed to—but I can tell you to be careful of whom you trust."

"What the hell do you mean by that?" He reminded me

of the twins, the way he twisted simple words into complicated riddles.

Dorian angrily thrusted a hand through his hair. The blond strands became even more disheveled with the gesture.

"I can't tell you," he muttered through gritted teeth. My already thin patience was splintering like cracked ice. First, he had the gall to sneak into my bedroom unannounced, and now, he couldn't even speak beyond cryptic riddles? If my bat accidentally connected with his balls, it would totally not be my fault.

"There are rules," he stated at last, voice teeming with frustration. I put my hand on my hip and cocked it to the side.

"And?"

"I promise that I'm telling you everything I can. Just don't trust everybody you speak to."

A headache was forming behind my eyes. A product, I was sure, of both annoyance and sleep deprivation.

"Is there any particular person you don't think I should trust?" I asked sarcastically. Surprisingly, he nodded.

"And can you tell me?"

"I'm not allowed."

Not. Freaking. Allowed.

Was he pulling my leg?

He must've seen the frustration on my face, because his own expression softened considerably. I thought, for a moment, he was going to give in and tell me. I could see the indecision flickering across his handsome features. He opened his mouth, shut it, and then opened it again. Finally, he clamped his lips together and turned towards the doorway.

He was going to leave.

He was going to leave without telling me what I needed to know.

"You can't just walk away!" I screamed, grabbing his arm and jerking him back. He glared at the spot I touched him, but I refused to lessen my ironclad grip.

"There are rules—"

"Why are you so damn anal about these rules?" I shouted.

"Because I don't want to die!"

We were both panting heavily, face inches from one another. I could see golden flecks in his eyes and a scatter of freckles across his nose.

"What?" I whispered, finally releasing him. His free hand immediately went to rub at the spot, eyes wide with wonder.

"Look," I said gently. "I feel like I'm losing my mind. So if you have answers, any answers, I will take them greedily. Please." My voice broke on that final word, that final plea, and tears sprang to my eyes unbidden. The wonderment in Dorian's eyes slowly contorted into horror.

"Please don't cry. I hate it when girls cry."

"Then tell me what I want to know," I quipped, shakily wiping away a tear. His eyes clouded over, expression changing and tightening until it was entirely unreadable.

"Imagine what it was like for me," he whispered at last. "I had no one. No one to talk to. No one to understand. No one. I tried to tell my parents, and do you know what they did?" He laughed, but there was no humor in it. "They accused me of talking to the devil."

"What?" I whispered, stunned.

"They sent me to priests, institutions, churches, until finally, they stopped." His eyes had a faraway look to them.

I swallowed.

"I am so sorry."

And I could understand, to an extent. It was for those reasons I refused to tell my own family about the nightmares plaguing me. I knew that they wouldn't react as badly as Dorian's parents obviously had, but I still feared they would look at me differently or judge me. Now, hearing Dorian's story, I realized that it was a viable fear.

"I told you what I could, but now I have to leave."

"Are you kidding me right now?" I screamed to his retreating back. And, as something occurred to me, I added, "And what about you? Can I trust you?"

My only answer was a waggle of his fingers before he disappeared around the corner.

It had never occurred to me how he could've gotten into my house in the first place.

## 22

The twins were uncharacteristically solemn the next morning. They both gave me quick hugs, eyes despondent. I hadn't realized that my disappearance would scare them so much.

At first, I'd refused their offer for a ride since I had to walk Karissa to school. She would arrive an hour before classes began, but my fathers refused to allow her to stay home alone. She had complained vehemently about being "babied" but eventually conceded to being dropped off at school early by the twins.

The ride was quiet on the way. The twins were lost in their own thoughts, and Karissa was fuming, her glare directed out the window.

She didn't bother to say thank you as she grabbed her backpack and stormed out of the car.

And of course…

Luke winced as the door was slammed, muttering something about his "precious."

Leroy merely stared after my sister with a quirk to his brow.

"She's a ray of sunshine."

"She's not that bad," I defended, though my voice betrayed my own thoughts. After a moment, I frowned and stared at her plaited black hair disappearing into the brick building. Conceding with a sigh, I reasoned, "She's a tween. Tweens always behave like they have sticks up their butts."

"I was the perfect tween," Leroy mused, and Luke snorted.

"Do you really want to talk about the goth phase?"

"Goth phase?" I was intrigued. Leroy always wore bright, vibrant colors and a fedora. I couldn't imagine him in anything else.

"Oh, yeah." Luke grinned devilishly at me through the rearview mirror. "I even have pictures."

"What?" Leroy asked, aghast. A delicate blush colored his cheeks.

And, oh yes, I most definitely wanted to see these pictures.

Luke glanced at me sideways, ignoring his brother's betrayed and slightly petrified expression. Smiling brightly, I rested my chin on Leroy's shoulder. He pinched my cheek affectionately, before turning his head to nuzzle my neck.

"I'll bring them tonight to your house." Luke paused, expertly steering the car into the school parking lot. His fingers tapped a staccato against the steering wheel—the only indication he was nervous. "Do you still want to meet up after school? I know after everything that happened..."

After everything that happened. After I vanished from school and appeared in the woods. After a search party was sent out to find me. After I lost hours of my life. As before, I tried to claw at the fragmented memories. They cascaded through my fingers like running water before I could entirely grasp them. There was something I had to remember. Something important.

Try as I might, the memory refused to make itself known.

"Yes," I answered Luke. "I want to figure out what's going on. There's something in the house...something evil. I want it gone."

"Have you been looking at the camera feeds?" Leroy queried. He swiveled in his seat to face me fully. We'd decided to keep the initial setup. There were cameras in almost every room, unbeknownst to my family, that connected back to two television screens in my bedroom.

"A little. I don't really know what I'm looking for."

It also felt slightly invasive to stare at the feeds when others were in the house. I tried to avoid any rooms my family members were in, as if that would somehow make the action of creeping less...creepy.

Luke opened his mouth to speak, but we were interrupted by a knock on the car window. All three of us jumped.

It was the twins who came to their senses first, simultaneous glares being aimed at the intruder beside me. Trying to steady my breathing, I finally turned to face the asshole who startled me.

Tyson stood there, separated by only a pane of glass. A beanie concealed his brown hair, and his leather jacket was unbuttoned to reveal a plaid shirt. On others, the outfit might've clashed, but on him, it was stylish and irresistibly sexy.

Reining in my irritation, I rolled down the window to flick his forehead.

"What the hell, Ty? You scared the crap out of me!"

He smirked, but it didn't quite meet his eyes.

"I just wanted to see with my own eyes that you're okay."

"You've seen her. She's okay. Now leave," Leroy said with a huff. Luke elbowed his twin in the stomach.

After leveling a glare in Leroy's direction, Ty turned back to me.

"Have you heard?" He absently rubbed at the back of his neck. A few tendrils of brown hair escaped its confinement beneath the hat, and he used his free hand to brush them behind his ear.

"Heard about what?" I asked, though I already knew.

Ali's face continued to haunt my dreams. Her wide, sightless eyes. The strange carvings on her chest. The blood pooling around her. The missing hands.

I took a deep breath to calm myself.

Calm. I didn't dare fall into the inky darkness of my depression and anxiety. I was afraid that I wouldn't be able to claw myself back out without losing bits and pieces of my already tarnished soul in the process.

"Ali," Ty said softly. His voice was tight, and his eyes were anguished. I didn't know the extent of their relationship, but I knew she had, at one point, meant something to him. If not as a romantic partner, then as a friend.

Reaching through the window, I squeezed Tyson's hand.

"I'm so sorry for your loss," I said sincerely, though I recognized how superficial those words were. "Sorry" wasn't going to bring the dead back to life. It was a word we used, a condolence we offered when other words failed us. What Tyson needed wasn't my pity, but the capture of the psycho who'd killed his friend.

I could only pray that psycho wasn't me.

"Did you know," Ty began, voice distance. His eyes were

locked on something above my shoulder. "That both Ali and Johnny gave away important intel to the Black Hawks?"

I blinked.

Black Hawks?

It took me a moment to connect that name with the little facts I held. It was the name of the Creepers' rival gang. I didn't understand gang wars and territories and this apparent "intel" that had been given away, but from Ty's tight-lipped expression, I figured it wasn't good.

Was he saying…?

Was he saying that Ali and Johnny were traitors to the Creepers?

Were their murders gang related?

I recalled my dreams. Some were hazy, distorted almost, but others were clear. It might have been wrong of me, but I hoped that the murders were gang related, if only to alleviate my guilt.

If the police were able to find the murderer…well, maybe my dreams were only that—dreams.

Clearing my throat, as if that could somehow clear my mind, I considered Tyson. His unruly brown hair escaping the dark beanie. The leather jacket with a skull on the back. His eyes, which were normally proud and willful, but were now soft and vulnerable.

I realized, with a startling clarity, that he had no reason to share any of that information with me. I wasn't an expert, but I was pretty positive that it wasn't normal to share gang secrets with outsiders. Was he telling me these things because my dad was a cop? Or for some other reason entirely? Tyson, I began to realize, was an enigma.

"Cami! Bitch! Get out of the car so I can hug your ass and then spank it!" A lilac head appeared beside Tyson's.

Her lips were pursed into a scowl, and her eyes were narrowed into thin slits.

Exchanging glances with the twins, I reluctantly left the safety of the car. Ty took a step backwards as Phoebe's tiny arms wrapped around me. I awkwardly patted her back.

"You fucking bitch! Do you know how worried I was? Fucking Colt was up all night having a panic attack because of you." She pulled back suddenly to glare at me. "Don't do that shit again."

"Sorry?"

"You better be."

Ignoring her brother and the twins, who exited the car to stand beside me, she linked her arm with mine and pulled me towards the front entrance of the school. I glanced helplessly at the guys, but they merely smirked, leaving me alone with the pissed off gang princess.

Assholes.

"Where are we going?" I asked Phoebe. She propelled us down the first hallway, teeming with students, and into a second one. This one was less crowded, with only a few groups lingering. She paused at a janitor's closet, opened the door, and pushed me inside.

Before I could snap at her, she slammed the door in my face.

What the hell?

"Cami?" a soft voice inquired, and I spun towards the person in the closet with me.

Ian looked different today. It took me a moment to pinpoint what that difference was. He was merely wearing a flannel shirt, the first few buttons undone. Without his Creepers jacket, he looked like an entirely different person.

Tamed, almost, though I doubted anyone would look at

this man and think he was anything other than a dangerous, beautiful predator.

"Ian?" I asked dumbly. The boy had a tendency to fry my brain cells. Maybe it was because I'd seen him naked. Hot naked boys tended to do that to hormonal teenage girls.

Two words—ass dimples.

Trying to think about anything other than the glorious specimen that was Ian, I stuttered, "W-Why are we in the closet?"

He smirked, the slightest curve of his lips. Add in his red plaid shirt, and he could've been a lumberjack straight from my fantasies. Not that I had fantasies, mind you, but if I did, Ian would be one of the stars. Along with a set of twins. And another asshole gang member. And a football player. And maybe even a neighbor...

"I was hoping to get my jacket back," he stated conversationally. His hand absently fiddled with the broomstick leaning against the wall. I watched his fingers, mesmerized, until I heard his sultry chuckle.

"Jacket?"

It took my brain a moment to catch up to his words. I had worn his jacket last night, after he'd found me. I remembered the distinct scent of cinnamon.

"I also wanted to make sure you were okay," he continued. His voice had lowered with that final statement, turning almost raspy. I wondered if he knew what he was doing to me—and every female in this entire world—when he used that specific tone of voice or if it was entirely accidental. The twins were cute. Dorian was pretty. Kieran and Ty were hot.

But Ian? He was sexy.

...And I was a slightly overweight, insane teenage girl who really had to stop lusting over every guy who gave her attention. Maybe, in some convoluted plot twist, I would actually get one of the men.

I also couldn't forget about Jaron. My boyfriend. My...love.

"Okay?" I parroted, rather intelligently if you asked me. Ian's thin lips crooked up even further. "I'm amazing. Swimmingly amazing. Is that a thing? I am beautifully, fantastically amazing. Five-hundred and twenty-two percent. Amazing. And sexy. You're sexy...I meant you're not sexy. You're the exact opposite of sexy. You're like a not-sexy person. And I'm just going to shut up now."

*Shadow Man, come out, come out, wherever you are. Please eat me. Or just drag me through the floor.*

I clamped my eyes shut as if that could somehow erase Ian from the closet—and, consequently, the last minute of that conversation.

I'd never had this problem with Jaron. My words, with him, were always eloquent expressions of love. Ian made me flustered in a way I couldn't explain—heart beating, butterflies in stomach, hands sweating type of flustered.

Ugh. Stupid libido.

"I could maybe pick up the jacket from your house? Tonight or tomorrow night?" Ian pressed. He sounded as if he was attempting to rein in a laugh. I could feel my cheeks flaming, but I refused to open my eyes.

If I didn't see it, see him, then maybe he would go away.

A girl could dream, couldn't she?

"Unless," Ian continued in that smoky voice of his, "you brought it with you to school?"

Was he seriously only talking about a damn jacket? Why did it feel like he was asking me to strip down naked?

I blamed his voice.

Voices could be immensely sexy. It was called an eargasm for a reason.

"Nope. I mean yup. I mean, it's not here. But yup, you can pick it up." My voice squeaked. Actually squeaked. I was so humiliated that I wanted to hibernate until next year.

"I'll see you, Cami," Ian said. There was the sound of the closet door opening and closing, and then I was alone. I allowed my breath to leave my body in a whooshing exhale. Alone at last, I hesitantly opened my eyelids. Thankfully, the tiny closet was empty.

Now I just needed to figure out a way to get a fake passport and move to England.

~

Kieran, surprisingly, was already in chemistry when I slumped down onto the stool beside him. The entire class period was an hour of work time for the lab project. Since Kieran and I were already done, we were allowed to do other homework.

Instead, Kieran produced a deck of cards.

"Go Fish?" he asked, and I couldn't help but smile in amusement. There was something alluring about a large, intimidating man asking to play Go Fish.

Nodding, I cleared the papers off my desk, and he began passing out the cards.

"I was worried," Kieran admitted gruffly after a moment of sullenly staring at his cards. "Any nines?"

"Go fish," I replied absently, turning over what he'd just told me. Kieran had been worried? I hadn't even expected him to realize I'd gone missing in the first place.

"What happened?" he continued.

I pursed my lips, surveying the cards intently as a way to get my thoughts together.

"Any twos?" I asked. He silently handed me a card from his hand, eyebrow quirked as he waited for my answer. Sighing, I dared to meet his penetrating gaze with a solemn one of my own.

"I don't know what happened. Sleepwalking, probably. One second, I was in the nurse's station, and the next, I was in the woods." I shrugged as if it weren't a big deal.

Kieran was silent for a moment. His eyes were trained fully on me instead of the cards in his hands.

"Why were you in the nurse's station?" he demanded, and I couldn't help but frown.

He was the first one to ask me that particular question.

"Fainted." I, again, lifted my shoulders in a small, nonchalant shrug. I was beginning to realize that shrugging was my standard response when faced with questions I didn't know the answer to.

His eyes narrowed, but he didn't ask me to elaborate. With a heavy, dramatic sigh, he resumed the game.

"How are *you* doing?" I asked tentatively after half of the deck was gone. Somewhere behind us, a student began to complain to the teacher about the project. I tuned them out and focused solely on Kieran.

His eyes were shadowed, dark bags beneath both of them and five o'clock shadow on his jawline. I yearned to reach forward and smooth out the worry lines between his eyebrows, but I balled my hands into fists to curb the irrational urge.

"Have you been sleeping?" I asked in concern. He looked, to be frank, like shit.

One of his hands held the cards, while the other scrubbed at his face as if that could somehow rid the evidence of his fatigue. When he didn't respond, I glanced down at his arm, obscured by his football jacket. He followed the direction of my gaze, eyes narrowing.

"I haven't hurt myself recently, if that's what you're asking." His tone was clipped, but instead of letting him bait me, I met his stare defiantly.

"That is what I'm asking." I held his stare with my own. I knew he could see the resolve in my expression. Finally, he ducked his head down, cheeks tinting pink.

"You don't know what it's like," he muttered, and I tried to control my temper. It wasn't Kieran's fault for being so obtuse. He didn't know me, so he didn't understand the struggles I continually faced. He didn't see the darkness churning low in my stomach, settling like years-old butter. It was better for everyone if he wasn't aware of those particular facts.

Schooling my features, I was shocked when my voice came out sharper than I intended it to.

"Don't know what it's like?" I asked in disbelief. When he winced, I grabbed his large, calloused hand in mind. "I know exactly what it's like to feel like you're not good enough, to feel like you're suffocating in your own darkness. I have it too."

His eyes were trained on my hand in his.

"Have what?"

"The darkness."

At that, his eyes flicked to my face. They traced over my features, the barest of caresses. Searching for what, I couldn't tell.

Steeling my resolve, I continued, "I have this darkness inside of me. I don't know how else to describe it. It's a part of me, but it also feels like an entirely separate entity."

I released my hand from his to fiddle with the hem of

my top. I didn't know why I was sharing such personal information with Kieran, my lab partner. Maybe it was because I recognized the darkness inside of him for what it was. Maybe it was because I was drawn to his kindred soul. All I knew for certain was that he was aching, losing the battle to his darkness, and I was desperate to help him. Save him.

His darkness, I knew, wasn't similar to mine. No two were the same. But it was still a darkness, still a voice, pounding against the edges of your mind and demanding release. The pull was almost seductive, and it was most definitely impossible to resist.

"I believe that we all have some darkness inside of us," I mused, watching as Kieran's throat bobbed as he swallowed.

"How do you deal with yours?" he asked at last. The rest of the classroom faded away, the squeals, the chatter, the squeak of stools being pushed back.

I considered his question.

How did I deal with my darkness?

The answer was simple—I ignored it. If I didn't acknowledge its existence, it wouldn't overwhelm me. I didn't dare start a battle against it, because I knew I would lose.

Instead, I blurted, "Do you know that a flame doesn't have a shadow?"

He raised an eyebrow.

"I want there to be so much fire, so much light, that not even a shadow can survive," I finished lamely.

I wanted...

What I would actually get, however, was an entirely different matter.

Kieran opened his mouth to speak, but the sound of my phone ringing cut him off. I smiled sheepishly at my chemistry teacher who gave me a disapproving head shake before turning once more towards the book on his desk.

I glanced at the unfamiliar number.

"I should probably take this," I told Kieran. His lips were pursed, but he nodded stoutly. I hoped that I hadn't already broken what little progress we'd made. We were venturing on a thin sheet of cracked glass, and we had to steady ourselves, support ourselves, or the glass would break.

I was afraid that I'd just broken the glass with my abrupt departure, especially when he was finally beginning to open up to me.

Stepping quickly out of the classroom, I held the phone to my ear.

"Hello?" I asked. The hallway was empty at this period. It felt almost ominous, that long stretch of white flooring and cracked, green lockers. For some reason, I kept envisioning Karissa moving down these halls, hair in two, long braids.

I remembered...

Well, I remembered nothing, really. I didn't understand where that thought about Karissa had come from. When would she have been at the high school? *Why* would she have been at the high school?

"Mrs. Rollings?" a clipped voice said in my ear. I jumped, momentarily forgetting that I was on the phone to begin with.

"Yes?" I said.

Wait.

Mrs.?

What. The. Hell.

Before I could correct her, the woman's strident voice sounded through the speaker again.

"I'm calling about your daughter, Karissa."

Daughter.

What. The. Hell.

I couldn't help but inwardly groan. She'd done this once before, last year, when she punched Tommy Davison for calling her a bitch. What had my firecracker of a little sister done this time?

"What did Karissa do?" I asked roughly. I was going to yell at her when we got home. I hated, absolutely loathed, when she put me on the spot like this.

There was a sister code that prohibited me from saying I wasn't her mother. However, there was a daughter code that urged me to tell my parents about this phone call. I decided quickly that I would evaluate what I would do based on what she'd done.

"It's her drawings..." The woman, whose name I still didn't know, trailed off.

"Drawings?"

That didn't sound too bad.

"They are...upsetting."

"Upsetting." Now I didn't even bother to phrase it as a question. I was more annoyed than confused.

"They're graphic, to say the least, and...well...you'll see them when she gets home."

I blew out a sigh in irritation. Was it too much work for her to explain what, in fact, Karissa had drawn? How could a drawing be bad? Were there not enough dots? What happened to artistic freedom?

"Right now," she continued on, oblivious to my growing frustration, "we are not going to take any disciplinary action. All we ask is that you look over the pictures and send a note to school saying that it has been done."

I rubbed at my forehead. My head was suddenly pounding.

"I can do that."

"Thank you, Mrs. Rollings."

Before I could respond, she hung up.

Rude.

"What was that all about?" Kieran asked as I slid back into my seat. I rubbed at my temples in annoyance.

"Apparently, I now have a teenage daughter."

He didn't question me again the rest of class.

## 23

Leroy and Luke did not seem too disappointed when I asked for a rain check on our monster hunting escapade.

"No problem, sweets," Leroy assured me.

Luke had even offered to drive me to the hospital when I said I wanted to visit Colt.

"I don't want to be a bother," I muttered anxiously. That was always my greatest fear—that I would be too much for someone to handle. Jaron and Fiona had made me feel that way constantly. If I were to ask a question that they deemed stupid, they would laugh in my face. I could never, not ever, ask them to give me a ride. They would just reprimand me for not getting my license when I turned sixteen.

Maybe I was better off without them.

Luke gave me a look that suggested I was ridiculous for even thinking that.

"It's fine. Get in."

Smiling gratefully, I slid into the backseat.

Phoebe had texted me during fifth period, asking if she could come with me to visit Colt. At the text, I felt the blood drain from my face and ice run through my veins. What type of sister was I?

I hadn't even considered visiting my older brother. Guilt weighed down on me heavily, but I pushed it aside. It would only add to the growing darkness if I allowed the guilt to consume me.

I'd agreed immediately and then texted the twins, asking if we could reschedule.

"You guys are great friends," I said as we pulled up to the impressively large brick building. The hospital looked old on the outside, almost unappealing. It was such a contrast to the high-tech, glass one I'd visited back in Chicago when I broke my wrist in middle school.

"The greatest," Leroy agreed. "Us ghost hunting freaks have to stick together."

"The only freak I see is you," I teased. Leroy grabbed his heart in mock offense.

"You have slain me, oh wise one."

"Wise one?" Luke piped in. He threw his brother a curious glance. Now it was my turn to pretend to be offended. I placed my hands on my hips and glared at him.

"Are you saying I'm not wise?" I quipped to Luke's abject horror.

Leroy turned to stare at his brother, slowly shaking his head. "You filthy wretch," he jested.

I snorted. I had yet to fully understand the twins' demented humor. Still, I found myself chuckling at the stricken expression on Luke's face and the giddy one on Leroy's.

The two were strange, for sure, but I was grateful I'd met them. They were quickly becoming close friends and confidants.

As they said, us ghost hunting freaks had to stick together.

"Bye, losers," I sang, sliding out of the car. Leroy rolled down his window to speak to me once more.

"You're welcome for our *hospital*-ity."

Luke grabbed his brother by the collar of his shirt and pulled him back into the car. Leroy muttered something beneath his breath about being manhandled before the car spun away.

Those boys.

Seriously.

I made my way inside the hospital, passing the security guard stationed near the entrance, and to the circular receptionist desk in the center of the lobby.

After quickly giving Colt's name, I was instructed to go to the second floor, down a hallway to the left, and into the first door on the right.

If the woman really expected me to remember all of that, she had another thing coming.

As I waited for the elevator to ascend, I thought of Karissa. I would have to deal with my little sister tonight. Papa had texted me and told me he would be at the station all night, and Dad was planning to stay with Colt at the hospital. It would be up to me to deal with my sister.

Releasing a breath, I followed the lady's instructions. After a few wrong turns, I finally found an open doorway.

The first thing I saw was Colt.

He was lying on a small bed, hair matted to his forehead with sweat. He wore a white hospital gown that stopped mid-thigh, the color seeming hideously bright beneath the synthetic hospital lights. His right hand was wrapped entirely in bandages.

The room itself smelled like bleach and disinfectant.

With the white walls, white ceiling, and white machinery, it was rather unwelcoming. The heart monitor beside him beat a steady pattern, and an IV ran down the length of his arm.

The second thing I noticed was Phoebe. Her lilac head was bent forward as she listened to whatever he was saying. Tears welled in her eyes, and she brushed them away with shaky fingers. Both of them hadn't noticed me yet, so it gave me an opportunity to observe them.

They looked to be in love, which was ridiculous. You couldn't fall in love in only a week. That was lust and infatuation, not love. That was one thing I hated about Shakespeare and romance novels—the instant love between the main characters. It just wasn't plausible.

But Colt was staring at her so tenderly, so wistfully, that it was impossible for me not to believe they had been lovers for years.

It bothered me.

Colt went through numerous girls a month, always searching for his "next piece of ass," his words. I had come to consider Phoebe a friend, and I would hate for our relationship to deteriorate because my brother didn't understand what being in a relationship meant.

It was Phoebe who spotted me first. A wide smile spread across her face, and she waved her hand eagerly. Unlike Colt, she didn't seem embarrassed at being caught in the midst of an intimate moment. My brother, however, was blushing crazily.

"Cami!" Phoebe squealed. I gave her a nod in greeting, but my entire attention was fixated on my brother. He looked pale, skin ashen and hair greasy. My brother had always been somewhat unkempt, but never to this extent.

Phoebe followed the direction of my gaze, and understanding dawned in her wide eyes.

"I'm going to grab some coffee," she said hurriedly, squeezing my shoulder before she left.

Alone with my brother, I tentatively sat down in the seat Phoebe had vacated.

"How are you feeling?" I asked softly. Instinctively, I reached a hand out to brush his blond, matted curls away from his forehead.

Colt gave me a small smile. To anyone else, to anyone who didn't know him as well as I did, the smile would seem authentic. But I could see the pain in his eyes as he fought a battle that he willed to remain hidden.

"Like I lost my hand," he admitted at last. He stared up at the ceiling, almost as if it pained him to meet my eyes.

"You don't have to hide from me." I kept my voice soft and soothing. But despite my attempts to get him to open up to me, Colt released a humorless laugh.

"What do you want me to say? That my future is over? That I might not be able to play an instrument ever again? That the only joy in my life has been ripped away from me?" While his words were bitter, his voice quivered. Unshed tears welled in his eyes, and I could feel my own eyes reciprocating.

"I am so sorry," I whispered.

He snorted. "It's not like it's your fault."

Oh, but it was.

I realized then the reason why I had been so reluctant to visit my brother. Guilt. Fear. Sadness.

It had been my fault. He might not have realized it, but I knew. I was stupid and thought that I could run away from my problems instead of facing them head-on. Now my brother was dealing with the consequences of my actions.

How could any normal being *not* feel guilty? It was so intense and potent that it practically contaminated the air.

Keeping my voice quiet, I added, "I was thinking that this town isn't good for us. For you. We should move."

I hadn't meant to say that. I honestly hadn't.

But all I could see were the tears in my brother's eyes, the bandage on his hand, the ominous message in my bedroom. We had to escape.

We had to.

Colt gave me a funny look.

"It's not that bad," he said. "I actually like it here."

"Colt..."

But what could I say? That I believed the house was haunted? That I believed the imaginary friend from my childhood was coming back for me?

Nope. That would get me locked up in the looney bin faster than you could say Shadow Man.

"Enough about me and my depressing life. Tell me about school."

We talked for the next hour about anything and everything, both of us pretending that life hadn't just fucked us both in the asshole. Phoebe joined us a few minutes in.

It was nice. Normal. It almost reminded me of the way I was with my brother years ago, before Jaron and Fiona had come into my life. I missed him. He'd been there physically but not emotionally. There had been distance between us, distance that we were just finally able to lessen.

"Oh, crap," I muttered, looking at the clock. "I need to head home for Karissa."

"Papa still working?" Colt asked understandingly, and I nodded, already climbing to my feet and stretching my taut muscles.

"And Dad wants to be here with you for your next surgery."

He rolled his eyes.

"You know, I don't always need him to babysit me. He has two other kids that he needs to look after."

I felt indignant on Dad's behalf.

"He knows that, but he also knows that you need him more than we do right now."

It was true. Colt had to spend night after night alone in the hospital. He may complain, but he enjoyed Dad spending the night more than he cared to admit.

"Be grateful that you have a father that cares so much about you," Phoebe scolded. There was something in her eyes that gave me pause, something laden with pain and suppressed emotion. I had the distinct feeling she didn't have a father who cared as much about her as Dad and Papa cared about us.

"Fine. I'll endure it with a smile," Colt said. Turning to me, he added, "Don't be a stranger this time. Come visit me."

I smiled sadly.

"I will. Love you, big brother."

"Love you too, little sister."

I kissed his cheek, said goodbye to Phoebe, and then called the twins to let them know I was done. As before, I'd argued profusely against them going out of their way to pick me up from the hospital and driving me back home. Like before, the twins had called me a "weed"—whatever that meant—and told me to stop being ridiculous.

They were already in the parking lot when I stepped out.

"Hey, dove twiddle!" Leroy greeted giddily, waving his hand through the lowered car window.

Dove twiddle? We really had to talk about these endearments.

Before I had even buckled myself up, Luke pressed a coffee cup into my hand.

When I raised my eyebrow in confusion, he hurried to say, "We stopped at the coffee shop while we waited for you and grabbed you a caramel apple cider. Your favorite."

My cheeks burned in tandem to his.

"Thanks," I muttered softly, taking the delicious drink. "How did you know?"

When Luke continued to blush a bright red, Leroy eagerly explained.

"You always get an apple cider from the school store. And I notice how you add caramel to it." He tapped his head with a finger. "See? Perceptive."

I felt warm and tingly. Not an unpleasant sensation, but something new. Different.

Strange.

I'd never felt this way before with Jaron. He'd never ordered me coffee, nor did I believe he knew what my favorite drink was.

"So..." Luke began as he turned out of the parking lot. "How is Colt?"

"Surviving," I admitted.

Leroy muttered, "Aren't we all?"

"He's struggling with everything. Music has always been his life, and he's terrified he's going to lose it."

"I can't even imagine," Luke said softly. I nodded mutely, biting my lip and turning to look out the window.

The sky was gray, and the dark clouds appeared bloated. It only took a few seconds for raindrops to begin pelting the roof of the car. I was grateful the twins had offered me a

*Gangs and Ghosts* | 251

ride. I couldn't imagine walking home in such horrendous weather.

Lightning streaked across the sky, and somewhere in the distance, thunder rumbled. I'd always loved storms. It might've been weird, but I found them calming and almost comforting. There was something pleasing about the patter of rain cascading down windows and the intermittent roar of thunder.

"Luke? Are you okay?" I heard Leroy ask. I turned, surprised, to see Luke gripping the steering wheel tightly. His breathing was shallow.

"It's okay, twin," Leroy continued. "Pull over, and I'll drive."

Without saying a word, Luke stopped the car.

"Is everything okay?" I inquired, concerned. His skin was so pale, I could see each distinct freckle on his handsome face. His eyes were wide, brimming with tears. "Luke?"

"I'm fine," he snapped briskly.

"You're not fine," I retorted. "What's wrong? Are you hurt?"

Leroy was already unbuckling both himself and his brother. For a moment, the car was silent besides Luke's panting as he pressed his face into the steering wheel.

"He's a little afraid of thunderstorms," Leroy admitted at last. He glanced fearfully at his brother before turning towards me.

My heart ached. Luke always put on a brave face, always tried to be the responsible one, that I hadn't realized he could even fall apart. But he was only human, and humans had a tendency to shatter. I could also tell he was embarrassed for breaking down so thoroughly in front of me.

"Luke," I said softly. "Come sit by me."

He froze, knuckles turning white where they still held the wheel.

"Luke," I repeated. There was a long moment of silence. I was almost afraid that Luke was going to reject my offer, though that thought was selfish to have.

Finally, he crawled over the console to move into the back with me, and Leroy slid easily into the driver's seat.

Luke was trembling as I reached for him. He came to me instantly, curling against my side with his head in my lap. I imagined that he hated this—this lack of control.

Fear was a funny thing.

"It's okay," I soothed, rubbing my fingers through his hair. "You're okay."

His shaking steadily began to subside, but he still didn't pull away from me. His eyelids fluttered shut with contentment.

Leroy met my gaze in the rearview mirror.

"Thank you," he whispered.

"For what?"

"For taking care of my brother."

With that, he pulled the car back onto the road.

## 24

Karissa was already home when we pulled up to my driveway.

She stood on the front porch, arms crossed over her chest and eyes narrowed on Leroy, still driving, and then on Luke, sprawled in the backseat. Being careful not to rouse the sleeping twin, I grabbed my backpack off the floor and gently detangled myself from his surprisingly strong arms. Leroy opened the door for me, rainwater drenching his fedora and trailing down his face like tears.

"You didn't have to do that," I muttered, an odd thrill going through me, especially when he held up an umbrella. Cheeks burning, I allowed him to walk me to the front door. Yup. I was turning into a blubbering, blushing idiot around these boys.

"Good afternoon, little miss. What's your name?" Leroy extended his hand to my sister once we were underneath the archway. Brows furrowed and lips pursed, she eyed his hand distastefully until he dropped it back to his side.

"Her name is Karissa," I filled in, stunned by my little

sister's rudeness. She directed her penetrating glare onto me at that comment. I met her gaze defiantly.

"Nice to meet you, Karissa," Leroy said brightly, seemingly unperturbed by her behavior. Then again, I didn't think anything could dampen Leroy's happy mood. He seemed to be one of those people that was constantly joyful and smiling.

It was almost nauseating.

Turning towards me, Leroy quickly wrapped me in his arms.

"You'll be okay alone?" he asked seriously. I nodded my head against his shoulder, a gesture I knew he felt rather than saw.

"I don't feel unsafe in the house," I admitted, unable to fully encapsulate what I felt. "Just scared."

"You shouldn't have to be scared," he whispered back.

In answer, I squeezed him tighter, his body heat thawing the ice surrounding me. When we finally released one another, I noticed that Karissa was watching us, eyes calculating. She quickly turned away when she caught me looking.

"See you tomorrow," I said, flicking the fedora on his head. A curly strand of orange hair escaped, and he immediately smoothed it back into its carefully constructed style beneath the hat. It was only as he was reaching up, body flexing, did I notice the swath of exposed skin on his stomach.

Covered in tattoos.

I blinked, wondering if I was imagining things. This was Leroy, for crying out loud. Cute, slightly nerdy, Leroy. My eccentric ginger twin. Yet, there was no denying the vibrant colors sketched into his pale skin, taking up every inch of available space.

*Don't drool, Cami. Don't drool.*

The last thing I wanted to do was drool over my new friend. The first rule of being friends with guys? Don't let them catch you checking them out. Seriously. Don't.

Fortunately, Leroy seemed oblivious to my less than friendly thoughts. Once he'd finished patting down his hair, he dropped his arm and offered me a brilliant smile. Not for the first time, I felt goosebumps erupt on my skin at being on the receiving end of such a smile.

What was wrong with me? I blamed it on the drink I'd finished in the car. Guys who knew your drink order were serious trouble.

"Yup. See you tomorrow," I muttered roughly. If he noticed my change in behavior, he didn't say anything. Then again, Leroy seemed to be in a continuous state of bliss and unawareness. I half wondered if he was on drugs the majority of the time. No normal person could be that happy, that energetic, every hour of the day.

I watched him run back to the car. He hadn't bothered reopening the umbrella this time. Instead, he allowed the rain to pelt his skin and clothes. I could see Luke's silhouette in the backseat as the car drove away, his arms raising as he stretched.

I wondered if he had tattoos as well.

No. I didn't wonder anything. Not me. Because friends don't ogle other friends' bodies.

Bad Cami.

"What was that?" Karissa asked, entertained, once the car had disappeared around a corner. I turned towards her innocently.

"Huh?"

"You looked as if you wanted to jump that boy."

"Did not," I scoffed. My face burned. Oh yeah. I totally did.

"It's fine." Karissa opened the door and gestured for me to enter. "He looked as if he wanted to jump you too."

"Karissa!" I squealed, slapping her shoulder. She merely shrugged, an amused smirk tilting up her lips.

"I only tell it as I see it."

"Speaking of seeing..." I began, though what I wanted to talk about had nothing whatsoever to do with seeing. Well, maybe it kind of did. You must have eyes to see art. So... seeing and art were related. Totally.

That was how I did the majority of my homework assignments—searching for connections and answers that didn't exist.

Shaking my head to clear my thoughts, I stared down at my little sister. I tried to look imperious and authoritative, channeling my inner badass, but I was afraid the final effect was kind of pathetic. I just didn't have it in me to look powerful, especially when Karissa was nearly as tall, if not taller, than me.

Nobody took a five-foot girl seriously.

Should I begin with a scolding? A question? A statement? How does one adult?

"What happened at school today?" I decided on at last. There. Simple and to the point.

"What are you talking about?" Karissa asked, walking into the kitchen. I followed after her in exasperation.

"You know damn well what I'm talking about. Your teacher. Calling me. Art. Ring any bells?"

She stuck her head into the fridge, perusing the choices, before straightening and turning back towards me.

"No bells rung," she replied slyly.

My hands clenched into fists by my sides. This girl was going to be the death of me.

"Karissa..." I warned darkly.

She huffed and rolled her eyes.

"It's seriously no big deal. I just made a stupid picture that she didn't like."

She grabbed a bottle of water out of the fridge and made a beeline towards the staircase. I followed a few steps behind her.

"Can I see this picture?"

"Nope."

Well, okay then.

I debated whether or not I wanted to press the issue. However, I knew that doing so would only push my sister further away. With her, I had to pick and choose my battles. A drawing the teacher deemed inappropriate? It wasn't a battle I was willing to fight.

In a sigh of resignation, I nodded towards the living room.

"Do you want to watch a movie tonight? Make popcorn? Have a girls' night?"

I waited with bated breath, pleading with my sister without words to say yes, to come downstairs and join me. We were so separated, so disconnected, that I scarcely recognized the little girl before me. I hadn't admitted to the twins why I'd wanted to reschedule our ghost hunt. I hadn't even admitted it to myself.

I wanted to—no, I *needed* to reconnect with my sister. We were two puzzle pieces with mangled edges. Maybe at one point, we fit together perfectly. But time had destroyed something beautiful, and I wasn't sure if it would ever be restored.

I wasn't surprised when Karissa muttered, "Not tonight," then hurried up the stairs.

I felt immediate disappointment, followed by self-loathing. Was it something I'd done? Was there something about me that made me so intolerable that even my sister didn't want to spend time with me?

With one last glance at the staircase, I reluctantly headed into my bedroom. I regretted not allowing the twins to stay. I needed someone to talk to. That truth hit me with a startling clarity.

I needed someone, and I had no one.

My phone beeped, and I pulled it out of my backpack.

**Jaron:** Why aren't you answering your phone?

**Jaron:** We need to talk.

**Jaron:** Answer me.

This was followed by numerous missed calls from my boyfriend. I considered calling him back but quickly decided against it. The last thing I wanted to do was listen to a three-hour lecture on why it was important for me to call him back. Apparently, I wasn't a "good girlfriend" if I didn't drop everything for him.

Why was it only now that I started to realize my worth? Why had I put up with his crap for all of those years?

The answer was simple—I had been lonely. I'd craved attention, any kind, and I had latched on to the first two people who'd offered it to me—Fiona and Jaron. They'd made me feel loved and wanted, even when my depression and anxiety told me otherwise. I hadn't realized that their love was conditional and our relationships relied on expectations I continually failed to meet. I could never be good enough for them. They made me believe I was a broken toy, a discarded scrap of clothing, instead of a human being. I'd lived my life under this preconceived notion that anything less than perfect was ugly. Wrong. Demented.

They made me feel ugly.

Wrong.

Demented.

Deciding quickly, I threw my phone onto my nightstand and crawled underneath the covers. I just wanted to sleep away the pain of Colt's injury, Karissa's rejection, and Jaron's treatment of me. Maybe when I woke up, I could pretend that none of those things had ever happened.

∼

I woke with a start.

The sky was pitch-black, the dark monotony broken apart by flashes of lightning. I must've slept longer than I'd expected, because the sky had still been grey when I'd finally settled.

But something had awoken me.

It took me a moment to pinpoint what, exactly, that was.

*Tap. Tap. Tap.*

The repetitive noise came from in my room. Was someone knocking on my door? My window? Those two seemed like the most logical explanations. As I strained my ears to hear the noise, I realized that it was coming from the closet.

I bolted upright, reaching blindly for the string on my bedside lamp. Immediately, light engulfed the room in a golden glow. It did little to diminish all of the shadows, all of the darkness.

*Tap. Tap. Tap.*

*I'm dreaming*, I thought dizzily. *I'm just dreaming.*

Somehow, that thought gave me the courage to push my blankets aside and venture closer to the ominous noise. It sounded as if someone was knocking their knuckles against the wall in a rapid succession. The closer I got to the dauntingly large closet, the louder the knock became.

*Just a dream.*

I tried to smother any fear I might've felt. If this was a dream, which it obviously was, I wouldn't be harmed. Dreams couldn't hurt you. This wasn't *Nightmare on Elm Street* or some other stupid horror movie. This was real life.

And I was just dreaming.

I repeated that in my head like a mantra as I crouched down and slowly moved aside my unpacked boxes.

*Tap. Tap. Tap.*

I pressed my ear against the wall, directly above the minuscule doorframe that led to the secret room.

*Tap. Tap. Tap.*

Holding my breath, I removed the peice of wall that separated the closet from the room. My hands were shaking uncontrollably, but I still did not stop.

*Just a dream.*

Poking my head through the hole, I was unsurprised when I was met with nothing but darkness. I really needed to invest in a small light or something. I could, potentially, make it into my reading cave.

Crawling back out, I reached for my phone, still on my bedside table.

*Tap. Tap. Tap.*

*Just a dream*, I reminded myself.

My resolve strengthening, I hurried back towards the closet, switching on my phone light as I did so.

There was nothing in the secret room. No murderers lurking in the darkness. No monsters awaiting me. I let out a sigh of relief.

I'd been imagining things.

*My dream-self has been imagining things*, I reminded myself. Because this wasn't real.

Right?

*Tap. Tap. Tap.*

I froze, light trained on the back wall of the hidden compartment. The noise, the persistent knocking, was coming from there. Didn't Luke tell me that it was hollowed? Was there a secret room behind the secret room? Fear strangled me. There were no words eloquent enough to describe how I felt at that moment. Iron clamped down on my heart, each rhythmic pump steadily becoming more erratic.

*Tap. Tap. Tap. Tap. Tap.*

The knocking was increasing in speed as I listened, horrified. The hand holding my phone began to shake. Someone—no, *something* was behind that wall, beckoning me.

*Just a dream.*

With a shuddering breath, I crawled farther into the dark, suffocating enclosure. The walls threatened to swallow me whole. There was too little room, too little space, and I felt like I was dying. My breathing was shallow.

Still, I pressed my ear against the hollowed wall.

The tapping abruptly cut off.

*Just a dream.*

*Just a dream.*

Why didn't those words seem true anymore?

Behind me, I heard a soft, continuous clank, as if a ball was rolling across the wooden floor.

My heart hammered, and my entire body froze.

*Just a dream.*

Slowly, as to not make any noise, I crawled back into the closet and turned towards my bedroom. A small, red ball, the source of the strange sound, was rolling in my direction. It stopped directly in front of me.

"Karissa?" I whispered softly. "Are you there?"

I heard a hiss, followed immediately by the shuffling of footsteps. Tears burned my eyes, but I willed them away.

*No. No. No.*

*This is just a dream, Cami. Remember that.*

I squeezed my eyelids shut and placed my hands over my ears. If I couldn't see or hear anything, it couldn't be real. It was only a dream.

*Wake up. Wake up. Wake up.*

I hesitantly released one of my ears to pinch my arm. The skin turned red, blood welling—my fingernails must've accidentally pierced my skin.

But I didn't mind the pain. I actually wanted it to hurt *more*. Maybe, just maybe, I would finally wake up.

More pain. I needed more pain.

"Cami..." a grotesque voice whispered. I heard what sounded like something being dragged across the floor, something heavy. Almost like...a body. "Cami, he's coming."

*Just a dream. Just a dream.*

Something—someone was scratching on the walls. The sound was ear-shatteringly loud.

I brought my knees to my chest and wrapped my arms around them. I was sobbing now, distantly aware of footsteps coming closer and closer and closer...

"What the hell are you doing?" Karissa demanded, frowning. She leaned against the closet doorframe.

"Kar?" I whispered, scrambling to my feet. I immediately grabbed her arm and pushed her behind me.

Something was here. Something malevolent was in the room with us. I had to protect her.

"Are you feeling okay?" she asked, attempting to step around me. I held out an arm to push her back. "I take that as a no. What the heck are you doing?"

I blinked at her wordlessly.

"I...I..."

The room behind her, my bedroom, had every light on. I didn't note anything out of the ordinary. No monsters. No dead bodies. No scratch marks.

My hand, numbly, released Karissa.

"I must've been sleepwalking," I murmured softly.

"Wow. You don't say?" she quipped sarcastically, rolling her eyes. I reluctantly followed her out of the closet, my hands fisted in preparation for a fight. My eyes scanned the cluttered bookshelf, the empty desk, and then my bed, the blankets pushed off to the side. Everything was as I remembered it, yet the uneasy feeling didn't lessen.

"I heard your annoying whimpers from upstairs," Karissa continued, oblivious to my growing inner turmoil. When I still didn't say anything or offer an explanation, Karissa huffed. "Whatever. I'm going."

When she was gone, I considered my room once more. There was no red ball near the closet, no figure hiding beneath my bed. I must've been dreaming.

I had to be.

Shaking, I considered going back to bed but immediately decided against it. The last thing I wanted to do was get pulled into another vivid nightmare.

No, what I really wanted to do was curl up into a fetal position in the shower while "All by Myself" blasted through my phone speakers. I figured that wouldn't be the most productive use of time, though.

*It was just a dream, Cami. A horrible nightmare. It wasn't real.*

I took a few deep breaths, calming my racing mind and heart, and nearly laughed at how ridiculous I was being. Had I really believed that a monster was in the room with me? Maybe I needed to cut down on the number of horror movies I binged.

Eventually, I decided to finish unpacking. I didn't have a lot of boxes to go through, but I knew I needed to start considering this place my home. My previous dreams of going back to Chicago and living with Fiona and Jaron were steadily diminishing. I didn't know if I would be accepted back, nor if it was what I even wanted anymore.

I steered clear of my shirts and dresses. The last thing I wanted to do was walk into that damn closet again. It was only as I was scanning through my huge collection of books that I noticed the black jacket draped across my desk chair.

Ian's jacket.

I eyed the fabric cynically. How could one article of clothing determine your entire future? It just didn't make sense to me. Of course, I realized that the clothing wasn't all of it, but it was a big part. It reminded me of my blonde wig —the ability to become someone else with such a superficial object.

I hesitantly traced a finger over the skull on the back. So stereotypical. Why couldn't there be something cool like a panda bear or a flamingo? I would have to have a long conversation with Tyson over the dos and don'ts of gangwear.

Grabbing the jacket, I headed back to the living room where I'd placed my backpack. I gently draped it over the couch, hoping that I would remember to bring it to school. The last thing I needed was Ian showing up again and...

*Way to talk yourself out of bringing it Cami*, I thought.

There was a loud thump from upstairs, as if something had been dropped. That was immediately followed by multiple bangs.

What the heck was she doing up there?

Squaring my shoulders, I decided it was time to be a big sister. I would confront Karissa, like I should've done earlier. With purposeful strides, I walked up the stairs and threw open her bedroom door. I didn't bother to knock.

What I saw made the blood drain from my face.

She glanced up from where she was bent over her desk.

"I have a message for you," she said, smiling. "From the Shadow Man."

## 25

There were drawings everywhere.

On pieces of paper taped to the wall. Painted onto the wall itself. On the bed. On the floor.

Each one showed an impossibly tall man shaded in black. In some, he was standing over a body. Red paint covered the majority of those particular pictures. In others, he held hands with two little girls. One I recognized as Karissa, and the other was...

Me.

"Karissa?" I whispered, horrified. She continued to scribble on a sheet of notebook paper.

"He misses you," she said at last. "He wants you to come home."

All I could do was repeat her name. My eyes latched onto the nearest paper. The Shadow Man, standing above a misshapen star. In the center of the star was a stick figure girl missing both of her hands.

Before I could stop myself, I ran to the trash can and vomited.

"What did you do?" All I could do was stare at my baby

sister, begging her to offer me some explanation. When she turned to look at me, her eyes were cold.

Dead.

"I did what he wanted me to do," she said at last, turning back towards her drawing. She tapped her pencil against her lips as she considered something. Smiling suddenly with satisfaction, she began to draw in vigor.

"What did he want you to do?"

I didn't want to hear it.

Half of me hoped that I was still dreaming, but the other half of me realized I was wide-awake. This was real. This was happening.

I let out a strangled sob. Even before Karissa answered, I knew what she was going to say. I knew.

"We took care of them. Those people that hurt you."

"No..."

"The Shadow Man and me."

"No."

Her words were running rampant through my head. The drawings. The impassiveness in her expression. It was all too much.

"Karissa." I trembled, unable to tear my eyes away from her small form. I remembered when we first adopted her, she was only six months old. I'd held her in my arms, and I knew that fate had brought her to me. To this family.

I remembered when she turned six, and I'd attempted to teach her how to ride a bike. After one fall, she began to cry and scream for Dad and Papa.

"Shhh..." I remembered telling her. When she continued to sob, I'd grabbed her shoulder and spun her to face me.

"Kar, you're so much braver than I was when I was your

age. I never dared to learn how to ride a bike. You're amazing."

Her tears had instantly dried up, and she'd climbed back onto the bike. She hadn't fallen since.

But now? Now, she had fallen, and there was nothing I or anyone else could do to help her. Life hadn't prepared me for this.

"Karissa..." I repeated, voice clogged with emotion.

Downstairs, the doorbell rang.

My body tensed as I ran through scenarios in my head. It could be one of the guys or even Phoebe, though I doubted they would come without texting. Even Kieran had learned his lesson.

Was it the cops?

Were they coming for Karissa?

"Stay here," I whispered to my sister harshly. She began to hum softly beneath her breath. It was one of those songs that I recognized but couldn't put a name to. The melody, however, seemed to be particularly eerie. I shivered, wrapping my arms around myself. "I'll be right back."

The doorbell rang again.

Plastering on a smile, I ran through everything I could say.

"What do you mean, Officer?"

"Karissa? No, that's impossible. She's been here with me."

"I won't speak without a lawyer or my parents present."

My hand was shaking when I finally unlocked the door and pushed it open. To be honest, my entire body was shaking.

"How can I help you?" I asked, still wearing my megawatt smile. I didn't recognize the figure in the doorway. He didn't wear the blue uniform of a police officer, nor did he look young enough to go to my school. His black hair was nearly identical in color to his piercing black eyes. His nose was too long in what might've been an arresting face otherwise.

I did, however, note the jacket he wore. A black jacket with a red patch on the shoulder.

"You must be Cami," the guy said, flashing me what he might've thought to be a friendly smile. He could smile all he wanted, but nothing could rid the coldness in his eyes.

"You have the wrong house," I said immediately, pushing the door shut. My heart was racing a mile a minute. Before I could fully close the door, he placed his foot in the threshold.

"I don't think I do," he said. His voice caused goosebumps to ripple up and down my body. There was something...off with it. Something malevolent in his tone that was infused into each husky word. "You're the girlfriend of Tyson, correct?"

"I don't know any Tyson," I lied through gritted teeth. I shoved ineffectually yet again at the door.

"Then of Ian?"

"Know no Ian," I said, then grunted. The door merely propelled itself off of his boot-clad foot. Using his weight, he pushed the door the rest of the way open, and I stumbled into the wall.

He stood in my foyer, eyes calculating as he took in the framed photographs. Those cold eyes paused when they rested on my living room couch.

Or more specifically, on the jacket draped over the couch.

Before I could run, the man had my body pinned against his.

"Don't know them, huh?" he sneered cruelly. His hands wrapped around my throat. "I hate liars."

I bucked, attempting futilely to rid myself of his weight. His hands only tightened around my throat. I gasped, seeing stars, and leveled a punch at his nose. I heard the satisfying crunch of bones snapping, and he released me to rub at it.

"You bitch!"

Using his momentary lapse of concentration, I kicked at his nuts and scurried out from underneath him.

I had to get to the phone. I had to call the cops. I needed my daddies.

A rough hand grabbed my leg, jerking me backwards. I screamed as pain radiated down my hip and to my calf. Fuck, did he break my leg? Fuck! Fuck! Fuck!

"Please," I whimpered. I was helpless against him. All I could rely on was some semblance of humanity still present inside of him. Some hope that I would make it out of this situation relatively unscathed. However, when his dark eyes met mine, there was no warmth. There was nothing resembling human in that reptilian gaze of his.

"I hate traitors," he hissed, pressing his arm against my throat. I sputtered desperately.

Breathe.

I needed to breathe.

"And I hate stupid bitches even more."

My vision was turning dark.

Dark.

So dark.

"Cami?" a hesitant voice whispered from the staircase. The man momentarily released me, flicking his gaze up to the descending figure.

"Run! Karissa! Run!" I gasped out. A sharp slap across

my face cut me off. Still, I hoped she got the message. I hoped she ran.

"I am going to enjoy this," he murmured with a moan of pleasure. And I imagined he would. I imagined that he was the type of person who got off on inflicting pain onto others. He was sick. Twisted. Demented.

And he'd found his next victim. Unfortunately, that victim was me.

I could feel water in my eyes, yet that was all I could feel. My body was growing numb beneath his tight grip. I only wished that I could see my parents and Colt one last time.

Darkness crept along the edges of my vision. Soon, it would consume me.

The man released me suddenly, and I desperately gasped for breath. I finally found that pocket of fresh air after tumbling helplessly through wave after wave.

The man...

Karissa...

I turned my head, unable to fully sit up due to the agonizing pain. I saw the man on the floor, Karissa standing over him. In her hands was my softball bat.

She hit his head.

Once.

Twice.

"Stop!" I croaked out.

Over and over and over...

"Stop!"

Blood splattered the walls, the ceiling, her face, my face. His head was unrecognizable, merely a collection of skin and bones.

Oh god. I was going to vomit.

Karissa turned towards me with a smile.

With. A. Smile.

Her face looked serene, almost excited, and her eyes were aglow with a hidden flame.

"What did you do?" I whispered. I couldn't tear my eyes away from the distorted body beside me. He'd been human only moments ago. Now he was anything but. "What did you do?"

She continued to flash that singularly beautiful smile.

"I took care of him. For you. For us."

I must've hit my head at some point, because it almost appeared as if there was a figure behind her—a figure shrouded entirely in shadows, nearly touching the ceiling.

"Don't worry," she said lightly. "The Shadow Man will take care of us."

The Shadow Man.

The Shadow Man.

The Shadow Man.

I, mercifully, passed out.

## ABOUT THE AUTHOR

Katie May is a reverse harem author, a KDP All-Star winner, and an *USA Today* Bestselling Author. She lives in West Michigan with her family, cat, and adorable puppy. When not writing, she can be found reading a good book, listening to broadway musicals, or playing games. Join Katie's Gang to stay updated on all her releases! And did you know she has a TikTok? Yeah, me neither. Follow her here! But be warned...she's an awkward noodle.

# ALSO BY KATIE MAY

Together We Fall (Apocalyptic Reverse Harem, COMPLETED)

1. The Darkness We Crave
2. The Light We Seek
3. The Storm We Face
4. The Monsters We Hunt

Beyond the Shadows (Horror Reverse Harem, COMPLETED)

1. Gangs and Ghosts
2. Guns and Graveyards
3. Gallows and Ghouls

Out of Sight (Prison Reverse Harem, COMPLETED)

1. Blindly Indicted
2. Blindly Acquitted

Kingdom of Wolves (Shifter Reverse Harem Duet, COMPLETED)

1. Torn to Bits
2. Ripped to Shreds

The Damning (Fantasy Paranormal Reverse Harem)

1. Greed
2. Envy
3. Gluttony
4. Sloth
5. Pride

Prodigium Academy (Horror Comedy Academy Reverse Harem)

1. Monsters
2. Roaring
3. Venom

Tory's School for the Trouble (Bully Horror Academy Reverse Harem)

1. Between
2. Beyond
3. Beneath

Kings of Grove Academy (Contemporary Academy Reverse Harem)

1. Mania
2. Psychotic
3. Pandemonium

Supernaturalette (Interactive Reverse Harem)

1. Introductions
2. First Dates
3. Group Outing
4. Game Night
5. Exes
6. Truth or Dare
7. Scavenger Hunt

## CO-WRITES

Afterworld Academy with Loxley Savage (Academy Fantasy Reverse Harem, COMPLETED)

1. Dearly Departed

2. Darkness Deceives

3. Defying Destiny

Darkest Flames with Ann Denton (Paranormal Reverse Harem, COMPLETED)

1. Demon Kissed

1.5. Demon Stalked

2. Demon Loved

3. Demon Sworn

Darkest Queen with Ann Denton (Paranormal Reverse Harem)

1. For Whom the Bell Tolls

Fae Revealed with Quinn Arthurs (Paranormal Reverse Harem)

1. Courting Darkness

2. Seducing Shadows

## STAND-ALONES

Toxicity (Contemporary Reverse Harem)

Not All Heroes Wear Capes (Just Dresses) (Short Comedic Reverse Harem)

Charming Devils (Bully/Revenge Reverse Harem)

Goddess of Pain (Fantasy Reverse Harem)

Demon's Joy (Holiday Reverse Harem)

Broken Howl (Wolf Shifter Reverse Harem)

## BOXSETS

Together We Fall

Manufactured by Amazon.ca
Acheson, AB